my daughter's baby

BOOKS BY KATE HEWITT

STANDALONE NOVELS
A Mother's Goodbye
The Secrets We Keep
Not My Daughter
No Time to Say Goodbye
A Hope for Emily
Into the Darkest Day
When You Were Mine
The Girl from Berlin
The Edelweiss Sisters
Beyond the Olive Grove
My Daughter's Mistake
The Child I Never Had
The Angel of Vienna
When We Were Innocent
That Night at the Beach
The Mother's Secret
In the Blink of an Eye
All I Ever Wanted
The Secret Between Us

FAR HORIZONS TRILOGY
The Heart Goes On

Her Rebel Heart
This Fragile Heart

AMHERST ISLAND SERIES
The Orphan's Island
Dreams of the Island
Return to the Island
The Island We Left Behind
An Island Far from Home
The Last Orphan

THE GOSWELL QUARTET
The Wife's Promise
The Daughter's Garden
The Bride's Sister
The Widow's Secret

THE INN ON BLUEBELL LANE SERIES
The Inn on Bluebell Lane
Christmas at the Inn on Bluebell Lane

THE EMERALD SISTERS SERIES
The Girl on the Boat
The Girl with a Secret
The Girl Who Risked It All
The Girl Who Never Gave Up

The Other Mother
And Then He Fell
Rainy Day Sisters

Now and Then Friends

A Mother like Mine

my daughter's baby

KATE HEWITT

bookouture

Published by Bookouture in 2025

An imprint of Storyfire Ltd.
Carmelite House
50 Victoria Embankment
London EC4Y 0DZ

www.bookouture.com

The authorised representative in the EEA is Hachette Ireland
8 Castlecourt Centre
Dublin 15 D15 XTP3
Ireland
(email: info@hbgi.ie)

Copyright © Kate Hewitt, 2025

Kate Hewitt has asserted her right to be identified as the author of this work.

All rights reserved. No part of this publication may be reproduced, stored in any retrieval system, or transmitted, in any form or by any means, electronic, mechanical, photocopying, recording or otherwise, without the prior written permission of the publishers.

ISBN: 978-1-83525-400-4
eBook ISBN: 978-1-83525-399-1

This book is a work of fiction. Names, characters, businesses, organizations, places and events other than those clearly in the public domain, are either the product of the author's imagination or are used fictitiously. Any resemblance to actual persons, living or dead, events or locales is entirely coincidental.

PART ONE

ONE

DIANA

When I get the call, I am so surprised I simply stare at the screen and don't answer it.

My daughter, my beloved Sophie, is calling me after eighteen endless months of total silence. You'd think I'd swiftly swipe to answer, my heart beating far too fast, my fingers trembling in my tearful eagerness, but I am too shocked.

Sophie... *Sophie*.

Eighteen months ago, she eloped with a man we'd forbidden from our home. A man my husband Andrew said he would not stoop to speak to. A man she chose over us, time and time again, first by running away with him and then every day since in her stony, stoic silence.

And now she's calling. *Me*.

My hand trembles as I try to swipe to take the call, but just as I do, it stops ringing, and the sudden silence feels like an accusation. I've failed her. Again.

I wasn't fast enough, kind enough, sensitive enough, *smart* enough to navigate the minefield that became our family life and led to the impasse we've been at for the last year and a half.

I feel that failure even more keenly now, as I stare at my phone, wondering if I should call back, if she'll even pick up.

I'm still overthinking all of this when a text flashes up on my screen... from Sophie.

I am standing in our backyard on a lovely April day, the kind of afternoon that feels like balmy springtime until the chilly breeze from the Long Island Sound cuts right through you. The trees are still bare of leaves, but the daffodils have already bloomed, banks of them waving in a sea of fading yellow all the way down to the water, their heads now bent and brown. I've been deadheading them for the last hour.

Since Sophie left, I've spent even more time in this garden, seeking solace in the blooms, my hands deep in dirt, my brain so busy with earth and plant that I can almost, *almost* forget how much I miss her.

Now, I lower myself into a chair on the patio, my phone in my hand. I need to swipe to read the text, but I'm afraid to because when it flashed up, I saw the first three words. *Diana, it's Tom.*

Not Sophie. Not my daughter, but her husband. The man we reviled, that my husband said could never darken our door again, and neither could our daughter until she'd left him.

The memory of that awful evening is still powerful enough, eighteen months later, to bring the taste of bile to my tongue and I swallow sickly, closing my eyes against it and the tidal pull of despair it inevitably brings. How can something go so disastrously wrong in the space of a single evening?

And yet that's what happened with our daughter. We knew she was dating someone, and even that he was special, judging from the smile that played about her mouth when she talked about him, the sparkle that came into her bright blue eyes.

We also knew, or at least I did, that it wasn't someone from our usual circuit—a son of neighbors, a college friend or one from New York, where she worked as a junior buyer for

Bergdorf Goodman, a job Andrew had arranged for her when she'd graduated with disappointing grades and few prospects. Once, he'd wanted her to follow in his footsteps at Yale, studying economics. She hadn't gotten in, and her four years in college had been a continual downgrade of expectations, one we valiantly tried to come to terms with, even though I knew Andrew had had such high aspirations for our only child.

The text flashes up on my screen once more, both an accusation and a warning. I need to read it, I know I do. What if it's urgent? What if something has happened to Sophie?

But I can't let myself think like that. The last year and a half has been hard enough without me catastrophizing more than I already have—waking up in the middle of the night, eyes straining in the dark, my heart racing as I wonder if Sophie is happy, if she's safe, or even if she's alive. I've spent far too many mornings simply staring into space, dreaming about my daughter, and afternoons falling asleep on the sofa after taking two Xanax, too weary in body and soul to face a tennis game or gardening club meeting, the staples of my cosseted and privileged life.

Eighteen months of total silence is, I've discovered, a very long time. It's a long time to consider what you could have done differently, not just on that one awful evening but through all the years stretching back to when I first held Sophie in my arms, shell-shocked from a grueling labor and then an emergency caesarean section, blinking this new life into existence, the mistakes I made all still in front of me. That moment was a blank page, and I was too tired and overwhelmed to realize what a fearsome and wonderful thing that is.

In any case, in all this time Sophie has never once reached out—not a postcard, not a phone call, and not a single reply to one of the texts I send her every single day.

Thinking of you, sweetheart.

Miss you, darling.

Knowing we're both enjoying the sunshine makes me smile.

I love you so much.

No reply every single time, and yet I've held onto hope that one day we can reconcile. Andrew will come around. Sophie will. And we'll finally learn how to be a family.

I let out a huff of sound, a fearful shudder of breath. The phone in my hand is damp with sweat, and my stomach swirls with anxiety.

I think some part of me already knows.

And so I swipe to read the text, the words dancing in front of my eyes as my swirling stomach drops right out.

Diana, it's Tom. Sophie's in the hospital and it doesn't look good.

For a second, I can't breathe and then the phone slips to the patio, clatters onto the smooth stones. I lean over, one arm wrapped around my waist, my forehead touching my knees, as I take in deep breaths to try to keep the dizziness at bay.

It doesn't look good. The words thud through my mind, my heart. What is *that* supposed to mean?

Of course, I know what it means, at least what it *usually* means. But I can't let it mean that now, not when I haven't seen my daughter in so long. Not when I told myself—the only comfort I could find in all these months of silence—that we still had time, that lots of families fell out with each other for a little while, and a reconciliation would be possible one day, maybe even one day soon. Sophie would come around. Andrew would. Something would happen, but not this, whatever *this* is.

Sophie... Sophie.

A shuddery sigh escapes me, closer to a sob, desperate and ragged.

Is my daughter in danger of *dying?*

No, surely not. My mind skitters away from the thought like a frightened animal. Maybe she has a broken leg, or bad pneumonia, or a bump to the head. Something that doesn't look good but doesn't mean *that*. I take a deep breath, willing myself to believe it. Needing to, because the alternative is impossible.

I stand, gingerly, like I've had a fall and I'm not yet sure how much everything hurts. Then I walk carefully into the house, to my little office—which is really nothing more than a glorified cupboard off the kitchen, and the room where I used to plan playdates and pay household bills. The house yawns emptily all around me, but for some reason I feel like I need privacy, a place to hide away.

I sit in the chair at my desk, my phone still in my hand. Outside my window, the lilac bush is just starting to bud, tiny purple blossoms ready to unfurl and release their heady scent. Andrew finds them a bit overpowering, but I love their sweetness.

I take a deep breath, and then I swipe to call my daughter's phone.

Tom answers after the second ring. "Mrs. Law... Lawrence?" He stumbles over my name, I suppose because we've never actually ever addressed each other before. He's my son-in-law, but he doesn't remotely feel like it. He's not even someone I know.

"Tom." My voice is croaky, and I clear my throat. "You said Sophie—"

"I'm so sorry." His voice chokes, and I freeze, staring into space, every atom of my being rejecting what that sudden sob reveals. "It all happened so quickly," he continues, his voice catching on nearly every word. "I would have called you sooner, but I didn't realize how serious it *was*."

"Tom... what happened?" The words whisper from me, barely a breath. My knuckles ache from how hard I am clutching the phone.

"She got sepsis... At first they thought it was just a fever, you know, because she'd been through so much, but then she seemed really confused, and she couldn't even remember stuff —like *any* stuff... but then they said there was an infection at her, you know, scar site... but that was only two days ago... two *days*... and all of a sudden she just got really, really bad..." He lets out another sound like a sob while my frozen brain tries to make sense of all the words—and rejects every single one.

Sepsis... scar site...

What is my son-in-law talking about?

"Sepsis can be treated," I say, sounding as scolding as a schoolteacher. "With antibiotics."

"It happened too fast," Tom says, and now he sounds like he's holding back tears, his voice clogged. "She just started swelling up... she looked so different..."

"Tom." I interrupt his pitiful musings, my voice like the rap of a ruler, each word an accusation. Why is he speaking in the past tense? "Are you saying Sophie is... that she's *dead*?"

"No." He sniffs, gulping back another sob. "She's in septic shock. They... they have her on life support, but they don't think she'll last very long. I thought you'd want to come."

I close my eyes as the world sways and shifts around me.

"Mrs. Lawrence?" Tom asks, and I realize it must have been some time since I've spoken.

I open my eyes, but I can't see anything. I feel numb, terrifyingly numb, yet also as if I am poised over an endless abyss and if I so much as look down, I will fall and keep falling forever.

"How long..." I have to force myself to say the words; my lips feel like they are buzzing. "How long do the doctors think she has?"

"A day—maybe two at most." Tom is silent, his breathing ragged. "Maybe not even that. I thought you should come."

I have so many questions, so many accusations, but I swallow them all down and simply say, "Where?"

"St Luke's Roosevelt," he says, naming a hospital on the West Side of the city. "In the maternity unit."

Everything in me screeches to a sudden and shocking halt at those words. *The maternity unit?* "Is... was..." I stumble over the words. "Is Sophie *pregnant?*" I ask incredulously.

"She had a baby boy two days ago," Tom confirms heavily. "He's in the NICU, because he had some trouble breathing at the start, but they think he'll be okay. I haven't even seen him yet because I've been with Sophie..."

My daughter was *pregnant*, and I didn't even know. She was pregnant and had a baby without telling me. And now she might be dying. It's far too much to take in. I feel lightheaded with the shock of it all, and I'm tempted to go upstairs and take a Xanax to steady my nerves, but I know I need my wits about me, even though I crave some blunting of the grief and horror that are already lapping at the edges of my mind, threatening to overwhelm me completely.

"I'll be there in an hour," I tell Tom, and then, because I can't trust myself to hold it together for a second longer, I end the call.

Alone in my office, I stare into space for several seconds, unable to hold onto a single thought, which is a relief, until my gaze rests on a Mother's Day card that Sophie made me at least fifteen years ago, stuck to the bulletin board above my desk. It's garish with glitter, and the bubble writing is loopy and uneven because she'd been practicing. I love it.

I love *her*, and now it seems I might never get a chance to tell her. To tell her *anything*.

I snatch my phone up, scrolling through the texts I've sent over the last eighteen months, one every single day. They stretch in a never-ending line on the screen, text after text after text, all unanswered. Many of them say that I love her. Now I wonder if she ever even read them, or if she'll have the opportunity to again.

Abruptly I rise from my chair. I head into the kitchen, grab my purse from the counter, my car keys from the hook by the door. I tell myself I'll call Andrew from the car.

I need to see my daughter before she dies. I need one last chance to tell her how much I love her, and how very sorry I am, but as I head outside, I don't know if it's already too late.

TWO

I decide to drive, even though I know as soon as I pull out onto our sleepy street that I'm in no state to do so. My hands are trembling on the wheel, my mind darting down dark alleys.

I don't like driving into the city, and when I go in for lunch or some committee meeting or museum exhibition, I almost always take the train. It's easy, just under an hour from Old Greenwich to Grand Central, but a cab from there to St Luke's Roosevelt could take another thirty minutes easily, and there isn't time.

I drive on autopilot, memories flashing through my mind like silver minnows, darting across the empty sea of my consciousness, gone before I can catch them to examine them properly.

Sophie, squalling as a baby, red-faced in her fury, because I was never able to get the hang of breastfeeding. My little Sophie at three, curled up on my lap, arms hooked around my neck as she promised me she'd never be too big for cuddles. My daughter at six, crying at her birthday party, presents piled in front of her, because she hated being the center of attention. Twelve-year-old Sophie, when she became obsessed with tennis, developed an eating disorder, and was so eager for our approval. Then eighteen-year-old Sophie, when she opened the letter from Yale that began with *We are so sorry...*

A sigh escapes me. Sophie was so beautiful, so lovely, so desperate, and ultimately so defiant. Always eager to please—until she wasn't. Her heart in her eyes until she hid it from us completely, and everything turned to darkness.

I gasp as I realize I am thinking about my daughter in the past tense.

I need to call Andrew, and so I swipe the car's screen to make the call. It flips immediately to voicemail, which I knew it would. Andrew doesn't like to be disturbed at work. He's an investment banker, every moment precious, or at least expensive. He's not going to waste his time on a personal call, even to me. Especially to me.

As I listen to his rather terse voicemail message, I struggle with what to tell him. How can I tell my husband our daughter is dying over voicemail? And yet if I don't, he might dismiss the message completely, assume I'm overreacting, as usual, or maybe not even listen to it at all.

"Andrew... it's Diana." Of course he knows it's me, he has my number in his phone. "I'm calling because of... Sophie. Tom called and she's... she's in the hospital. Andrew, he said she was... that it didn't..." My voice chokes and my throat tightens, so I have to squeeze the words out. "He said that it doesn't look good," I force out. "And that we should come as soon as we can. She's at St Luke's Roosevelt. I'm on my way there now. Please... please come."

It's not until I end the call that I realize I didn't mention Sophie was pregnant, that we have a *grandson*. I haven't thought about that myself yet, not properly. I can't. Right now I can only think about seeing my daughter.

I use the valet service for parking, practically hurling the keys at the driver before running into the hospital, already breathless with anxiety. I have no idea what I must look like; I went out without brushing my hair or even washing my hands. There is still soil under my fingernails from working in the garden.

I ride the elevator to the maternity ward with my eyes squeezed shut, as if I can deny the reality of what's happening, the very fact that I'm here. As the doors ping open, I open my eyes and am startled by my reflection in the mirrored side of the elevator—my silver-streaked brown bob is uncharacteristically disheveled, my deep blue eyes like black holes, dazed and haunted, the wrinkles I refuse to Botox like so many other women my age are compelled to do seeming carved even deeper into my forehead. There is a streak of dirt on my cheek.

I wipe it off as I head down the hall. At the locked entrance to the maternity ward, I press the intercom and then haltingly explain who I am here for before being buzzed in, the moment seeming utterly surreal.

"The third room on the left," a nurse tells me from the station at the center of the ward. Her tone is too compassionate, her face full of pity.

I walk to the door in a numb daze, forcing myself to put one foot in front of the other, although part of me feels like I'm floating.

This can't be happening. It simply *can't* be. I won't survive something like this, so therefore it can't take place. I am still thinking that as I push gently on the door that is mostly, but not completely, closed, and step into my daughter's hospital room.

My first thought is that this is the wrong room. That it has to be. This bloated body, lying so still and supine in a hospital bed surrounded by beeping machines, is not my daughter. I don't even recognize her. Her skin is pale and flecked with red spots, and her arms and legs and face have all swelled up, so she looks as if she's been inflated, her blond hair lank and thin against the starchy white hospital pillow.

It's not her. There must have been a mistake. Then the man sitting by her bed stands up and stares at me.

Tom.

I take in his guarded expression beneath a dark blond buzz cut, the tattoos up and down both arms and across the knuckles of both hands, all which still make me uneasy. Andrew had been horrified by the sight of him, back when Sophie had brought him home; we didn't socialize with people with such tattoos. Something small and artful, *maybe*, but not a full sleeve of them, or gothic-looking letters across his hands like some *gang* member.

Which, unfortunately, wasn't far off the truth. When we first met him, Tom had been a drug dealer. An *ex*-drug dealer, according to Sophie, to be fair, and one who had served his time in federal prison, but considering he'd reeked of cannabis when he'd come to our house, Andrew and I both had our doubts about just how reformed a character our daughter's new boyfriend was.

Eighteen months later, I still have no idea what he's like. He stares at me, his brown eyes dark, his expression completely flat, like I'm a stranger he couldn't care less about, which might not be all that far from the truth.

"Tom," I say faintly. His name sounds strange on my lips. Even though I've thought about him endlessly over the last eighteen months, I've only called him by his name a handful of times, on the night I met him.

He doesn't reply and I turn back to my daughter, because of course it *is* her. I think I knew that all along, even if I wanted to try to convince to myself, for a few desperate seconds, that it couldn't be.

"What did the doctors say?" I whisper.

"They say there's nothing more they can do, because of the septic shock." It's what he said on the phone, but it jolts me again now, a constant, unwelcome surprise. Tom's voice is hoarse, and when I turn to look back at him, I see how bloodshot his eyes are, how stark the bones of his face are beneath several days' stubble. He looks like he hasn't slept in a week. "Her organs are starting to shut down," he explains in a voice that sounds numb with shock. "The bloating is from all the liquid she's retained because her... her blood vessels are leaking." I give a little shake of my head; I can't bear to hear this. "They're keeping her going so people can say their goodbyes," Tom finishes heavily. "But after that..."

He trails off without saying anything more, slumping back into his chair, his shoulders bowed, his hands laced loosely in front of him so I can see the letters on his knuckles. *Hold Fast*, they read. I don't think I'd ever made out the words before.

I shake my head again as if to clear it and then stumble my way to a chair at the end of her bed and collapse into it. Even after what Tom said on the phone, I prayed it wasn't going to be this bad. I let myself believe it couldn't be.

But now he's basically telling me my daughter's death is imminent.

"I called Andrew," I say into the silence, and my voice has the same distant quality as Tom's, as if neither of us can believe this is happening, as if we're not fully present in this room, in this reality. "He'll want to come."

"*Is* he coming?" Tom asks after a moment. His voice is neutral, dealing in facts, but I don't think I'm the only one remembering how he and Andrew last interacted.

If I see you in or near my house again, I'm calling the police, do you understand?

Andrew had frog-marched Tom to the front steps while Sophie had trailed after them both, sobbing. Tom had been in our house for less than an hour, and in that time, we discovered that he'd spent three years in prison, was high, *and* had stolen a Royal Worcester Pekingese dog figurine from the guest bathroom that had belonged to Andrew's mother. He'd chucked it at my husband's head after being ejected from our home. Fortunately, it hadn't hit Andrew, but had landed on the front stoop, shattering into tiny fragments.

That moment might have been weirdly funny, if it hadn't felt so utterly dreadful. As she'd clung to Tom, Sophie had screamed so many hateful things at me and Andrew, things I hadn't realized she'd felt, although perhaps I should have.

I hate you! You both are the snobbiest, most stuck-up and unforgiving people in the whole world. All you care about is appearances, not what a person really is. Why can't you give him a chance? Oh, I know, because you never gave me one.

That last jibe sticks with me the most, I think, maybe because I'm afraid it might have been true, at least in the tumult of Sophie's mind in that moment. As Andrew has told me many times, we gave her everything.

And yet, to Sophie, it was far, far too little.

It's hard not to feel like a failure as a parent, in light of an accusation like that, and the ensuing year and a half of silence.

But for it to end like this?

"Mrs. Lawrence?" Tom prompts quietly, and I realize I haven't answered him.

"I left him a message on his phone," I say, and then wince as I realize how that sounds. Like Andrew doesn't care but also like *I* don't. "I don't know how else to get in touch with him," I admit. "His secretary won't take my calls."

Tom's eyebrows rise at this, but I choose not to enlighten him. There was a period in my life, a very brief period several years ago now, when I may have harassed my husband's secretary. I can't justify it, only say that I'm ashamed of myself and at the time I was deeply unhappy for a variety of reasons.

But not as unhappy as I am now, staring in disbelief at my dying daughter. I long to take her into my arms, but with all the tubes and wires, I'm afraid even to touch her.

"*Sophie,*" I whisper, hoping she'll hear me, but she doesn't stir. Her eyelids don't flicker, her labored breathing doesn't change, nothing at all happens, even though part of me even now is expecting a miracle, because the alternative is simply too terrible to accept.

It's too late, I realize numbly, for a reconciliation, which was the only thing I had left to hope for. My daughter is too far gone; if her organs are failing, she won't even know I'm here. Will she? A sob escapes me, an unruly sound, and I clap my hand over my mouth as I gaze down at my once-beautiful blond girl, now nearly unrecognizable.

"I'm so sorry," Tom says, and I wonder what he's sorry for. Marrying my daughter, and causing the huge rupture in our family? Getting her pregnant, so she ended up like this? Or the simple fact that she is going to die, and I never got to tell her I was sorry, save by texts that she never replied to and maybe never even read?

Another sob slips through my fingers, and I scrunch my eyes closed, willing myself to claw back control. The last thing I want to do is lose it in front of Tom West.

"I don't understand how this happened," I finally whisper as I open my eyes.

"Sepsis cases can progress really quickly." Tom sounds like he's repeating verbatim what some anonymous doctor said, his voice hollow and dazed. "Within hours. They were treating the infection pretty much right away, but it was still too late."

I take my hand from my mouth as I gaze at my daughter, trying to see her as she was, rather than the woeful and even grotesque figure she is lying in this hospital bed, so different from the vibrant, beautiful, funny, and shy daughter I knew and loved.

Sophie... Sophie.

At twelve, insisting on setting up a lemonade stand on our driveway even though it's a gated community and nobody comes by.

At sixteen, so in love with her first boyfriend that it made me unable to sleep or eat from anxiety, because I could tell right off the bat that he didn't remotely feel the same way about her. And then at nineteen, exchanging her velvet headbands and Lily Pulitzer dresses for grungy T-shirts and baggy jeans; Andrew was more amused than anything else, insisting it was just a phase, which it inevitably was. I suppose he thought Tom was a phase, too, but then, just six weeks after our disastrous meeting, Sophie eloped with him. She sent us a text with a picture of her left hand, the middle finger pointed upwards, the fourth with a wedding ring. No message.

Marriage wasn't, I'd thought then, meant to be a phase, and so after that, I suggested to Andrew that we should change our tactic. Try to make amends, find some kind of way forward, but Andrew was adamant. He wasn't going to be the one to break first.

Well, we're all broken now.

"Do you want some time alone with her?" Tom asks, and now he almost sounds gentle.

I glance at him, this man who has been the absolute bane of my existence. Without Tom, I'd still have my daughter. She'd be alive and she'd love me, and I'd have seen her nearly every week. We'd have gone shopping and watched trashy TV together and she'd have come over for family dinners and late afternoon cups of tea. On weekends she'd lug home her laundry, and Andrew would take her out in his sailboat, and I'd make something delicious for dinner, and we'd all be happy.

Instead, I have a stranger in a hospital bed who hasn't spoken to me in eighteen months, but whom I have never stopped adoring.

After a brief hesitation, I nod my acceptance. Despite my complicated feelings for this man, I recognize that it's a thoughtful gesture, a generous one, and I want Tom to know I appreciate it. "Thank you," I whisper, and he nods back and then, without another word, gets up from his chair and leaves the room, closing the door softly behind him.

Slowly I walk toward my daughter's bed. I sit in the chair Tom just vacated and then carefully, tenderly, I reach for Sophie's hand. Her skin is cool and clammy, and it feels lifeless; there is no twitch of acknowledgment, no curling of her fingers into mine, no warmth or vitality like I expected, like I am used to. It feels like a disembodied limb, separate from my daughter. I glance down at Sophie's face, trying to ignore all the aspects that aren't my daughter—the paleness, the bloating, the speckled rash. Signs of the sepsis, but not of my Sophie. Not who she was. Not who she *is*.

"I love you, Soph," I whisper, and saying those simple words makes my eyes fill with tears, so for a moment I can't see, can't speak. I simply hold her hand as the tears drip down my face and off my chin. I want to sob, to howl and rail against *something*—God, fate, the world, *this*—but I keep it all back as I hold my daughter's hand and do my utmost to make these last moments matter. "I've always loved you," I tell her softly. "I know I haven't gotten it right all the time, and sometimes I got it really, really wrong. Too many times. I know that." I sniff, the sound like a shudder, and then keep going. "But you really have been the light of my life, always. Your smile. Your dimples. That laugh you have when you find something really funny, deep down from the belly. It makes me laugh too, every time."

I stop again as my voice turns ragged, and I have to take several breaths before I can continue.

"I love everything, Sophie. Absolutely everything about you. I know you sometimes felt like you were a disappointment, and like you tried too hard but it was never enough, but I want you to know that it *was*—that it always was. Maybe we didn't say or show that enough, but please believe me, darling, that it was. That you were. That your dad and I both loved you so, so much, exactly as you were. Always."

I stop again, and then, amazingly, I feel her fingers twitch in mine. Did she hear me? Was she acknowledging what I said? Hope balloons crazily inside me, even now, when I should only feel despair.

"Oh, Sophie." My voice breaks. "Sophie... what am I going to do without you?" My voice rises tremulously, and I know I'm in danger of breaking down completely. I suck in a hard breath. "I've missed you every day these last eighteen months," I tell her. "Every day. I don't know if you ever read my texts, or if they seemed shallow or thoughtless, maybe they did, but I *meant* them. I think about you every single day. Every single *minute*. You're always there, you know, in my mind. My heart. You always have been. You always will be."

Again I feel her fingers twitch and even tighten on mine, and it gives me the strength to continue, my voice turning fierce.

"I love you, Sophie. I love you. I love you so, so much—"

I stop abruptly as she lets out a gurgling sort of breath that doesn't sound right, and then she goes completely still. I stare at her, my face streaked with tears, and despite how lifeless she seemed before, this feels far worse.

The door opens, and I turn to see Andrew, harried, more disheveled than I've ever seen before, rush in.

"Sophie—" he gasps before he falls silent, as he realizes what I already have, the monitor that was beeping steadily now emitting the long, steady flat note of a heart that has stopped beating.

Our daughter is dead.

THREE

Andrew stops, staring at Sophie, and then he takes a few staggering steps toward her bed, one hand outstretched hopelessly, as the monitor continues its remorseless drone. I can't speak, can't think; there are tears on my cheeks and my chest aches with a pressure I feel will never lessen. I will never lose it or be able to let it out.

This is the rest of my life, I think dully. *The rest of my life without Sophie.*

Stricken, Andrew stands at the foot of the bed and simply stares at our daughter, and right there in front of my eyes I see him turn into an old man. His shoulders slump, his face sags, and his skin turns gray. His outstretched hand falls limply to his side.

"What... what happened?" he whispers hoarsely.

I can only shake my head, because how can I even begin to explain? I don't entirely know myself how we ended up in this awful place, with both of us estranged from our dead daughter.

Tom slips quietly back into the room. He stiffens as he catches sight of Andrew, but before any of us can react to what I know could quickly become a volatile situation, he hears the endless drone of the monitor and I see the realization flash across his face. He doesn't cry out or gasp or make any sound at all. He simply walks over to her and takes her hand, the same one I was holding moments before, and presses it to his lips, his eyes closed, almost like he is at prayer.

Neither Andrew nor I speak.

Then Tom lowers Sophie's hand, placing it carefully across her chest as he bows his head. A shudder rips through him and then he takes a quick, steadying breath. Still none of us speak. I glance at Andrew, and see that he is staring stonily at Tom, his mouth set, his eyes hard. I look away again, wanting to break the silence but having no idea how.

Tom lifts his head and turns to me. "When?" he asks, and I blink, my dazed mind struggling to grasp what he's asking. *When did Sophie die?*

"Just..." My voice comes out faint and scratchy. "Just a moment ago."

He nods slowly, and before any of us can say anything more, although I don't know what we could possibly say, a nurse slips into the room. She turns off the monitor and then goes to our daughter's body, checking the pulse, which hurts me somehow, because she's so clearly dead and it doesn't need *checking*, and yet at the same time I can't suppress a wild lurch of hope that maybe somehow we're wrong and she isn't.

Then the nurse turns to Tom.

"I'm so sorry," she says directly to him, and my hurt suddenly turns into a towering rage, so my hands form into fists. Tom has known my daughter for less than two years. *I'm* the one who carried her, who had her ripped from my body after twenty-three hours of grueling labor, who pumped milk for weeks because we couldn't figure out breastfeeding, who rocked and sang and cuddled and comforted her every day of her childhood.

I'm the one who went to every one of her tennis matches for

three years, who stayed by her side through even more years of battling an eating disorder, who cooked healthy food and tried to make weigh-ins a game and who comforted and cajoled and encouraged and wept when things were hard, and they were hard a *lot*.

Why isn't this nurse saying those words to me?

But of course I know why she isn't.

Tom nods slowly. "Thanks," he says quietly.

"Would you like to be alone with her?" the nurse asks. She's still only talking to Tom, as if Andrew and I aren't even in the room, and I must make some kind of small, protesting sound, because she glances at me, lips pursed and eyes narrowed, and then her gaze flicks away. I've been dismissed, I realize with shock, almost like she knows Sophie and I were estranged. Like she knows how I let my daughter down. Like someone told her.

The thought that she might know that, that I've been judged and found wanting as a mother when my daughter is *dead*, sends a prickly flush over my body, and I have to blink rapidly several times. I don't know why I care in this moment, when something so much worse has happened, but it hurts all the same, ripping open old wounds I'd hoped had long since scabbed over.

Even this nurse knows what kind of mother I've been.

Andrew still hasn't spoken, hasn't even moved.

"I think I'm okay," Tom says, "but..." He glances questioningly at both of us, his expression veiled.

"I think we'd like a moment with our daughter," I say stiffly. I don't really want to be with Sophie like this, when she's so clearly *gone*, but it feels like the right thing to do. We're her *parents*. I need someone to acknowledge that, to understand just how much it means.

The nurse nods without looking at either of us. "Of course you can have a few moments," she says, and slips out of the room.

Tom remains, looking back and forth between us, and it feels like one of us should say something, but no one does.

Then he murmurs something inaudible and follows the nurse out of the room. The door shuts behind him, and the silence feels like concrete poured over us, hardening all around. Neither Andrew nor I speak.

I make myself look at Sophie, but then I look quickly away again. She looks even less herself than she did before; she looks *dead*, her skin already turning gray, although maybe that's just my imagination, but I can't bear it. For a second, I think I might pass out or scream. A hitching sob escapes me, and I press my hand to my mouth. Andrew finally looks at me.

"How did this happen?" he asks hoarsely. "What... what did she die of? And how could we not have known?" His voice rises stridently; I know it's always been easier for him to be angry rather than sad.

Slowly I lower my fingers from my mouth. "She was in septic shock," I tell him. "From her incision."

"Her incision?" he barks. "What incision?"

"A... a caesarean section."

Andrew's eyes widen. "*What—*"

I nod jerkily. "She was pregnant. Tom said she... she had a little boy..."

I can't believe my little girl was pregnant and she didn't even tell me. Didn't feel the need or desire to tell me. I could have talked her through morning sickness, told her how eating bananas helps with leg cramps, given her some of the maternity clothes I saved, classic pieces. I could have had the ultrasound photo of my grandson on the fridge; I would have given her the *best* baby shower. I would have been right here in the delivery room, if she would have let me, cutting the cord if Tom didn't want to.

I would have done it all, gladly, and more. I would have helped her through those first few weeks that feel like they go on forever; I would have told her she was doing a great job when, like me, she felt like a failure. I would have been by her side through it all. I would have found a way to make it work with her marriage to Tom, with all of it. I would have... save for my husband.

"A boy?" Andrew repeats in a dazed voice. He looks stunned, his mouth agape as he blinks several times. It's so unlike him; he's a man who has always exuded authority and charisma, with his thick head of silver hair, bright, penetratingly blue eyes, the ready smile that can slip so quickly, too, although maybe I'm the only one who sees that. I know how much I have wearied him, over the years.

"That's what Tom said," I affirm uncertainly, because already I'm starting to doubt myself. What with all the shock and grief of these last few hours, I am questioning whether he really said that. Whether my daughter really had a baby.

"Where is he?" Andrew asks. His voice is harsh, and his eyes look bright and wild. "Where's the baby?" he demands, his voice rising. "Where's our grandson?"

Grandson. Did I really lose a daughter and gain a grandson in the space of a single day? A grandson. Can I really be a grandmother? And am I even still a mother?

"In... in the NICU," I reply, the snippets of my conversation with Tom coming back to me as if I have to fish them out of deep water. "I... I think."

Abruptly, Andrew wheels toward the door.

"Andrew... *wait.*" My voice chokes. "What about Sophie?"

He glances back at her, and for a second his face collapses in sadness. "She's gone," he tells me quietly. "She's not here, Diana." He draws a quick, steadying breath. "I'll call a funeral home to... arrange things."

I turn back to my daughter. I can't make myself look at her, but at the same time I don't want to leave her alone in this room. When I walk out of here, I'll never be able look on her face again. Yes, she's dead, but she's still *here*. At least in a way.

"*Diana.*" Andrew's voice sharpens, and then he sighs. "Honey," he says, gentling his tone, "we've said our goodbyes."

Have we? I don't feel like I got to say hello, never mind goodbye, and Andrew certainly didn't, yet already his hand is on the door. He's moving on, a man with a mission, while I am still in a fog of grief, blundering through every moment blindly. I have no idea what comes next, what we're meant to do in this situation. Are there forms to fill out? Doctors to see? Do we really just *leave* her alone in here?

And what about Tom? How on earth are we meant to relate to him now, when we've never related to him at all?

Because we have to, I realize numbly. Because there's a baby involved. Our *grandson*.

On stiff legs I walk to the door. Andrew puts his hand on the small of my back as he guides me from the room. I feel like I should look back, but I don't, and as the door closes behind us, I wonder if that is another thing I'll always regret.

Tom is waiting in the hallway, and he steps toward us, his arms folded across his chest, biceps rippling. It feels like an aggressive stance, but maybe it's just a defensive one. I really don't know this man at all. We spent maybe two hours with him, in total, which was, shamefully, enough for us to completely reject him—and for Sophie to then reject us.

I don't know how he got into drug dealing and whether he's truly stopped, if he has family to support him or if he ever truly loved my daughter. He is a complete unknown, a wild card whose possible actions I can't even begin to predict, which seems particularly volatile in this situation.

"We want to see our grandson," Andrew states firmly, and I see Tom's jaw bunch. It feels like we have already turned this into a battle, and surely it didn't need to be. Not yet, anyway, even if that's how it is likely to end up.

"The nurse just told me he's out of the NICU," Tom says. His voice is low and gravelly, surprising me, because I realize I have barely heard him speak. That fateful night, he said no more than a handful of sentences. They were enough to condemn him. "They've moved him to the nursery."

"And where is the nursery?" Andrew practically barks.

Out of the corner of my eye, I see two nurses standing at the station exchange glances. Andrew and I are the bad guys, I realize, and I understand why. Tom's been here for days, the grieving husband and new father, downtrodden and despairing, while we breezed in moments before our daughter died, wearing designer clothes and demanding answers. I think if I was one of those nurses, I'd see us as the bad guys, too. Even if we're not the person who has been to *prison* in this situation.

"Why don't we all go together?" I suggest quietly, a ragged edge of desperation to my voice. I don't know who I'm trying to appease—Tom, or the nurses whose opinion I stupidly still care about.

Tom is already shaking his head. "You guys can see him on your own. I have stuff to do here, forms to fill out." He glances at the nurses, and one smiles kindly back.

The other one says in what is a decidedly cool tone, "The nursery is on the end of the hall, on the right."

"Thank you," Andrew says stiffly, and no one replies as we start down the hall.

Doors along the hall are ajar, and I glimpse new mothers in beds, with helium balloons and bouquets of flowers and teddy bears decorating their rooms—*It's a Girl!*, *Congratulations*, *New Parents*. All of it makes my stomach churn. Why didn't they move Sophie to a different ward, when they knew it was serious? It feels like an affront, to be here among all these joyous signs of life, when my daughter is lying dead in the next room.

Dead. The word echoes through me. I still can't believe it. I won't let myself.

We stop in front of a plate glass window that overlooks the nursery, a small sea of plastic bassinets, with half a dozen of them occupied.

The nurse on duty smiles at us and opens the door.

"Who are you here to see?" she asks cheerfully, because of course everyone is excited on a maternity ward. There should be nothing but good news here.

"Baby Boy West," I reply after a second's hesitation. My voice sounds strange to my own ears. Of the six babies in the nursery, four have pink knitted caps and two have blue. The smiling nurse, clearly oblivious to our situation, scoops up one of the blue-capped babies. He has a red, scrunched-up face and he's swaddled tightly, his curled fists up by his cheeks. I stare at him, trying to find something familiar, some hint of Sophie in his newborn features, but I can't. I could be looking at a stranger's baby, or even a doll. I feel nothing inside, even though I want to, and I feel that I should.

Andrew, however, is clearly having a different experience, judging by the rapt look on his face as he stares at the baby.

"He has my nose," he whispers.

I look at Baby Boy West. He has a little dot of a nose, a perfectly normal newborn nose, and not my husband's distinguished one, straight and sharp.

"Can we hold him?" Andrew asks.

The nurse, who has been smiling so benevolently at both of us, hesitates.

"Well, normally we have Mommy or Daddy around..." she begins, looking down the hallway as if said parents will materialize.

"My daughter died a short while ago from septic shock and my son-in-law is understandably still reeling from it," Andrew replies, his tone turning flat and hard. I don't think he's ever called Tom his son-in-law before, and he certainly hasn't cared whether he's reeling or not. "Please," Andrew says stiffly, a demand rather than a request, "may I hold my grandson?"

The nurse, startled and clearly apologetic, hands over the baby without a word.

I watch Andrew cradle this baby with an expertise I don't think he ever exhibited with Sophie. He wasn't so great with the bottle feeds or dirty diapers, and in any case, he was far too busy with work. When she was about four, he told me she'd finally become interesting. To be fair, though, he spent a lot of time with her after that.

But now? He supports Baby Boy West's tiny head, his hand cradling his skull with a tenderness that makes my eyes sting, although it doesn't take much to set me off right now. I am limp with emotional exhaustion, overwhelmed with all I have yet to absorb, and I am trying not to think about anything, even this baby, precious as he is.

"Diana." Andrew's voice is hoarse with emotion and full of wonder. "Look at him."

I take a step closer while the nurse looks on, sympathetic but also, I think, a little wary. Clearly we're the wild cards in this situation.

As I gaze down into this baby's face, I feel a flicker of... something. A stirring of remembrance, like an echo whispering through me, a longing I always found it so hard to trust. My arms begin to ache.

"Do you want to hold him?" Andrew asks, and I look at the nurse, as if for permission. She gives a little nod, granting it, and I take him from Andrew, my arms remembering instinctively how to hold a baby, one hand cradling his skull just as Andrew was, my other arm coming around his tiny, swaddled body as I bring him into my chest, a warm, sleepy bundle whose very presence in my arms causes all sorts of emotions to tumble through me.

I could be holding Sophie, I think, although I know that at

this stage one baby is much like another. Still... this is Sophie's son. She might never know him, but he's hers. It's hard to absorb that fact, to accept it, when I didn't even know she was pregnant. I never saw her cradle her bump or proudly show me a grainy ultrasound photo. Really, I think, this little boy could be anyone, could belong to anyone. How do I even know he's Sophie's?

I want my *daughter* back, I think, not this stranger's child. Tears blur my eyes, and I start to hand the baby back to the nurse, but Andrew intercepts me.

"Let me hold him one more time," he says, and wordlessly I pass the baby off.

Andrew gazes down at his little face, his own face suffused with both tenderness and grief. I take a few steps away, my head bowed as I struggle to contain the sorrow that sweeps over me.

"I'm very sorry for your loss," the nurse says quietly, and I can't bring myself to reply, so I just give a jerky nod. My heart is like a weight dragging me down. If I let myself think about Sophie for so much as a second, I know I will crumble into pieces, and I might never find a way to put myself together again.

"We should probably check on Tom," Andrew murmurs, and I lift my head, shocked that he is considering Tom's feelings... until I realize he isn't. His expression is bland, but there's a shrewd look in his eyes I recognize as he gives me a meaningful look.

The nurse steps forward. "Shall I put him back?" she asks, her tone cheerful but, I fear, pointed. Do all the nurses know that we were estranged from our daughter? Are they all on Tom's side, or am I being paranoid, because I feel my own guilt and regret so keenly?

We never should have arrived at this place, the villains in this tragedy.

It isn't until Andrew has let go of Baby Boy West and we are walking back down the hallway that I wonder why I'm thinking in terms of sides at all.

FOUR

Halfway down the hallway, Andrew takes hold of my arm and draws me toward the wall.

"We need to have a plan," he says in a low voice.

I take in his intent expression, his mouth set in determination, his fingers digging into my arm. "A *plan?*" I repeat. I feel like my mind is full of all the things I don't have the strength to think about, and there's too much to hold onto a single coherent thought, not that I even want to. "What do you mean, a plan?"

"*Diana.*" Andrew's fingers tighten on my arm. "Tom could walk out of here with our grandson *tonight*, and we might never see either of them ever again. Right now, he has that right, and there's *nothing* we can do about it."

I blink, absorbing that possibility, but it bounces off the blankness in my brain, so I end up just shaking my head. It's so hard to accept *any* of this—Sophie's death, my grandson's birth—because it's all so new and shocking. A few hours ago, I didn't know I even had a grandson. A few hours ago, I didn't know my daughter was dying. I'm not ready for us to make a *plan*. I don't even know what that means.

"He's not fit to be a father, much less a *single* father to our grandson," Andrew continues in a low hiss. "We have to make sure he doesn't disappear before we sue him for custody."

"*Custody?*" I repeat. I am still drawing blanks, and irritation flickers across my husband's face. He needs me to keep up, to be on board, but he's leaping ahead, and I do not have the mental or emotional energy to match his pace. "Andrew... we need some time to think about all this," I say. "*Sophie...*" My voice chokes. We'll have to plan her funeral, I realize. Will Tom even let us? How does any of this *work*, when a family is so hopelessly estranged? We have to find a way to work *with* him, not against him, but I can't see myself convincing Andrew of that. I'm not sure I can even convince myself.

"That baby is Sophie's son," he says in a low voice. "He's *our* grandson. I am not letting that *drug dealer* walk away with my own grandchild. Not if I can help it, and I *can*."

"You don't know that he'd do that—" I protest, and Andrew cuts me off, his voice sharp.

"What have the last eighteen months looked like?" he demands.

"But that was because of *us*," I argue feebly. "We were the ones who cut off contact first."

In truth, *Andrew* was, but I'm not brave enough to point that out to him in this moment. I don't usually stand up to Andrew, although I used to. When I was young and sure of myself, I argued with him about all sorts of things, sometimes just for the hell of it. We bounced off one another in a good way, sharpened each other's edges, but it's been a long time since I've felt we related to one another in that way. Right now, I don't have the strength, but for Sophie's sake as well as Tom's and their child's, I try.

"Tom might be willing to be reasonable," I say to my husband. "And considering his situation, he might want our help. If we go in their guns blazing about gaining custody, we might lose the chance of having a relationship with him *and* our grandchild."

Andrew frowns, like he hadn't thought of that, and I nearly sway on my feet. I'm so tired, and I cannot get my head around having sole custody of a newborn right now, and all that would entail. The bottle feeds, the sleepless nights, the crying and fussing, the *endlessness* of it, wondering if I'm getting any of it right. It was incredibly challenging the first time round, and I have never shaken the feeling that I failed, and never more so now. Can I really consider doing it again? Can Andrew?

In any case, there surely must be a few steps before we even *think* about taking that mammoth one.

"Let's talk to him," I urge Andrew. "See if we can... find a way to reconcile." Even if it's too late to reconcile with our daughter, it might not be too late to at least try with Tom.

"I don't want to *reconcile*," Andrew flashes back. "Diana, do you remember what he did? He was in prison for three years for dealing *cocaine*. He was *high* when he came to meet his new girlfriend's parents. He *stole* from us—"

"I know, I know..." Briefly I close my eyes against the sight of my husband's flushed and furious face, before opening them up and staring at him resolutely. "But it's been eighteen months, Andrew, and suing for custody could take months or even years. We'd have to find evidence of him being an unfit parent, which would be difficult, considering we have no idea what he's been doing for the last year and a half." My long-ago experience as a paralegal before I got married holds me in good stead now, and it gives me a flash of uncharacteristic courage. "We have to find a way to work with Tom for *right now*," I emphasize. "And we can decide whether we want or need to start a custody battle later."

Andrew's frown deepens; he knows I'm right, but it's clear he doesn't like it.

"Let's talk to him," I urge. "At least see where he is and

what he's thinking before we do anything else." Even if I am dreading that conversation. I have no idea what to say to the father of our grandson, the widower of our daughter.

Widower. It slams into me all over again, that Sophie is gone. When will it stop being a shock that leaves me breathless? How long does that take?

"Fine." Andrew lets go of my arm. "But I don't want to give him the opportunity to slip away from us again."

I think of Andrew standing on our front step, telling Tom in no uncertain terms that he was not welcome in our home ever again. I don't think that was much of an opportunity to *slip away*.

Tom is still standing by the nurses' station when we return, cradling a paper cup of coffee and looking exhausted. There are hollows in his cheeks and purple shadows under his eyes, and I see a look of wariness come over his face as he catches sight of us. He straightens his slumped shoulders, putting his cup down on the counter of the nurses' station.

"How is he?" he asks.

"How are *you*, Tom?" Andrew replies. He leans over and claps a hand on Tom's shoulder, making him stagger just a little. "You must be exhausted."

Tom is clearly startled by Andrew's change of tone, and it's no wonder. My husband has gone into genial mode, all confident charisma, his head cocked, his blue eyes so bright in his face.

He won me over this way, when I was just twenty-three years old, working as a paralegal in the city and living in the Bronx. We met at a weekend in the Hamptons, when my rich friend Taylor invited me along, even though I was broke. I accepted because it was a free vacation, but I can't say I enjoyed the weekend, even if I was eventually and reluctantly charmed by Andrew Lawrence, up-and-coming investment banker who knew the power of his charm and unleashed it relentlessly on me, day after day.

"I am tired," Tom admits cautiously. "It's been a hell of a couple of days." He pauses and Andrew removes his hand from his shoulder, putting it his pocket and rocking back on his heels.

"Are you heading home?" he asks. "Can we give you a ride?"

Tom glances at the nurses, and then between the two of us. "Umm... well, we need to decide what to do with... with Sophie," he says uncomfortably. He glances again at the nurses by their station; none of them are even trying to pretend not to eavesdrop on our conversation. "I can't afford a funeral," Tom states bluntly. "But they told me that the state can collect the body..."

I flinch, because I do not want to think of my daughter as *the body*, and I certainly don't want the state collecting her. Andrew clearly feels the same, because, for a second, his genial mask drops away, and he simply looks old and shaken.

"We can take care of all that," he finally says, after a short pause. "We had a great funeral director for my mother. Very sensitive, very thoughtful. I'll give him a call and make the arrangements." His tone does not leave room for discussion, but I don't think Tom is interested in arguing the point.

"Okay," Tom replies, and then adds uncertainly, "thank you." It's obvious he doesn't know how to deal with us, and the feeling is mutual. We are hostile strangers flung into this most painful and intimate situation, and it all feels impossible to navigate. Somehow we have to overcome the impasse of the past.

"And what about the baby?" Andrew asks. "When were you thinking of taking him home?"

For a second, Tom looks flummoxed, like he doesn't know what we're talking about. Has he even *thought* about his own child? I wonder. Were he and Sophie prepared? Had they bought baby clothes, a bassinet, a car seat?

"They said he can come home tomorrow or the day after that," Tom tells us. "Depending on how he's doing. I... I haven't thought..." He trails off, shaking his head, and I realize Andrew is right. This man, grieving and alone, is not prepared to take care of a newborn infant.

But are we?

Am I?

"Let us help you," Andrew suggests coaxingly. "I know we haven't had the easiest relationship before." Tom's eyes widen at this, and no wonder. We haven't had *any* relationship, and our one interaction was the domestic equivalent of a cage match. "But it's obviously very different now," Andrew continues in the same smooth, cajoling tone. "The truth is, we've always regretted the way we left things."

He lets that sentiment hang in the air for a few seconds, and I wonder if he is waiting for Tom to agree, maybe even apologize. But he doesn't. He simply remains silent, waiting for whatever else Andrew intends to say.

After another uncomfortable second's pause, Andrew resumes. "Why don't we give you a ride home, and then we can meet up in the morning? Have breakfast, discuss a way forward that works for everyone?" He raises his eyebrows in friendly but determined expectation. "This is a very difficult situation, and we need to work through it together."

Tom gazes between us, his expression blankly exhausted. Like me, I suspect he can't think past his grief. He certainly can't keep up with my husband's plans, which I know come from a place of grief as well, but right now they feel relentless.

"All right," Tom finally says with a little shrug. Then he adds, another afterthought, "Thanks." Considering the nature of our past interaction, gratitude doesn't come easily, and I can't really blame him.

It feels surreal to simply walk out of the hospital into a cool spring evening, leaving our daughter behind, but that's what we do after Andrew has made some calls to the funeral director. Not one of us talks in the elevator or while we wait for the valet to fetch the car. Andrew came in on the train, so we'll have to get his car from the Old Greenwich Station. I have the sense of having forgotten something important, like when I've gone on a trip and wondered if I remembered my toothbrush, my wallet, my phone.

In this case it's my *daughter*, and I have a painful jolt of surprised recollection. I wonder if the reality of her death will ever stop shocking me, a punch to the gut every time.

"Where to, Tom?" Andrew asks as he slides behind the wheel of my car. Whenever we're together, he drives, without any discussion; I'm grateful now, because I know I couldn't cope driving through the city as I am.

Tom mumbles an address in Baychester, in the Bronx, not far from where I once used to live and not the nicest of areas, either. When I think of the one-bedroom apartment we paid for, for Sophie, on the Upper East Side, with a doorman and in view of Central Park, it feels like a long way to fall.

Andrew puts the address into his phone, and we all remain silent as he starts driving up the West Side Highway. It's only a little after seven o'clock, just past dusk, but it feels like the middle of the night. I lean my head against the window and close my eyes against the blur of city lights.

I think of Sophie back at the hospital, lying motionless in that bed. Have they taken her from her room—and to where? The *morgue*? Has she been zipped up into a body bag? I picture a blank-faced nurse pulling the zip over her face and I scrunch my eyes tight, wanting to block out the awful image.

After a few minutes, I open my eyes. In the darkness of the car, I gauge Andrew's determinedly bland expression, his knuckles white on the steering wheel. In the backseat, Tom is staring out the window, his head turned so I can't see his face. If Sophie were here, I think, she'd have her arm looped through

Tom's as she scooted forward, her head hanging over the back of the seat, to talk to us in the front. She could be such a chatterbox, I think with a pang of bittersweet nostalgia. She'd talk my ear off when I drove her to tennis lessons, a constantly running monologue about school, friends, clothes, anything.

It was only later that I realized her chatter was a coping mechanism, rather than the lighthearted banter of a girl without a care in the world. The real Sophie was beset by anxiety over so many things—her weight, her grades, her tennis ability, her popularity in school, whether boys liked her, whether we did.

When she was eighteen, just after getting rejected from Yale, she had what Andrew calls a *blip*, and I consider a mental breakdown. She spent six weeks in a high-end facility for girls with eating disorders and other mental health issues. During that whole time we were only allowed to visit her once, a painful hour sitting on a sunny terrace with nothing to say when there was so much that I wanted to.

Sometimes I wonder if our alienation from our daughter started then and there, or maybe even before, rather than five years later, with the arrival of Tom. Instead of bringing her into the bosom of our family, caring for her ourselves in her weakest moment, we farmed her out to strangers who, we found out later, had been telling her how toxic parents could be. At least, according to Sophie, they did.

You know a lot of issues stem from my childhood? I didn't realize it before I had therapy, but all this performance-based parenting... it's toxic, you know? You *are*.

She flung those words at us the first Thanksgiving she was at college. I'd been so excited to have her come home, had cleaned the house top to bottom, fresh flowers in every room, baking every treat and delicacy she'd ever even hinted at liking. Her words felt like a slap in the face of everything I'd ever done or even been.

Of course, I knew teenagers say unkind and even cruel

things, and that any sensible parent doesn't take such reckless words to heart. I also knew there was, as there so often is, a grain of truth to her words, even if I didn't want there to be. Yes, we had always wanted Sophie to do well. Andrew would have loved for her to go to Yale, and we were both thrilled with her tennis achievements, made sure she knew we were proud of her. But was our love dependent on those things? No, of course not. It certainly wasn't for me, and I don't think it was for Andrew, either.

But did Sophie believe that? It seemed as if she didn't. And now it's too late to fix it.

The car slows down, and I realize we've pulled up to a dilapidated and anonymous-looking brown brick building. There's trash blowing around the uncut grass out front, and when Tom opens his door, I hear traffic from 95 roar past. Has my daughter really lived here for the last year and a half?

"Why don't we pick you up tomorrow, around nine?" Andrew suggests, as if we are all friends and he's not horrified by where our daughter has been living. "Then we can have breakfast and talk, before heading over to the hospital."

Tom stares at him wordlessly before nodding, and then he closes the car door and walks toward the apartment building without saying goodbye.

We watch him go, swallowed up by the darkness, the only sound the rumble of traffic on the highway we can still hear even with the car doors closed.

When Tom is finally inside, Andrew reverses and starts back down the street, his face determined once more. "I'll call Ken tomorrow," he says, mentioning our lawyer.

"About custody?" I ask. "Don't you think we should talk to Tom first?"

"I just want to know our options. It's always good to be prepared."

I choose not to reply. I am thinking about Sophie and the

last time I saw her before that awful evening with Tom. She'd come home for the weekend and I was standing at the kitchen island, slicing red peppers for dinner and she was on a stool, snagging the odd pepper to munch on, which I pretended to mind even though I didn't. It was a game we'd often played; she always knew I was pleased she was eating, but if I'd acted like I was, it would have annoyed her. We both participated in the charade, for our mutual benefit.

I suspect a lot of life is like that. Maybe we should have been that way about Tom, even though it felt impossible at the time. If we'd kept the door open even just a crack, perhaps we could have avoided this outcome—even if she'd stayed with Tom, even if she'd gotten pregnant... if we'd been in touch and involved, maybe we could have influenced things, made sure she had better care...

It's torturous thinking this way, but I can't keep myself from doing it.

In any case, that weekend, the one before everything went wrong, wasn't entirely unsullied itself. Sophie told me about Tom, and the alarm bells had already started ringing.

"I just don't want you to judge him," she'd said then, her expression both tense and earnest. "Because of how he looks or what he's been through, because that's not who he is."

"I try not to judge anyone," I'd replied, although I was already feeling deeply apprehensive. What parent wants to hear that kind of caveat about their daughter's new boyfriend?

"He's been through some really hard times," Sophie continued, "and people have let him down in so many ways. His life's been really unfair, but he's the most amazing artist. I met him at a gallery showing in Brooklyn. He does these *incredible* ink drawings."

"Oh?" I'd tried to smile, although everything she was saying was making me feel nervous. Sophie had already had several damaging relationships. I didn't want to watch her embark on another. "Can you show me one?" I asked.

"Let's see..." Sophie reached for her phone and started to scroll. "Now, don't judge," she told me severely, before handing me the phone.

I glanced down at a black and white ink drawing of a butterfly with its tattered, blood-spattered wings outstretched in front of a gaping-mouthed skull. It was well-drawn but also disturbing, and not the kind of art I'd ever get excited about.

"It looks like the design for a tattoo," I remarked at last, because it was the only thing I could think of to say that wouldn't somehow be seen as critical.

Sophie beamed at me. "It is!" she exclaimed, clearly pleased. "He designs his own tattoos."

That little nugget of information did not make me feel much better.

I didn't tell Andrew about our conversation, although in retrospect maybe I should have warned him. Maybe then he would have been more prepared for meeting Tom in the flesh, with his tattoos and his buzz cut and his drug-induced state. If I had, maybe he might not have reacted so dramatically.

"You've not even given him a chance!" Sophie accused me that night, cornering me in the kitchen when I went to collect the tray of drinks and nibbles. "Just because he doesn't *look* the way you want him to. Because he doesn't have a trust fund and an Ivy League degree like all the other jerks you've tried to set me up with."

That didn't feel fair, since I didn't think we'd tried to set her up with anyone, although I suppose we'd introduced her to various young men we liked the look of. "We're trying, Sophie," I told her calmly. I'd felt as if I were walking a tightrope of expectations, balancing my husband's alarm and anger with my daughter's desperate desire to be accepted and loved, along with her boyfriend. Of course I was going to fall off. "But I have to ask... is he... *on* something?" I'd queried tentatively. "I'm just concerned, Sophie. For you."

Sophie had glowered at me, her hands on her hips. "All right, he might have smoked a *little* bit of weed before coming here, but only because he was nervous. But it's *legal*, Mom, and he's been out of prison for over a year. Smoking weed is no big deal these days."

Another nugget of information that did not help. Out of prison for over a year was hardly a ringing endorsement, and in any case, the fact that he was high right then didn't help.

A sigh escapes me now. If I could go back and do it all again differently, would I? The trouble is, I don't even know. Back then, despite how angry Andrew seemed, we were both just *afraid*. We were trying to do the best for our daughter, by protecting her not just from her ex-con drug-dealing boyfriend, but from herself. We'd seen how Sophie could get into toxic relationships—not just with *us,* at least according to her, but with friends, with boyfriends, with everyone. She was a desperate people-pleaser, to her own detriment, and we'd had to step in before, for her own sake.

The college roommate who stole her clothes. The boyfriend who cheated on her. The friends who always made sure she paid for everyone when they went out and then talked about her behind her back. Sometimes stepping in was just comforting her when it all went wrong, and at other times, it was taking a more proactive role, like when her tennis coach told her to lose ten pounds and Andrew had him fired.

I think we both thought Sophie would drop Tom when she realized what was at stake. It was a tough-love decision that blew up in our faces, and while I know I would have chosen a more softly-softly approach, I didn't really begrudge Andrew his hardline stance. At the time, Tom's behavior seemed to warrant it.

But if I'd known it would lead to this... if it indeed *did* lead to this. Can I really draw a direct line from point A to point B? If we'd been able to reconcile with Sophie, to figure out a way forward... maybe she still would have died.

There's no point in wondering about the what-ifs, but it's so hard not to.

Andrew drives to the station to pick up his car, and I slip behind the wheel. It feels both a relief and a terrible loneliness to be by myself, after the events of the day. I follow Andrew's car back home, trying to focus on only the mechanics. Foot on the gas. Turn signal. Turn left.

Back at home, Andrew pulls the car into the garage and walks into the house without waiting for me, which doesn't surprise me but still hurts. I park my own car and then follow him in, not bothering to turn on any lights, so the house yawns, a vast darkness in every direction that I drift through, feeling like a ghost in a stranger's home.

Our housekeeper Carmen has left something in the oven for supper, with a Post-it note stuck to the counter. I turn the oven off without even checking what's inside, because I know I can't manage so much as a bite.

I wander through the darkened downstairs rooms, my gaze flicking from photo to photo—the three of us sandy on the beach in Montauk when Sophie was two, her hair a golden, curly halo about her tanned face; at her first piano recital, beaming proudly at six, a space between her teeth and her blue eyes shining; the oil painting we had done of her for her sixteenth birthday, over the dining-room fireplace, looking both elegant and uncertain.

She looks lovely in her debutante's dress, her hands folded sedately in her lap, her expression, I fear, a little resigned. I had to ask the portrait artist not to make her so thin.

Her graduation, the three of us smiling stiffly for the camera; Sophie had just tossed at Andrew that she knew he wished we were at Yale, and he'd snapped something back while I'd retreated into myself, as absent from that moment as I had been from much of Sophie's college years, after that first Thanksgiving.

I thought I'd get myself back once she was safely settled, but instead, numb from the anguish of walking with her through all the trauma of her eating disorder and ensuing anger, I'd shut down emotionally for far longer than I should have. I wish I'd been stronger, but sometimes you just can't be.

A sigh escapes me, long and low and weary. Every parent's history is littered with mistakes; it is, I suspect, the nature of such an intense and important relationship. I just wish I didn't feel them all so deeply now, each one carved into my soul, scars that never heal.

I find Andrew in his study, slumped in a chair, a tumbler of Scotch next to him, the photo album of Sophie's school years opened on the coffee table in front. I glimpse a picture of her on Father-Daughter Day in third grade; they are both beaming.

I stand there for a moment, and neither of us speaks. I know Andrew is grieving as much as I am, and that he just shows it differently—with action and anger, determination and focus, whereas I remain mired in the swamp of sorrow and regret. I *know* that, I've lived it, but it still makes it hard to bridge the chasm that has yawned between us, seeming to grow wider with every passing year as he buries himself in work and I feel the weight of my failures.

I try to think of something to say, some sort of overture that acknowledges we are both grieving, but I can't think what it could be.

"She always loved you," I finally say, helplessly, and Andrew doesn't reply as he reaches for his drink and takes a sip.

After another moment, I turn away and then head up to bed, by myself.

FIVE

By eight o'clock the next morning, we are in the car, heading back toward the Bronx.

Andrew has already spoken to our lawyer, who referred us to Claire, a colleague in family law. She's on the speakerphone now, taking us briskly through our options as the bright green trees that line the Hutchinson River Parkway flash past. It's a beautiful spring day, warmer than yesterday, the kind that promises so much, but I feel utterly leaden inside.

I resisted taking something to help me sleep last night, knowing I needed to be sharp today, and the result was I barely slept at all and now I feel gritty-eyed and aching, my limbs heavy with fatigue. When I gazed at my reflection this morning, I looked far closer to sixty than fifty, even though I'm only fifty-two. My eyes, a darker shade of blue than Sophie's, look tired, and my hair, also darker than my daughter's, has faded from a chestnut brown to a dishwater gray. As a small act of defiance, I've refused to color my hair or engage in any "medical aesthetics," but staring at the sight of my deeply lined face and silver-streaked hair this morning, I wonder if I should have.

All the women of my acquaintance keep meticulous care of

themselves, with regular Botox injections, hair coloring, waxing, and who even knows what else. They look like aging Barbie dolls, perfectly preserved but still invariably getting older, because no amount of injectables can keep you looking like a nubile twenty-two-year-old.

I didn't get on that relentless treadmill because I knew I wouldn't be able to keep it up, and also because I wanted to be different. I've conformed to Andrew's way of life in so many ways, but the care of my own body felt like one area I shouldn't have to change. Not that Andrew ever asked me to; he's always been accepting of my gray hair and lined face.

But, like Sophie, I have felt the weight of his expectation, or maybe it was just my own. We're always hardest on ourselves—something I've told Sophie but which she never seemed to believe, and I'm not sure I've ever believed it, either.

Now I do my best to tune into the lawyer's sharp, matter-of-fact tone. "It's not unheard of, of course, for grandparents to successfully sue for custody, but it's certainly an uphill battle," she states. "In order to have an involuntary termination of parental rights, you'd have to prove the biological father's general unfitness to be a parent—either through neglect, abuse, addiction, mental incapacity... there are a number of ways."

"I think we can prove just about all those," Andrew interjects, sounding almost jocular, but the lawyer continues without acknowledging his remark.

"To prove that," she says, "you have to amass a *considerable* amount of evidence, documenting a history of abuse, addiction, or whatever it is you've deemed as cause for a custody suit. And, I should warn you, these cases are weighted heavily toward the parents, understandably." She barely pauses to take a breath before continuing, "However, there could be another way forward that might be more amenable to both parties, and far more straightforward, which is a voluntary custody agreement, where the biological father relinquishes some or all parental rights to the child. If you went in this direction, the court would be examining the case to make sure there were no issues of coercion, but you could potentially share custody—"

"I do not," Andrew states flatly, "want to *share* custody."

"Andrew..." I murmur in protest, shooting him a worried look. I thought we'd agreed yesterday to talk to Tom first, figure out what he wants and is willing to do, or not do, before we started a custody battle.

"My daughter's husband spent *three years* in prison for dealing cocaine," Andrew tells the lawyer, his voice turning hard. "When we met him for the first time, he was high on cannabis. He also stole an item from our property and was violent with me when we asked him to leave our home. I think that covers just about all the elements you mentioned in terms of deeming unfitness as a parent, don't you?"

Claire is silent for a second before she gives a short, sharp sigh and says, "Not necessarily. You're talking about a single occurrence. Any judge will want to see a *pattern* of behavior, with evidence of repeated history of addiction or physical or emotional abuse, before even considering granting custody to grandparents."

Andrew's breath hisses between his teeth. "Considering our grandson is only a few days old, we don't have that history," he tells her with exaggerated patience. "And we certainly don't want to start one, by allowing our son-in-law unfettered access to our grandchild, without knowing what he might do, what he is capable of."

Another brief silence ensues, and Andrew flexes his hands on the steering wheel, a deep line bisecting his forehead. I think he wanted this to be a lot simpler than it's going to be.

"That's understandable," Claire finally says, "but custody cannot be granted based on merely potential scenarios. I think, at this point, the best chance you have is working with your son-in-law to come to a mutual agreement regarding custody of this infant. You might be surprised at how much he is willing to negotiate and even accede, considering he's a single father who, according to your description, is not particularly well-resourced."

"Thank you for your time," Andrew says through gritted teeth, and ends the call.

I turn to look out the window. I am not surprised by this outcome, and I basically said as much as the lawyer just did last night, but I also know that when Andrew wants something, he usually gets it. It's why he's so successful in business. It's how he married me.

We met that weekend in the Hamptons, when I was freeloading off my friend Taylor, sleeping in the second bed in her room in a house share where everyone else was swimming in money and privilege. They used to play roulette with their credit cards for who would pay for a dinner out, with the bill often brushing four figures, thanks to the flowing wine and sixty-dollar steaks. I refused to participate, since I invariably had the cheapest thing on the menu, and I definitely did not have the money to pay for an expensive dinner for eight people. It earned me the nickname Cheapskate, laughingly said, but I'm pretty sure they all meant it. None of them could understand just how poor I, a normal middle-class girl with a normal, middle-class job, was.

Andrew was fascinated with me. I was pretty back then, in a wholesome way—deep brown hair, dark blue eyes, an athletic figure. I played a good game of tennis, but I didn't care about it the way everybody else did. Their Lilly Pulitzer dresses and Gucci sunglasses didn't impress me, either; back then, I didn't even recognize the brands.

The first time Andrew asked me out, I said no, and I think that whetted his interest far more than a simpering acquiescence would have. I was so much more confident at that age, so much surer of myself and my place in the world. I could simply say no to someone like Andrew, amused by his determination, unbothered by it. Eventually, it became a way to flirt; his invitations more dramatic, my refusals more laughing, with both of us silently acknowledging the inevitable endgame.

When I finally said yes, he surprised me by not taking me to one of the expensive restaurants we all went to, as a matter of course; instead we had a picnic on the beach, with sand getting to the tub of hummus and our plastic cups of wine tipping over, much to Andrew's chagrin. I was charmed, not by his good looks and money, but by the earnestness and vulnerability I sensed underneath. They were far more appealing to me, and they were what had me agreeing to a second, and then a third date.

Twenty-seven years later, I still don't know if I'd been deluding myself as to both qualities.

"I suppose we'll just have to see what Tom's thinking," Andrew finally says, his jaw still set. "He might not be ready for this at all. Maybe it'll be a relief, if we take this baby off his hands." He glances at me. "This pregnancy surely couldn't have been planned."

"We can't know that," I protest quietly.

It took me years to get pregnant with Sophie. Maybe Sophie had been worried that she'd have similar problems, so they'd started trying early. I wish I could have talked to her about it, shared my experiences. I'd have bought her prenatal vitamins, added folic acid to anything I'd made her. I would have hugged her when the pregnancy test came up with only one mocking line month after month, just as it did for me. And I would have warned her about how hard it can be after the beloved baby is born, when you've gotten everything you thought you ever wanted.

"It would have been insanity, to try for a baby in their situation," Andrew declares flatly. "Did you see where they were living? We don't know if Tom is even working."

"We don't know that he isn't," I reply. When we first met him, Sophie told us Tom was interested in art and worked in construction. Is there any reason to think he's stopped either? But if he *is* working, I wonder, how will he take care of his son? I don't like the prospect of my grandson in full-time daycare, and I'm not sure Tom could even afford it.

And what about his own parents? I don't recall Sophie saying anything about them, but that doesn't mean they aren't around. There could be another set of anxious grandparents waiting in the wings, hoping for access, battling us for visitation rights. The thought makes me feel uneasy. There's so much about this situation, about *Tom*, that we simply don't know.

"Let's talk to him," I say again, wearily now. "And take it from there."

"Yes, but we need a *plan*, Diana," Andrew replies, an edge entering his voice. "We can't just *wing* this. If we want custody of this baby—"

"But do we?" I burst out.

Andrew falls silent in a way that feels censorious as well as disappointed. I have prodded the elephant in the room, in our lives, of my own failure as a mother.

"I just mean," I try to explain, already backtracking, "Tom should have *some* rights, surely, as the father? And as for *raising* a baby, Andrew..." I can't make myself remind him, not that he needs it. We both know—have always known—how little I was able to cope after Sophie's birth. How for weeks, and even months, after I failed in her care. It's something we never talk about but which can feel like the subtext to every single conversation. "You're fifty-five," I point out. "I'm fifty-two. We're not as young as we were..."

"This is Sophie's *son*," he replies flatly, and I don't miss the emphasis. I'd always suspected Andrew had been hoping for a boy, and now maybe I know.

I fall silent, accepting the reality that Andrew is not going to give up on this baby. And do I even mean what I say? This little boy is my last link to my daughter. Of course I want to be involved in his life. I just don't want to make the same mothering mistakes all over again... and experience the same kind of heartache. I don't want to fail this baby the way I once failed Sophie. But maybe, I tell myself, not truly believing it, this can be a redemption. If I can be strong enough this time, even if I wasn't before.

Andrew parks the car in front of Tom's building and we both walk over to the door. Tom buzzes us through without saying anything, and we head inside. The floor of the lobby is littered with old flyers for restaurants and drycleaners, and there is a forgotten feel about this whole place that makes me feel sad, to think of Sophie living here. I can't imagine her climbing these stairs, living in these small, airless rooms, when she was used to so much more. So much *better*.

After a few minutes, Tom comes downstairs, freshly showered and smelling of soap. His buzzcut puts the bones of his face into sharp relief, reminding me of a skull, like the one he drew with that torn butterfly, and his tattoos look darkly inked against his pale skin. I try to imagine him looking different—without the tattoos, his blond hair grown out, wearing a Polo shirt and khakis instead of a tight white t-shirt and ripped jeans. Looking more like someone from my world, from Sophie's world. Someone we could, potentially, fit into our lives.

"Hey," Tom says in that low, gravelly voice that still jolts me with its unfamiliarity.

"Hey, Tom." Andrew is back to being genial. "Have you eaten? Why don't we head out to breakfast? There's a pretty good diner near the hospital."

Tom shrugs. "Sure, okay."

And that's all the conversation we have before getting back into the car and heading to the West Side.

It isn't until we're seated in a deep vinyl booth with cups of steaming coffee and large laminated menus in front of us that Andrew speaks again. He laces his hands on the table in front of him as he leans forward.

"This is so hard for all of us," Andrew begins, dropping his voice in a confidential and sympathetic manner. "And especially for you, of course, with a baby to consider. What I want you to know, Tom, is that we really would like to let bygones be bygones." He manages a rueful smile that makes me tense. "We didn't get off to a good start, we can all acknowledge that, but we want to be helpful now. We want to support you, and of course our grandson, whatever that looks like. However we can." He pauses to let Tom absorb the import of those words, their unfathomable generosity.

Tom stares at him without saying anything, and then he picks up his coffee mug and takes a considering sip. I glance at Andrew, noticing the flash of annoyance in his blue eyes at Tom's silence, which doesn't feel entirely friendly, and certainly isn't the stammering gratitude Andrew was undoubtedly hoping for. I'm not sure what I was hoping for, but I know I feel uneasy.

"What are your thoughts?" Andrew finally asks, holding onto his kindly tone, if only just. "I know these are early days, but how do you see us all going forward, especially in terms of our... your son?" He corrects himself quickly, smile still in place.

Tom lowers his mug. "I haven't really thought about it," he says after a moment. "With everything happening so fast, I haven't been able to..."

"Well, that's understandable," Andrew murmurs. He swallows, looking down at his laced fingers. "If Sophie had lived..." For a second, with his gaze still lowered, his throat works, and he can't speak, and I realize he's struggling not to cry. My Andrew, always so stoic, brought to near weeping over our daughter.

I reach over and touch his hand, barely brushing my fingers

against his. Andrew lifts his head and gives me a watery smile, and I try to smile back, but I'm too close to tears myself.

If Sophie had lived... if only, if only. We are united in our grief, at least, if not much else.

"Was she planning to stay home with the baby?" Andrew asks, a hoarseness to his voice. "I don't actually know what you do for work—"

"I was in construction, but I got laid off a couple of weeks ago."

Andrew and I are both silent, absorbing this news, trying to figure out what it might mean.

"And our lease is up at the end of this month," Tom continues. His tone is matter-of-fact but with, I fear, a slight hint of aggression, and I wonder if he thinks we owe him something. Then I wonder if we do. "We were going to have to move out," he explains, "but we didn't have a place lined up yet, and you know, what with the money for a deposit, I don't know if we could have swung it, especially with the baby..." He trails off, reaching for his coffee mug again as he leans back against the booth. "So, yeah, you could help us out." He takes a sip of coffee and then lowers the cup, meeting our gaze directly in a way that feels like a challenge; his eyes look very bright, more golden than brown, and the blond stubble glints on his jaw. Everything about him feels strange and also a little menacing, but I don't know if that's just my unease.

"I was thinking," Tom tells us, his chin jutting upward a little, "that maybe the baby and I could come and live with you. Just for a little while, until I get back on my feet, figure something out. You know." There is a hint of defiance in his eyes, as well as vulnerability. I can't tell if he wants something from us, or he's reluctant to ask for help. Maybe it's both, because all I know is this situation feels hopelessly complicated, but maybe it doesn't have to be. If Tom lives with us, we can be closer to our grandson.

But we'll also be closer to Tom.

I don't know if that's what *I* want, but I'm almost positive it's not what my husband does.

"How does that sound?" Tom asks, and I wonder if we really have any choice in the matter.

SIX

The next day, I am folding tiny blue onesies into the drawer of Sophie's old nursery dresser.

Tom's suggestion that he move in with us certainly wasn't what either Andrew or I were expecting, but in retrospect I realized, reluctantly, that it made a terrible kind of sense. There was no reason for us to be going back and forth to the Bronx day after day to help out with the baby, and we had plenty of room, even if we didn't welcome the idea of our son-in-law, such as he was, living with us.

The whole thing made Andrew furious.

"He knows he has us over a barrel," he fumed on the drive back home. We'd had breakfast, been to the hospital, and arranged to pick up Baby Boy West the next morning, before moving both Tom and him here. "He knows we want access to our grandchild, so we have to accept anything, including having him freeloading off us."

"We're helping him out," I protested. "It doesn't have to be anything more than that."

"Well, I'm locking up the silver," Andrew informed me darkly. "And my Scotch."

I didn't bother to reply to that, because I couldn't help but feel it was probably wise.

After Tom had made his suggestion, and we'd both been stunned silent for a few seconds, neither of us having anticipated this turn of events, his eyebrows had lifted, his mouth twisting as he'd said, "Or maybe you just want my kid to come and live with you? And not me? Is that what you'd prefer?"

A silence, twanging with tension, had stretched between us while we'd just stared, trying to figure out the best way to respond.

"If—if you need a place to stay," I'd finally stammered, "then of—of course we'd be happy for both of you to be with us." It was only after the words were out of my mouth, that I realized how grudging I'd sounded—but could he really blame me? We didn't know him, and what we did know had been a cause for serious alarm. But that had been eighteen months ago.

Tom's mouth had curved into a cool smile in return. "Thanks," he'd said, and he'd lifted his coffee mug in what I'd feared was a mocking toast.

Now, as I fold the baby clothes we've bought, I wonder just what the future will look like, and more importantly, how it will feel. I gave Tom the guest room next to Sophie's old nursery; we didn't have time to redecorate, but the cream walls and Noah's Ark theme work for a boy, I think. The rooms share a bathroom and they're two doors down the hall from us, which feels a little too cozy, but the only other option was the in-law suite downstairs off the kitchen, and that felt too far away.

I don't want Tom prowling around our downstairs, looking for the silver or the Scotch or anything else, not that I really think he will. At least, I certainly hope he won't. Still, it's uncomfortable enough having him here at all, although I'm trying to tell myself that there are bound to be some growing pains as we all get used to one another. The important thing is to have the right attitude, one of acceptance and understanding and patience.

Right now, those feel like nothing more than words. I'm trying not to feel nervous or even scared, but the truth is, I'm both. I wonder if we're making a big mistake... but what choice do we have, when it comes to our grandson?

I hear footsteps down the hall, and then Andrew appears in the doorway. He took the day off work for this, which is a big deal for him. I can count the number of days he has taken off for anything other than life-or-death scenarios on one hand. Even after Sophie was born, he was back at his desk the next day. To be fair, he'd hired a night nurse to help out, and offered a nanny, as well. It wasn't as if he'd left me alone, even if I'd felt like he had.

"Are you almost ready?" he asks, before looking around at the nursery that I had Carmen clean from top to bottom yesterday afternoon. "I don't think I've been here in years."

"No, nor have I." When Sophie was three, we moved her to a bigger bedroom. Sometimes, in the following years, I'd come in here and sit in the glider, torturing myself with what-ifs, but at some point I closed the door on it at all and pretended this room didn't exist, which felt far easier.

We are both silent, acknowledging the weight of the years, or maybe just the reality of this room and all its expectations and disappointment. Then Andrew clears his throat, the precursor to him making an announcement.

"We'll need to meet with the funeral director today or tomorrow," he says, leaning against the doorframe. "I thought we could have the funeral at Christ Church. I talked to Father Matthew, and he's willing to have it there."

"All right." Christ Church where was his mother's funeral was, seven years ago, a big, splashy affair, Greenwich socialite and matriarch that she was. Even then, Andrew was back at work the day after, but then, as he said, why shouldn't he be? It wasn't as if there had been anything else to do.

"I thought we might as well do the same hymns and readings," he continues. "Make it easier on ourselves."

I frown at that. "Won't people remember?" Cut-and-paste doesn't feel like the right attitude for our daughter's funeral. "Maybe we could pick a song Sophie liked?" I add, a catch to my voice at the thought. I already know, whatever it is, will reduce me to tears right there in the church, and that will horrify my husband, who has always been much more stoical than me, in so many ways.

"A hymn?" he asks skeptically. "Did Sophie know any?"

We have not been the most dedicated of churchgoers, even though Andrew's mother did the flowers for Christ Church for over thirty years.

"It doesn't have to be a hymn," I say. "Maybe just a song?"

"A pop song or something?" Andrew frowns. "In church? I don't know..."

"Maybe something meaningful, like 'Scarlet Ribbons'?" I suggest. It's an old-fashioned ballad that Andrew used to sing to Sophie when she was little, her standing on his feet as they shuffled around the room.

To my surprise, my husband's face suddenly crumples. He puts his hands up to cover it as his shoulders start to shake.

"Oh, Andrew..." I murmur, brought near to tears myself. I put down the onesie I was folding and go to put my arms around him. For a second, we simply stand there as he weeps and I blink back tears that slip down my cheeks anyway. Sometimes I forget that the earnestness and vulnerability I glimpsed in my husband on that first date really are there. It's just that he hides them so very well.

"*Enough.*" He draws a shuddering breath as he steps out of my embrace. "We need to go," he adds, averting his face from me as he swipes at his cheeks. I know we'll both pretend this moment never happened—and also that I'll need to keep reminding myself that it did.

Andrew puts the car seat we bought yesterday into the back and then we head toward Manhattan. It all still feels so surreal—thinking about funerals and births, the loss of one child and the gaining of another. And *Tom*... how is Tom going to fit into all this?

It was hard enough, navigating the relationship between Andrew and Sophie during her high school years, when things were so tense between them. He was baffled by her, and she was hurt by his seeming disappointment.

But this... it feels impossibly harder. I don't even know if I want to defend Tom against Andrew, or if it will come to that. I don't know him well enough to like or trust him, but he's in our lives and we need to make the best of it... not just for our sakes, or his, or even this baby's, but for *Sophie's*. She chose this man. She married him and had a baby with him. I can't change the past, but I can try to shape the future... the future my daughter should have had, if only she'd survived.

We've arranged to meet Tom at the hospital, and he's waiting up in the maternity ward when we are buzzed in. Someone has clearly just had a baby, because there is a crowd of people in the room next to the nursery, laughing and exclaiming, pink balloons bobbing in the doorway. *It's a Girl*, reads one in silver glitter. It's almost enough to set me off, and I draw a quick breath to steady my nerves. The future. I need to focus on the future.

"Hi, Tom," I say in as friendly a voice as I can muster. He still seems tired, hollowed like a husk, but I'm pretty sure I look similar. This morning I couldn't rouse myself to put on any makeup, even though I saw in the mirror how gaunt and pale I was. Andrew, too, doesn't look great—bloodshot eyes, his jawline sagging. We are all still bowed under the weight of our shared grief.

"I've just been signing the paperwork," Tom tells us. "They'll be back in a minute, and then we can get him and go." He gives us a crooked, uncertain smile, although his eyes still droop with sadness. "I guess he needs a name."

"Have you thought about that?" I ask, and he shrugs, running a hand over his bristly hair.

"Honestly, I don't know. Sophie liked the name Henry..." He trails off as Andrew makes some small noise. Henry was his father's name and is his own middle name.

"I like Henry," I say with a smile. "And if Sophie did..."

Tom doesn't reply, and I decide to leave it there.

A few minutes later, a nurse is wheeling the bassinet down the corridor, giving us all a compassionate smile. I suppose every nurse here knows Sophie is dead. Their sympathy feels suffocating, making it hard for me to breathe. I focus on the baby in the bassinet, swaddled tightly with a cap on his head and scratch mitts on his little fists so he is no more than a reddened, scrunched-up face.

Henry, my grandson, I say to myself, and the words feel like marbles in my mouth. They don't fit; they don't make sense.

"I brought a car seat," Tom says, and I see a brand-new one, resting at his feet. We'd assumed he wouldn't have thought of that, or have the money to buy one, and I make a mental note to put the one currently in the back of our car in the trunk before he can see it, and realize we'd underestimated him.

Andrew folds his arms across his chest, widening his stance as Tom gently scoops the baby from the bassinet. The nurse guides his hand to cradle the tiny skull, and he lets out a shaky laugh, flashing us a shamefaced look.

"I haven't actually held him before," he admits, and Andrew draws a sharp breath, and then lets it out without saying anything.

I watch as Tom draws the baby to his chest, one hand cradling his head, the other splayed across his back, so the letters tattooed across his knuckles are in bold relief. I read them again. *Hold Fast.* I wonder what it's meant to mean, and when he had it done.

Andrew notices the tattoos, too, and his eyes narrow. None of this is going to be easy.

"Do you need help with the car seat?" the nurse asks, and Tom flashes her a wry smile.

"Yeah, I might," he admits, and with an answering smile—Tom is clearly a hit with the nurses—she takes the baby from him and puts him in the seat, then shows him how all the buckles and straps fit together. I would have offered to help myself, but I'm not sure how these fancy new car seats work, and the last thing I want is to fumble with anything right now.

I watch Tom buckle the strap across the baby's chest, a look of intense focus on his face, and I feel a pressure in my chest. No matter what Andrew or I want, and in the privacy of my own mind I can admit I'm not sure I even know what that is, Tom is this baby's father. He has rights.

Finished, he straightens, and then, amazingly, it's time to go. Tom holds the car seat by the handle as we head downstairs, walking carefully, his arm out at an angle. "If we could swing by my place on the way back," he says when we're in the elevator, "that would be great. I've got some stuff."

"Of course," I murmur. Last night, Andrew and I discussed the details of Tom living with us—would he get a job, should he pay rent, who is actually going to be the one caring for this baby? The last question felt the most fraught.

"We can get a nanny," Andrew told me. "Like we did before."

When Sophie was three months old, Andrew employed a hatched-faced woman called Teresa as our nanny. I was terrified of her, tiptoeing around her, deferring to her stern judgment in every possible way, feeling even less of a mother than I already had.

She stayed for six endless months before Andrew and I agreed I could cope on my own. And I *did,* but the trouble was, it all felt far too late.

In any case, now we are both conscious of how little power or authority we truly have in this situation, and also how little knowledge. Neither of us knows Tom at all, and the thought of letting an ex-con former drug-dealer into our home is more than a little alarming—something I voiced to Andrew, who frowned in response.

"If you don't feel safe, we could hire someone, maybe," he said. "Someone to keep an eye on things..."

The thought seemed over-the-top, considering our interactions with Tom so far had not been more than an average amount of fraught, and in any case, I didn't want another person looking over everything I did. "No, I don't think that's necessary," I replied quickly.

"I suppose you have Carmen in the house, at least," Andrew offered, as if our housekeeper will defend my life armed with a toilet brush and a bottle of cleaning spray. Somehow, even if pressed, I didn't think she would—not that it would ever come to that.

"I'm not *afraid* of him," I said, not entirely truthfully. "I just wish we knew him better."

"I don't," Andrew answered flatly. I knew he saw Tom as only a means to an end—getting custody of our grandson. "I'll work from home for the next week," he decided. "Keep an eye on things."

"Well, be discreet about it," I suggested. The lawyer, Claire, had reminded us when we spoke to her again yesterday afternoon that we have to make sure we don't do or say anything that could make us appear coercive, which is hard when every single question or offhand remark feels like it could be taken that way.

I get to the car first, but not in time to remove the car seat. Tom notices it, and I try for a light laugh. "We weren't sure if you would bring one," I explain, "but it's good to have two, because then we can keep one in each of our cars."

"How many cars do you have?" he asks as I wrestle the car seat from its buckle and into the trunk. I pretend I don't hear his question, because there seems no good way to answer it when we have four.

The awkwardness doesn't ease on the way to Tom's apartment, or when he goes up to collect his stuff, having refused Andrew's offer of help.

Alone in the car, Andrew lets out a shaky breath as he passes a hand across his face.

"Good Lord, this is difficult," he says, before dropping his hand and pressing his lips together. "I think we should ask him for a voluntary custody agreement sooner rather than later. I don't think it's good for either of us to have him in our home for more than a short amount of time."

"Let's give him a chance," I say, and Andrew turns to give me a hard look.

"Diana, what for? So he can show he's not a fit parent? I don't want him *damaging* our grandson. I'm sure you don't, either."

There's a meaningful note to his voice that makes me wonder what he is implying. If we're going to talk about fit parents... I push the thought away as I recall how carefully Tom buckled his son into the car seat. It's a small thing, but I feel like it matters.

"You don't know that he will be unfit," I say. "And as he'll be living with us, we'll be able to keep an eye on him and the baby. Make sure he's doing his best."

"And you really want to be the police for this guy?" He sighs, leaning his head back against the seat. "Watching his every move?"

"No..." That sounds both stressful and exhausting, and I already know it's what Andrew will be doing, what he'll expect me to do, even as I know I won't be able to do it. "But maybe we should at least try to get to know him," I suggest tentatively. "Sophie married him, Andrew. She lived with him for a year and a half, and she had his baby. Those facts should weigh more than the *one evening* when we met that didn't go well."

He lets out a huff of hard laughter. "That's an understatement."

"Is it?" I ask, and Andrew frowns at me. I don't usually push back this much against his directives, at least not for many years. I've had far too many reasons to doubt myself, but I feel in my bones, in my *heart*, that I might be right about this. This is what Sophie would have wanted.

Andrew doesn't answer, and then from behind us we hear a snuffling sound and we both turn in surprise. I think for a few moments we both forgot there was a baby in the car with us. Our grandson. We stare at him dumbly as he squirms in his seat, his little mitted hands batting his face, and then he lets out a bleat of distress which causes my heart rate to skitter in alarm.

"What do you think he wants?" Andrew asks, and I realize afresh how unprepared we are for this. I flailed so badly during my first experience with a newborn—struggling to breastfeed, feeling like a failure, never able to stop Sophie's crying, getting so upset myself making more mistakes than I can bear to remember. Twenty-five years later, and I feel just as unprepared and inadequate.

"He might be hungry," I offer uncertainly. "Did the hospital provide bottles?"

Andrew shrugs in reply. Babies are a mystery to him. He wants our grandson in our lives, but does he know how to feed him, change him, care for him?

Do I?

The question reverberates through me, reminding me of all the ways I failed before, and I'm pretty sure Andrew is remembering them too, which hurts all the more. We both know I am going to struggle.

"We'll ask Tom when he comes back," I say, but I am pretty sure he won't know either.

Already, I think, we're in over our heads... in so many different ways.

SEVEN

By the time we get home, I am exhausted and on edge. Henry cried the whole way, and nothing any of us could do helped. Tom tried to give him his pacifier, patted his arm awkwardly, and admitted that while the hospital had given him a six-pack of formula, he hadn't bought any bottles.

We stopped at a Walmart, and I ran in and got a starter feeding kit—bottles, sterilizer, even a cleaning brush and dishwasher basket. All things I probably should have thought of buying before, but it didn't occur to me—or, obviously, to Tom. I added several packs of newborn diapers and wipes, as well, before hurrying back to the car, where Henry was still screaming bloody murder and Andrew and Tom were both grim-faced and silent.

Now Tom is standing, seemingly helpless, in the middle of our kitchen while I unbuckle Henry from his car seat. His face is crimson with distress, his little body soaked in sweat, causing anxiety to skitter through me, an echo of everything I felt when Sophie was small.

"Do you want to change him?" I ask, and Tom looks taken aback.

"Uh, no, you can do it," he says after a second's pause. "I don't know how…"

I consider suggesting he watch me and learn, but I'm not ready for that yet, and I don't think he is, either.

Andrew has already disappeared into his study to check his messages, and as I head upstairs alone I realized I had been anticipating—and dreading—this very scenario.

I'm not good with babies. I wasn't with Sophie—doubting my every move, feeling like I was doing everything wrong. I felt like the sleepless and fussiness and trouble with feeding were all my fault, and I also started to resent her for turning me into a cross between a zombie and a ghost. I know it's how a lot of new mothers feel, and when I tried to explain it to my doctor, she laughed and told me it was totally normal.

But I didn't *feel* normal. I felt scared and strange and *wrong*, as well as afraid that if anyone saw the thoughts that flashed through my mind they might even take Sophie away from me… and eventually they almost did.

And those old emotions and memories are rushing back as I carry Henry, only snuffling now, seeming too exhausted to scream anymore, up to the nursery and lay him down on the changing table carefully, like he's a priceless antique.

"All right there, buddy," I say in a singsong voice as I start to unwrap him from his swaddling blanket. "It's all right…"

My fingers tremble as I unsnap the buttons of his sleepsuit and gently take his tiny limbs out of it. He feels so fragile, but then so do I. I wish I was one of those briskly competent matriarchs who could take care of a newborn with confident ease, but I'm not. I never have been, although when I was younger I thought I would be. I think I thought motherhood would be easy and instinctive, that I wouldn't make any mistakes, or if I did, they wouldn't matter. The arrogance of the young really can be breathtaking.

Now, for a few seconds, as I change his diaper, Henry

simply stares at me with those dark, liquid newborn eyes, the darkest blue I've ever seen. I try to smile at him, but I can't quite manage it.

I'm thinking of Sophie as a baby, as a little girl, as a young woman who turned away from me, and then, most horrifyingly, as a body in a coffin, only twenty-four years old. *I'll never see her again.* Why can't I wrap my head around that fact?

My fingers tremble as I get out a fresh diaper and Henry gazes up at me, solemn-eyed.

"Okay," I say, breathing out in relief when I've finally changed his diaper and buttoned his suit back up. Success, of a sort, although it feels like so little. I do my best to swaddle him, although it's not as tight or neat as the nurse did. Still, it will have to do. *I will.*

Because it seems this precious little baby is going to have to depend on me... a thought I find utterly terrifying.

When I come back downstairs with Henry quiet in my arms, Tom is in the living room, wandering around, which makes me uneasy.

Obviously, this is his home for now and I'm not going to forbid him from certain rooms, but I am conscious of a lot of different things as I stand in the doorway: his prison sentence, the fact that he's already stolen from us, the expensive artwork and antiques that decorate this and every other room of our house, and that right now we're more or less alone.

"You must be hungry," I say, a little too loudly, as I come into the room.

Tom turns, letting out a huff as if he knows what I was thinking. "Yeah, I could eat," he says.

"I can make us some sandwiches," I offer hesitantly. "While you feed Henry?"

"Oh, uh..."

I keep his gaze, willing him to say yes. Part of me agrees with Andrew that it might be easier if we followed Tom's lead and didn't have him involved with his own son. He's obviously inexperienced and uncertain, and cutting him out subtly but completely would help us get to the voluntary custody agreement Andrew wants.

But that doesn't feel right or fair to me, and in truth I have my own dark doubts that I can cope with the full-time care of a newborn, especially in my current state. It feels as if everything is up to me, and I know I'm not strong enough. I've proven that before, to my own shame.

"I guess I could," Tom says, and I smile, relieved even as I remain apprehensive. How can I trust this man? And yet I have to. For his sake, as well as Henry's and my own.

"Great," I tell him, and head into the kitchen, hoping he'll follow, which he does. "Why don't you hold him while I get a bottle ready?" I suggest.

"Oh..." I don't give Tom a chance to refuse or deflect as I hold Henry out, basically forcing him to take his son into his arms which he does—clumsily, a grimace of concentration twisting his features, a shadow of fear in his eyes. I feel a surge of sympathy for him, because I wasn't any better with Sophie. In fact, I was worse.

It doesn't help that Henry starts wailing the minute Tom holds him in his arms.

"Oh, shit," he blurts, and then hangs his head. "Sorry..."

"I'm pretty sure he's just hungry," I tell him, and for once I sound—and maybe even feel—certain, which gives me a little swell of confidence. "Do you know when he was fed this morning?"

Tom shakes his head. He's holding Henry incredibly awkwardly, his elbows stuck out with Henry held aloft and basically horizontal. As he starts to flail, kicking his little legs free from the blanket, I'm worried he might roll right out of Tom's arms onto the floor.

"Why don't you try cradling him closer to your chest?" I suggest, and then step forward, putting one hand on each arm to guide him into that position.

Tom stiffens under my touch, and I can't blame him, considering I don't think I've ever touched him before, and now I'm standing close enough to feel his breath fan my cheek, my hands on his arms, Henry screaming between us.

I let out a little apologetic laugh. "Sorry, I'm just..."

"No, it's okay," he says quickly, and I laugh again, uncertainly, because this situation is so surreal, and also so sad. If Sophie were here...

But I can't let myself think like that.

"There," I say, and step back.

Tom is holding Henry a little more securely now, but he still looks incredibly awkward, his arms stiff, his body tense, and his expression pained, like he can't wait until this is over.

"I'll make the bottle," I tell him.

I fumble with the kit I bought, tearing off the plastic and hurriedly scanning the directions while Henry continues to wail and I *feel* Tom's tension, as well as my own. Where is Andrew in all this, I wonder, even as I recognize I'm glad he's not here, because his presence would surely make things worse —judging Tom, and judging me.

"Sorry about this," I say with an attempt at a laugh that sounds closer to a sob. Already, minutes in, I am out of my depth. I knock over a couple of the bottles, sending them spinning across the marble countertop, and I swear under my breath. "I haven't prepared a bottle in a long time..." I explain, hoping I don't seem as useless as I feel.

"Yeah, well I never have," Tom replies, and he almost sounds wry, which makes me smile as I finally manage to unscrew a bottle top and wash it out.

"It's not as hard as I'm making it look," I quip, and he chuckles softly, which heartens me. I wasn't expecting this level of camaraderie, tentative as it is, but it is so very welcome. "Okay," I say, once I have the bottle washed and dried and I've filled it with readymade formula and heated it in the microwave. I do the standard drop-on-the-wrist test and hope it's not too hot, although I can't even remember what that temperature should be. Already I'm second-guessing myself as I've done so many times in the past, mired in doubt, but Henry is still screaming, and we need to *do* this. "Why don't you sit down," I suggest, "and I'll do my best to show you how to feed him?"

Tom perches on a kitchen chair, still cradling Henry clumsily in his arms, and once again I have to redirect him as I do my best to position Henry more comfortably, his head in the crook of Tom's elbow, Tom's arm braced against his body.

"They're so little," I murmur, "but you'd be surprised at how heavy they can get. Now." I put the bottle into his free hand. "This has a slow-release nipple, so he shouldn't choke or dribble too much to begin with, but it's okay if he does." I sound like an expert, but I certainly don't feel like one. I'm just parroting the directions I hastily scanned. "Give it a try."

Swallowing audibly, Tom fits the bottle's teat into Henry's mouth. For a second, he jerks away, still screaming, still furious, and Tom gives me a questioning look.

I smile, nod, remembering exactly how that kind of rejection felt. "Keep trying."

He fits the bottle into Henry's mouth again, jiggling it up and down a little so a drop squeezes out. Henry's eyes widen and for a second his whole body stiffens before he starts to suck eagerly, greedily, so much so that he splutters, and Tom swears out loud.

"Sorry... sorry..." he says quickly. "That just surprised me."

"It's okay," I assure him. "He's getting the hang of it, just like you."

"Yeah, I think he's a quicker learner than his old man." Tom lets out a shaky laugh, and I smile.

"I think you're both doing great," I say firmly, and then go to take some things out of the fridge for sandwiches.

Henry continues to drink his bottle, and I am conscious of Tom watching me as I move around the kitchen, getting the bread from its bin, a knife from the drawer. He doesn't say anything, and despite the warmth I felt toward this man moments before, now I'm feeling uneasy and uncertain again.

I try to think of something to say, something kindly and innocuous, but nothing comes to my mind. My tongue feels thick in my mouth and my hands are clumsy as I reach for a knife.

"Ham and cheese okay?" I finally ask, my voice a little strangled.

"Yeah, yeah." Tom's voice is gruff. "Whatever is fine."

Another silence. I concentrate on spreading mayonnaise across a piece of bread, before I realize I didn't ask him if he wanted mayo. I decide it doesn't matter.

Several torturous moments pass as I make the sandwich in silence, the only sound Henry's steady *glug glug glug*, which is comforting in its own way. I remember that sound from Sophie, how it filled me with satisfaction that I finally felt like I was doing *something* right.

"He sounds like he's gotten the hang of it," I manage as I put the sandwich on a plate and bring it over.

"Yeah." Tom smiles faintly and then nods toward the sandwich. "Thanks."

I know I am reading way too much into these simple interactions, but I am craving some kind of reassurance that we did the right thing in inviting Tom into our home, into our lives. That we can handle having him here, along with Henry.

Gingerly I take the seat opposite him. "Was Sophie excited about the baby?" I blurt, my hands tucked between my knees. "How was her pregnancy? Did she have morning sickness? Leg cramps? I had terrible leg cramps..." I fall silent abruptly, feeling as if I've breached some unspoken, agreed code not to talk about these things.

Tom has turned guarded, and his hand slips on the bottle so it falls out of Henry's mouth, causing a spray of formula and a furious baby.

"Oh, whoops..." He glances down, taking an inordinate amount of time to situate Henry again, bottle firmly clasped in his little mouth.

I feel like he's avoiding answering my questions, and I consider apologizing, offering to take it all back, but then I don't because I really do want to know.

"Yeah, she was excited," he finally says in a low voice. "Even though it was an accident."

An accident. I don't like to think of Henry that way, even though I know it makes sense.

"I was wondering about that," I murmur. "Since you hadn't been married very long..."

"Yeah." He pauses before lifting his gaze. "As for the other stuff, I don't think she had too much of that. Leg cramps and that kind of stuff. I don't really know."

I am silent, wondering how he could not know. When I was nauseous, Andrew brought me saltine crackers slathered with peanut butter, which for several weeks was the only thing I could think about eating. When I woke up in the middle of the night with excruciating leg cramps, he massaged my calves until I fell back asleep. He has always, in his own way, been a very supportive husband.

It's just that I have not always been a very supportive wife.

Henry starts spluttering again, and I see that he has almost finished his bottle.

"He's probably had enough for now," I tell Tom. "He'll need to be burped. Shall I show you how?"

He shrugs his assent, and I reach for the baby. The feel of him in my arms is becoming more familiar, a small yet solid weight that speaks to my heart. Maybe, this time round, I don't need to doubt myself so much.

Smiling, I drape him over my shoulder and pat his back gently, waiting expectantly for the gas bubble to emerge, but Henry just squirms and starts to cry. The mirage of my expertise is already vanishing like a vapor.

I try him on my other shoulder, managing a little laugh. "When they're this small, it's not always easy to get the gas up," I explain, and Tom shrugs and reaches for his sandwich.

As I watch him eat, his gaze moving around the kitchen, it's obvious that he is not as invested in his son as perhaps he should be, although I know I need to cut him some slack considering what he—and all of us—have been through. Still, it's something which will no doubt give Andrew a sense of hope that a voluntary custody agreement is certainly possible and maybe even desirable on Tom's part, but it only makes me feel sad.

I don't think this is what Sophie would have wanted, her husband seemingly uninterested in their son's life. And I don't know that it's what I want, even if Tom's presence still feels like an unknown.

Just then, Henry lets out the most enormous burp; it echoes through the room and Tom and I exchange startled glances.

"Wow," Tom says, shaking his head in wonder, and then we both laugh.

At that moment, Andrew comes into the kitchen, sees us laughing together, and glares—at me.

EIGHT

Christ Church is a mammoth stone church on a ten-acre plot in the center of Greenwich, a bastion of holy prestige and wealth. A hundred years ago, the pews had little gold-plated plaques with names on them for the parishioners who sat there—and paid for the privilege. Now the plaques have been removed, but the sentiment is the same. This a church for the wealthy and well-connected. It's where Andrew's mother had her funeral service, and where Sophie is having hers today.

It's been a week since she died, five days since we brought Tom and Henry home to live with us, and it all still feels surreal and strange. When Andrew came in on Tom and me laughing in the kitchen that first night, I felt his displeasure rolling off him in waves, and I could tell Tom sensed it too.

"Henry just did the biggest burp!" I exclaimed, trying to lighten the ominous mood, but Andrew didn't even crack a smile.

"Tom, I have some paperwork for you to look through," he said, turning to face our son-in-law, his tone somewhere jarringly between jocular and steely.

"Paperwork?" I couldn't help but interject. "Andrew, I don't—"

"Regarding *Sophie*," he emphasized, giving me a quick, quelling look, and I fell silent, because whatever this was, it wasn't about custody. Was it?

Tom put down his sandwich, looking wary again. "Okay," he said after a moment, and followed Andrew out of the kitchen without a word.

It was only later that I found out what the paperwork was for. "I told him about the trust fund," Andrew explained tersely as we got ready for bed, the curtains drawn, the door locked. We were speaking in whispers, conscious that Tom was only two doors down. I'd given Henry his nighttime bottle and settled him in his crib while Tom had watched, seemingly ambivalent about being involved, and when I'd mentioned he would most likely wake up in a few hours, he'd looked even more so. I was pretty sure I was going to be the one to get up for nighttime feedings, a thought that filled me with dread, because I hadn't handled the lack of sleep all that well last time we had a baby in the house.

"What about it?" I asked Andrew. His mother had bequeathed a trust fund of two hundred and fifty thousand dollars on Sophie, that she would have inherited on her twenty-fifth birthday, which was in three months. I hadn't even thought about that money, or what it could mean for us all now.

"Sophie died without a will," Andrew explained briefly. "The trust stipulates that upon Sophie's death, any children she had would become the beneficiaries of the assets. If she had no children, any monies would go to us, as her closest relatives. Spouses were precluded."

So Tom couldn't get his hands on Sophie's money. Surely that was a relief? But Andrew was looking grim.

"Okay..." I said cautiously, waiting for more.

"My mother was envisioning a scenario where Sophie died

in old age," Andrew said on a heavy sigh. "Not... not *this*." He paused, his expression shuttering as he struggled to compose himself, and I ached for my husband who so clearly did not know how to handle his grief, but then I didn't think any of us did. We were all trying to deal with it by ourselves, and that made it even worse. "Until Henry is of age," he continued after a moment, his voice steady again, "the money needs to be managed by a guardian. The guardian wasn't stipulated in the trust, but I think we can make a very strong case that it should be us."

"But legally..." I began, knowing there had to be more, and that it wouldn't be good, or at least not easy.

"At this moment, as Henry's father, Tom could be considered his guardian, both in terms of the trust and generally." Andrew gave a little shake of his head, as if in denial. "He's not entitled to any of the money himself, but obviously he could abuse that if he became Henry's guardian, in terms of the trust. I wanted to avoid that if possible, so I suggested to Tom that he allows us to become guardians of the trust, and we would give him a monthly stipend from it in return."

"That seems... reasonable," I ventured. I couldn't help but be a little hurt that Andrew hadn't thought to mention any of this to me before putting it before Tom, but I wasn't particularly surprised. He had always handled our financial affairs, and, to be fair, I had never professed much of an interest. "So what did Tom say?" I asked.

"He refused," Andrew replied shortly. "Said he wasn't about to sign anything without talking to a lawyer first." His face twisted in a grimace as he tossed his cufflinks onto the top of his dresser with an angry little clatter. "Arrogant little twerp."

"*Andrew!*" My voice came out in a pleading hiss. If Tom heard him, that wouldn't help anything—not our relationship with our son-in-law, or the possibility of becoming guardians of either Henry's trust or Henry himself.

For a moment, I pictured Tom crouching outside our door, glowering as he listened to every word, and I had to suppress a shiver. I wasn't sure whether I was being unfair or not, but despite our brief moments of camaraderie, I still didn't feel entirely comfortable with him in our home.

"If it goes to court, we'll win," Andrew replied in a low voice. "We're sure to. A legal aid lawyer representing a convicted felon and former drug addict? And I don't even know if he *is* former." Andrew shook his head, his expression darkening. "You two might have been *cozying up* in the kitchen, but this is a case of keeping our enemies closer, Diana. We can't trust him. We're letting him live here so we can keep an eye on him. And I don't want him alone with Henry, *ever*."

I stared at him. "How am I supposed to manage that?"

Andrew frowned. "I know it's difficult, but I think it's reasonable to hire some part-time help, maybe a few hours every afternoon, or a nurse to deal with the nights? I don't want you to shoulder the burden alone."

I swallowed hard, feeling the indictment of those words, and his expression gentled as he came over to rest a hand on my shoulder.

"It was different back then," he said quietly. "*We* were different. I remember how hard it was. But it doesn't have to be like that this time."

I nodded, although I didn't entirely agree with him. It *was* different, but not necessarily in a good way. And Andrew reminding me of it felt like another accusation.

After Sophie's birth, I didn't just have a burst of baby blues that my sister-in-law, Elizabeth, assured me, impatiently, was normal. I struggled with a depression so deep that days went by when I had to force myself to get out of bed, a darkness swamping my mind, my life. I had no interest in my daughter, even though I wanted to, desperately. I wanted to hold her and feed her and love her, but I simply couldn't summon the will. I resented her and her constant tears, the way she arched away from me when I tried to feed her, and at the same time scared me with her endless needs. I felt woefully ill-equipped for any of it, feeling so unmaternal while longing for my own mother, who had died only weeks before.

I tried to hide all my struggles from Andrew, but eventually it came to a point where I couldn't, to my own everlasting shame.

When Sophie was six weeks old, I ended up on the psychiatric ward of a hospital, and when I came out, fragile but determined, I discovered that Andrew had hired a nanny, Teresa, a battle-ax of a woman who emanated disapproval of me, the mother who couldn't cope at all.

All of it felt like failure, and I worked so hard over the next years, and even decades, to make it up to Andrew, as well as Sophie herself. To show them both, and myself, that I was a better mother than I had been at the start.

Considering all that has happened since, I don't think that I ever convinced anyone. And now I was afraid of failing not just Sophie, but her son.

Because even though it *was* different, I really didn't know if I could do better—*be* better—now. Once again, in the midst of life, I was struggling with grief, and this time it felt even darker, heavier, even more overwhelming.

And then there was the added stress of Tom in our house, in our lives, and what he might or might not be capable of. I didn't feel *unsafe*, not precisely, but I certainly wasn't comfortable, and I seriously doubted whether I could manage *any* of this.

I didn't say that, however, because I could already sense that Andrew didn't want to hear it, and I certainly didn't want to admit to it. I'd spent the last twenty years pretending I could cope. I couldn't stop now, especially because I knew we would never gain custody of Henry if I, his own grandmother, wasn't up to the job of taking care of a baby—again.

"Okay," I said at last. "That's a good idea. I'll look into hiring someone tomorrow."

Right then, as if on cue, I heard Henry's thin wail coming from the nursery, and I felt my shoulders slump. Then, to my surprise, Andrew said, "I'll go."

"You will?" I couldn't keep the disbelief from my voice. I don't think he ever offered to tend to Sophie in the night, although, to be fair, we had a night nurse for the first few weeks, and then of course the intimidating Teresa. After she'd left, I insisted I could manage on my own and did everything within my power to make sure I did.

"I know I didn't always pick up the slack when Sophie was small," he admitted stiffly, "and I certainly should have, especially when..." Thankfully, he left that thought there, but it hung between us, like a thickness in the air. "But you know how demanding my job was back then," he said instead. "I was working all hours, trying to make VP. Maybe I shouldn't have been so... driven, but it's different now."

Was it?

I finished getting ready for bed as Andrew went to see to Henry. I heard a murmur of voices in the hall, and knew he was talking to Tom, but I couldn't make out what they were saying. I slipped into bed, straining to hear more, but all was silent—whether peaceful or ominous, I couldn't tell. I closed my eyes, the events of the day pressing down on me, pulling me into exhaustion, which felt like a relief. I didn't want to have to think or remember anything anymore.

I'd fallen asleep by the time Andrew came back; he'd been gone over an hour.

"Is Henry..." I mumbled as he pulled back the covers.

"Asleep. Finally." He lay down next to me and closed his eyes, and I let sleep drag me back under. I didn't wake again until five in the morning, when I heard Henry crying once more, while Andrew snored softly next to me.

I stumbled out of bed and went to get him, but when I got to the doorway of the nursery, I saw Tom standing by the crib, wearing just a pair of boxers as he held Henry to his bare chest.

"Oh..." The syllable slipped out of me involuntarily.

Tom glanced up, his face shrouded in darkness so I couldn't read his expression.

"Do you think he's hungry?" he asked, and there was a note of vulnerability in his voice that tugged at me, spoke straight to my heart.

Already, I noticed, he was holding Henry more comfortably, without his elbows sticking out like he didn't know what to do with them. "Probably," I told him. "Babies need a lot of feeding." I hesitated and then suggested, "I can make a bottle, if you like?"

Tom nodded, cuddling Henry closer, his head bent over the baby. "Okay, thanks."

And despite what Andrew had told me just a few hours ago, I left him alone with Henry to go make the bottle. After hovering for a few minutes to make sure he could feed him properly, which it seemed he could, I left him alone again to give it to him and went back to bed, uneasy and anxious but also relieved. It was good Tom was taking an interest, I told myself, even if Andrew wanted to keep him at a distance. How could we, when he was Henry's father?

When I woke up, Andrew was in the shower and Henry and Tom were both asleep. Somehow, we had all survived the first night.

I hired Mia, a night nurse to come from ten o'clock until six to manage Henry's nighttime feeds. She lets herself in and out again, and we barely know she's there, but it means we all get a decent night's sleep.

I'd asked Tom about it, and he seemed only relieved to have

some help. With the pressure off the nights, I tell myself I can handle the demands of the days, even if sometimes they've felt like too much. Henry isn't particularly fussy, but he still has his moments, and every shriek or sob reminds me of Sophie—the days pacing the nursery, tears running down my face as she screamed in my arms. The times I left her in the crib and put a pillow over my head so I couldn't hear her cries. And worse than that, memories I can't let myself think about, even now, all these years later.

Especially now, when grief hovered over me, blotting out all light, all hope, so I wonder how I can do anything at all, and yet I do; I get up, I get dressed, I take care of a tiny newborn baby, I make dinner, I ask Andrew about his day. On the outside, I am coping, maybe even marvelously. But inside, all I can think about is Sophie and how I'll never see, or speak to, or touch her again. I'll never hold her in my arms, breathe in the scent of her shampoo, sling my arm around her shoulders...

As for Tom... it's hard to know what he thinks or feels about Henry, or even anything. At times, he seems happy, or at least willing, to take care of his son, giving him a bottle or changing his diaper. At other times, he seems apathetic and indifferent, lying around on the sofa or closeted in his room. He's polite, in his own way, but he's also reserved, and on several occasions he's gone out for hours at a time—first to empty his apartment, and then, ostensibly, to look for work, but he came back smelling like beer and cigarettes, and I didn't think he'd done much looking.

I thought Andrew would be furious, but he almost seemed pleased; such things, I suppose, will help our custody case, should it come to that, and as the days passed, I feared that it would.

But I am not thinking about the custody case, or even Henry, who is back at the house with Mia, as I walk into the church on Andrew's arm.

Sophie's casket—white with gold handles and heaped with white roses and trailing ivy—is at the front of the church, which is packed with mourners. There are friends from school, from college, from the country club and Andrew's work, as well as a handful of relatives, Andrew's sister, a couple of cousins—and I feel everyone's sorrowful and speculative gazes on me as I walk down the aisle in my mourning clothes, a simple navy-blue sheath dress I pulled from my closet, my head held high and my gaze distant and unfocused. I can't bear to meet anyone's eye, to catch a glimpse of the pity and judgment I fear will be reflected there.

Most people know, or at least suspect, that something went wrong between Sophie and us. Even though we never spoke of it, I know rumors swirled about our estrangement, her marriage that we didn't attend. Over the last year and a half, I fielded cautious questions, people probing for news under the guise of sympathy.

A few friends have called since her death, but I haven't been able to bring myself to answer my phone, or return any of their messages. Somehow, though, people still find out things. I'm pretty sure they know about Tom as well as Henry. That's the nature of a small, enclosed community like Old Greenwich, where people go to the same exclusive club and their children to the same private schools; where we run into our neighbors at the olive bar of King's Food Markets, or on the beach, where we wave our resident passes for Tod's Point with airy, and slightly bored, confidence.

Tom, at least, has cleaned up fairly well. He's wearing a suit Andrew bought him, and it covers all of his tattoos, save the ones across his knuckles. Even in an expensively tailored suit, though, he looks rough, somehow; maybe it's just the way he walks, something between a stride and a swagger, or the jut of his chin, the set of his mouth. I feel the ripple of speculation as he follows behind Andrew and me to the first pew, reserved for family, and we all sit down.

The service washes over me in a wave of words I barely take in. I stand when I'm meant to stand, and I sit when I'm meant to sit. I even sing when I'm meant to sing; we went with the same hymns as Andrew's mother's, with no song of Sophie's choice like I suggested. It's just as well; I don't think I could handle hearing something I knew she loved. It's hard enough to go through the motions; I feel too fragile to fully engage in any of it, even though I know I should.

Afterward, there is a reception in the church's grand fellowship hall, with champagne and canapés, all of it arranged by the flower guild, who were Andrew's mother's friends, not mine. I had nothing to do with any of this, but I feel like I should have, because isn't that what a mother does? Shouldn't I be the one picking out what Sophie wore—I don't even know—or her casket and flowers? Instead I showed up to my daughter's funeral like a distant relative or a casual acquaintance, a mere spectator, not knowing or having done anything.

Even the display of photos of Sophie through the years was made by someone else—I don't even know whom—and I stand in front of it, staring at a photo of her in her tennis whites, swinging a racket, beaming with pride at winning the Under Thirteen regionals. She's only twelve, but she already looked too thin.

"Aren't these photos wonderful?" A woman I only vaguely recognize comes to stand next to me, nodding in approval. "They did such a good job."

"They did," I agree, even though I don't know who "they" are, and the fact that I don't feels humiliating as well as shameful. Where did *they* get all these photos? It feels deeply wrong, somehow, that a stranger put together a collage of my daughter's best moments, without even asking me.

"It must be very hard," the woman continues, dropping her voice to a murmur. "How is your little grandson?"

"He's fine." I narrow my eyes, trying to place this busybody. Someone from the club? She speaks as if she knows me, as if she knew Sophie, which I suppose she must have, for her to be here. But she's not important enough for me to recognize, although right now I wonder if *anyone* is. I am surrounded by the people who are meant to be closest in my life and I feel utterly alone.

"And... Sophie's husband?" The woman's tone turns both delicate and probing. "He's living with you, isn't he?"

"Yes, for now," I reply stiffly. "It seemed easier..."

"That must be difficult, as well, though," the woman says, her mouth drawn into a moue of sympathy. "Considering—"

My polite expression turns into a frown. I've had enough of these gossipy suggestions, and two glasses of champagne have made me unusually bold. "Considering *what*?" I ask, my tone sharpening.

"Oh, just..." The woman shakes her head, backtracking instantly, but with a knowing gleam in her eye. She's clearly enjoying this. "Jessica mentioned that Sophie had told her that they were having some, you know, *marriage* troubles."

I stare at her, trying to make sense of the words. *Jessica. Marriage troubles.* Then I realize this must be Jennifer Stanton, mother of Jessica, an old school friend's of Sophie. But how would Jessica know about my daughter's marriage, troubled or otherwise? I didn't even know she had stayed in touch with my daughter since they left for different colleges. Jessica, as I recall, went to law school at Yale.

"Everyone has marriage troubles of some description, at one time or another," I finally say, stiffly. "And Tom is Henry's father. We're making the best of it."

Jennifer waves a hand in apology, but already I am sure she's going to repeat what I've said to all and sundry, and probably make a meal of it, too. *Making the best of it* is hardly a ringing endorsement. "Of course, of course, I understand...it's so admirable, really, what you're doing, especially considering..." She stops, delicately, and I feel myself go icy-cold. I have, of course, suspected that my friends and acquaintances, especially the longtime ones, know about my bout of depression, but no one has ever dared to say anything to my face, and I don't think I can stand Jennifer Stanton doing that now.

And so I turn away blindly, plucking a glass of champagne from a tray even though I know I shouldn't have any more. I've barely eaten, and my head and stomach are both already swirling. I bolt it down in one desperate sip.

Marriage troubles. Were Sophie and Tom really having such troubles, and if they were, how bad were they? And, more painfully, why did Sophie confide in an old school friend I didn't even think she'd kept in touch with, and not in *me*, her own mother?

Of course I know why, because she'd cut off all communication with me and Andrew after that terrible night, but *when* will that fact stop hurting?

I put my empty glass down and head for the bathroom. I need to be by myself, away from all these stares and suspicion, where I feel like my every word and move are being examined and then torn apart. I imagine I can hear their whispers, like the scuttling of spiders.

Such a shame Sophie quit tennis like that. She basically went off the rails, and Andrew and Diana just couldn't handle it.

You know she had an eating disorder? She was hospitalized for it, even...

I always thought Diana was a little... passive... about things.

Oh, I know, Diana never could hold it together. Remember when Sophie was a baby? She's really such a mess...

All things I've heard before, in one context or another, and pretended not to. Are they saying even worse things now?

How on earth is Diana going to cope with a baby now, when she couldn't the first time round?

That son-in-law will run rings around them. I hope they're not putting that innocent little baby in danger...

Really, that family is a dysfunctional nightmare. Always has been.

Those are the whispers I imagine, and although I haven't heard anything, I know such sentiments are not out of the realm of possibility, and the thought makes my stomach cramp. How have I made such a mess of everything, *again*?

I stand in front of the bathroom mirror, staring at my pale face, my wild, dilated eyes, my silver-streaked hair lying in rigid, hair-sprayed waves. Somehow, over the last twenty-four years, I've become a shadow of my former self, and I don't even know how it happened, or why I let it. It was a slow creep of self-doubt and sorrow, a crumbling of the person I thought I was, to be replaced by something I still don't even recognize.

Who is this wild-eyed woman with trembling lips and a fear of letting everyone down, most of all herself? How, when I once considered myself so savvy and strong, did I become this pathetic shadow? And how do I become something—someone—else?

When you're young, I reflect, you're so certain you can face anything, but at the same time you can't believe you'll ever have to. You think your youthful confidence will protect you from life's tragedies, but it won't. It never does.

I didn't know it back then, but I was woefully unprepared for all the challenges fate threw at me over these years. My mother's death, when I was eight months' pregnant with Sophie. The traumatic birth of my daughter. My postnatal depression. The years of her eating disorder and hospitalization. The blank space of her college years, when I finally thought I'd breathe easier, *be* the person I wanted to be, and instead spiraled into paranoia and apathy. And now my *daughter's* death...

A choking sob escapes me, and I close my eyes against the sight of my pale, grief-stricken face.

I need to be stronger. I *want* to be stronger.

I fumble for my bag and open the change purse. Carefully I take out two Xanax and, ignoring the rush of guilt this little act gives me, I slip the little blue pills under my tongue. I know I shouldn't, not on top of three glasses of champagne, but I can't help myself.

I really am that weak.

It only takes a few minutes for the lovely, light feeling to slip through my veins like liquid silver. My head goes fuzzy and it feels as if my bones are melting. A sigh escapes me in a long, low shudder as I brace my hands against the sink, my head hanging down. I feel as if I could slip to the floor right here, curl up like a puppy and go straight to sleep, which right now is all I want to do. Slip away into oblivion and forget absolutely everything, if for just a few minutes...

I'm already starting to slump when the door to the bathroom opens, and I hear a sharp intake of breath.

I straighten immediately, my head swimming, my vision blurring. I really should not have taken two Xanax on top of three glasses of champagne. My regret is instant and total.

"Diana... are you all right?"

It's my sister-in-law Elizabeth, who is five years older than Andrew and has always intimidated me. When I suffered from depression, she was impatient, telling me all new mothers got the "baby blues" and I needed to *snap out of it*. When Sophie had an eating disorder and was dangerously thin, she told me I needed to be a stricter parent and simply *make* her eat. When my mother died and I felt like I could barely function, she stated that when we are adults, our parents get sick and die, that was the natural and expected order of things and *really* shouldn't come as such a surprise, and maybe I needed to find some hobbies to distract myself from moping so much, the way I had before.

I've taken all her advice with a murmur and apology for being the way that I am, which does little to appease her, or me. We have always pretended to get along, but the pretense has worn paper-thin over the years, and it's bare to both of us now.

"I'm fine," I say, but the words come out slurred and I can tell Elizabeth notices, her mouth pursing up like a prune as her eyes, the same electric blue as Andrew's, flash with both irritation and disgust.

"Good gracious, have you *taken* something?" she demands, and there is so much censure in her voice, as well as smug knowledge. She's remembering my postnatal depression, as well as when my mother died, those days and even weeks a blur of sadness, failure, and regret.

I can't go back to those dark times, not again, even if this hurts more.

"I'm fine," I say again, and Elizabeth presses her lips together, her expression holding nothing but scornful condemnation.

"I'll go find Andrew," she tells me, and I know this is a threat. She has always enjoyed running to Andrew with whatever misdemeanor of mine she stumbles across—whether to have one up on him or me, I don't know, but I don't think it matters. The result is the same—my shame and Andrew's disappointment.

"No, you don't need to find him." I think my words are clearer now, but I'm not sure. "I'm fine," I insist for a third time, and then I push past her into the hall, stumbling through the doorway so I nearly pitch forward, about to fall flat on my face, but then someone catches me in their arms, holding me steady.

"*Mrs. Lawrence!*"

I look up, groggily blinking Tom into focus. "Tom..." I say

weakly, but I can't manage much more than that because my tongue feels so thick in my mouth.

He stares at me for a moment, his hands gripping my forearms, his dark gaze scanning my face in troubled concern. "Have you taken something?" he asks in a low voice. It's the exact same question my sister-in-law asked, but Tom sounds so much more sympathetic, and I guess he would, being a former *coke* dealer.

For some reason, this makes me start to laugh—a high, wild laugh that even in my current state I recognize is totally inappropriate for this moment, and yet somehow I can't stop. The sound keeps coming from me, something between a cackle and a shriek, and as much as I want to clamp my lips together and find *some* kind of decorum, I just can't.

Tom doesn't say anything, just puts his arm around me and then ushers me toward the back door, away from the guests milling in the hall.

"Where are we going?" I ask, and now I recognize that my voice really does sound slurred. I trip in my heels, and he puts his other arm around my waist to steady me.

"Home," Tom replies, and wordlessly, utterly helpless, I let him guide me away.

NINE

I wake up with a dry mouth and a pounding head.

I am lying on the sofa in the family room adjoining the kitchen, and Tom is sprawled in a chair across from me, Henry asleep on his chest, his little legs splayed out like a frog's. I remember when Sophie used to sleep like that, my hand resting on her back, our breaths following the same sleep-steady rhythm. Just the thought is enough to bring tears to my eyes, and so I close them again, as if I can shut out the memories inside my head of then, of now, of everything.

"Are you awake?" Tom asks in a low voice.

Slowly, I open my eyes again. He is staring at me, a look of concern on his face mingled with a telling sympathy, and it makes me feel even more ashamed. I never expected Tom West to feel sorry for *me*.

"I'm sorry," I mumble. "I don't..." I can't finish that sentence. I don't know how.

"It's okay."

"What... what *happened*?" A sense of impending dread swirls in my stomach as snatches of the last few hours flash through my mind. Downing champagne, taking the Xanax. Elizabeth walking in on me, threatening to tell Andrew. "Where's Andrew?" I ask Tom.

"He's still at the church. People are staying for a while, I guess."

I force myself to a seated position, even though it makes my head spin. "What time is it?"

"A little after five. You've been asleep for about an hour."

My hair feels sticky and stiff from the hairspray, and I do my best to shove it out of my face, which also feels sticky. My mouth is terribly dry. "And Mia...?"

"She left when we got back."

I can't remember that, not even vaguely. My last coherent memory is leaving the funeral with Tom's arm around me. The realization makes me wince. "How... bad... was I?" I force myself to ask, even though I don't want to know.

Tom smiles wryly. "Well, I've seen worse."

An unruly laugh escapes me like a hiccup. "I don't know how comforted I should feel by that."

"Probably not that much, to be fair," he admits. He adjusts Henry on his chest, fingers splayed across his back in a way that looks natural. Already he seems more confident than he did a few days ago, handling his child with an ease it took me months, if not years, to feel. "Look, you were clearly out of it, but it wasn't that bad. You stayed in the taxi while Mia left, and then I carried you in here. She didn't see anything, if that's what you're worried about."

"*Carried* me..." The thought makes me blush.

"Yeah, walking wasn't your strong suit, at that point." The wry smile returns, and I look away.

"I'm so embarrassed," I admit in a squeezed-out voice. I want to tell him I don't normally act this way, that this episode is entirely out of character due to the overwhelming nature of my grief, but I can't bring myself to lie. It's been a while, yes, but I've been here before, in one way or another.

"Yeah, well you've had a tough day. A tough week." He pauses. "Hell, a tough few years, maybe. I'm not going to judge you, Diana."

"And yet we've judged *you*," I blurt, and then wish I hadn't said that. Admitted to it, even if it was glaringly obvious from the one night we'd spent in his company.

"Yeah, well." Henry lets out a snuffling sound, and Tom hoists him a little higher on his chest, one hand still resting on his back, the other cupping his backside. He's starting to look like an expert. "I get why you did."

I don't know what to say to that, and yet I feel I should say *something* about that night we've never talked about that affected so much.

"I wish things had happened differently back then," I finally say, and Tom nods.

"Me, too." He lets out a sudden laugh, almost like a snort. "I was so messed up that night. No wonder you guys were freaking out."

There is no good reply to this except the truth. "Yes," I agree. "We were." I pause before daring to add, "And you were."

He laughs again, the sound subsiding into a sigh. "Yeah," he admits. "I really was. It was because I was so nervous."

"Nervous?"

"About meeting you guys. Knowing you were from..." He gestures to the kitchen yawning all around us. Outside, the sky is turning to violet twilight and I can just about glimpse the indigo stretch of the Sound below the lawn. "This big fancy life. I thought I'd smoke a little weed to relax me—not the best idea I know, but..." He shrugs. "Well, I've had a lot of not-so-good ideas like that, I guess." He lets out a snort of laughter. "And you thought I'd stolen that little dog..."

"The Pekingese," I remind him. "It belonged to my mother-in-law."

"I wasn't *stealing* it," he tells me, sounding earnest. "I was just looking at it. My grandma had a dog like that. I'd forgotten..." He sighs. "But yeah, I know what it looked like. What it always looks like."

I am silent, absorbing this statement, what it means.

"I don't actually know anything about your life," I tell him finally. "Besides the fact that you were in prison." I wince apologetically, wondering if I should have mentioned it, but he seems unfazed, giving a grimace of acknowledgment.

"Well, that's kind of a big part, isn't it? Especially for you guys, although, honestly, it was pretty big for me, too." He sighs, his gaze turning distant as he absently strokes his son's back, the gesture seeming far more natural than it did even a few days ago.

"That's understandable on both counts," I allow, "but it doesn't have to define who you are. Or who we think you are."

He reflects on that for a moment, his gaze turning distant. "I feel like a lot of things have defined who I am," he says finally. "And I don't know if that's on me. Maybe I shouldn't have let them."

And yet how can we keep the events of our lives from making us who we are? I think of my own life, the disappointments and sorrows that feel as if they shaped every choice I've ever made. Then I remind myself to focus on Tom. This is a chance to get to know him, and I want to take it.

I settle into the sofa, tucking my legs under me, more than a little curious about this man I never got to know. "Like what?" I ask. "What do you think has defined you?"

He shrugs. "Just... stuff." I wait, and he admits after a moment, "My dad left when I was fourteen. That messed me up pretty good."

"I'm sorry," I say quietly. "That must have been hard for you and your mother."

He lets out a laugh, this one hard and sharp, and it startles Henry, so his arms and legs flail out like a starfish before he tucks them in again. "Sorry, buddy," Tom murmurs, patting the baby's back gently, before looking back at me. "My mom wasn't around then, either. She was off saving the world."

I stare at him in confusion. "Saving the world...?"

"She worked for this NGO, Crisis Action. Always flying off to an earthquake or flood or whatever, to be on the ground to help with disaster relief in some godforsaken shithole. She loved it, but it meant it was just my dad and me most of the time. She'd come back for six weeks or so, every few months, but it wasn't much."

Somehow this is not the kind of backstory I imagine Tom having, although admittedly I never put particulars to it. But if I'd been pressed, I would have assumed he had some socioeconomically-deprived childhood, broken home, abusive relatives... Something of a stereotype, or maybe even a caricature. Not a mother who worked for an NGO, something that is surely admirable, even if she abandoned her family to do it.

"And then your dad left you?" I ask, feeling my way through the words. "While she was away?"

He nods. "Yeah, he just walked out and didn't come back. No note, no text, nothing. He'd been depressed, I guess, and it got to him. He killed himself a few weeks later."

My mouth drops open and I gape at him soundlessly for a few seconds. "Oh, *Tom*..."

"And when he left, my mom was in Tajikistan, so..." He shrugs.

"But your mom must have come back as soon as she heard," I state, not a question, and he shrugs again.

"She was out of cellphone signal on some rescue trip in the mountains, so I couldn't get in touch with her at first. And I guess I was kind of angry with her, too, because she hadn't been there, so I didn't try as hard as I could have." He shrugs. "A week went by and then one of my teachers figured out I was living alone, because I missed the bus and couldn't get to school, and they called social workers in. And it kind of spiraled from there." He sighs as he rests his head back on his chair. "So yeah, my dad walking out kind of defined my life bigtime. But everybody's got something, right?"

I am trying to imagine the sort of mother who would leave her son alone for so long, without any way of contacting her... and then I realize I know *exactly* what sort of mother that is.

"What happened when your mother finally was able to be contacted?" I ask.

"It took a couple of weeks, and then..." He pauses. "Well, it was another week or so before she came home. And by that point, I was living with a foster family, and I was still pretty pissed at her, so I told her I wanted to stay with them, and she let me. She was off somewhere else soon enough, and it seemed to work out better for both of us."

I am horrified, and unable to keep from openly showing it. "Oh, Tom..." I say again. I have no other words.

"Everybody's got something," he repeats, and now he sounds almost angry. He doesn't want my sympathy, and I understand that, but he already has it.

And yet...

"So, how did you get from living with a foster family at fourteen to going to prison for drug dealing?" I am compelled to ask.

He sighs and leans his head back against the chair as he closes his eyes. "By having a couple of those not-so-good ideas, I guess." He doesn't sound like he wants to say more, and I decide not to press. We've come a long way in the last half-hour, in terms of learning about each other. At least, I've learned about him. All he's learned about me is that I may have an addiction to benzodiazepines and I am still struggling to cope with real life.

"I'm sorry you went through all that, at any rate," I say after a moment. "And I'm sorry I put you in a difficult position today."

"You didn't, not really. I wanted to get out of there." He

lifts his head and opens his eyes. "Not my crowd, you know? I felt like they were all looking at me like I was some freak show."

I sigh. "I felt that way, too." I pause. "I feel that way a lot of the time, actually."

"Not your crowd then, either?" Tom guesses after a moment.

"I didn't grow up this way," I reply with a nod of agreement. "I was solidly, boringly middle class, no ponies or boarding schools or Cotillion dances for me." I sigh. "I don't think I've ever felt like I really fit in." I also don't think I've ever admitted that to anyone. Why am I telling *Tom*? How can I trust him not to use anything I say or do against me? And, thanks to my behavior today, he already has so much to work with, should he choose to do so. "I don't think I've ever wanted to fit in, either," I continue, still compelled to a painful honesty that is probably unwise. "And that, I suspect, has always been part of the problem."

A smile crooks the corner of Tom's mouth. "You're your own worst enemy," he tells me. "That's what my social worker used to say to me when I was doing all kinds of crap, and she was right. Still couldn't do anything about it, though. You can know you're messing up, but you can't always keep yourself from doing it."

Story of my life, I think wryly. I never expected to find such a point of commonality with my daughter's husband.

"How did you meet Sophie?" I ask when I realize I don't know. I am, suddenly and uncomfortably, reminded of what Jennifer Stanton said to me about *marriage troubles*. I don't know if Tom will tell me anything now, but I want to know more. "I think she said something about an art gallery..."

"Yeah, I was working on a construction site out in Brooklyn and when I got off shift, it was pouring rain, so I ducked into this art gallery to get dry. She was there, you know, looking around at the pictures, which were pretty bad, if you ask me. All this modern crap."

He chuckles softly while I try to smile. I'd assumed, from Sophie's telling, that he'd been there for the art, maybe even had his own work displayed. Not that it makes a difference, but in my mind, back then, it sort of did.

"Anyway," he resumes, "she asked me what I thought about one of them and I told her the truth and she *laughed*..." He trails off, his gaze going distant, his expression soft. "She had such a nice laugh," he says quietly. "Like, right from her belly, kind of weirdly deep. It made me laugh, just to hear it."

Tears prick my eyes at this poignant detail. "Yes," I whisper. "Me too."

We are both silent for a moment, the memory of Sophie like a shimmering in the air between us. I feel as if I can almost hear the echo of her laugh, see her eyes sparkle...

Then Tom sighs. "So, yeah. I asked her if she wanted to get a drink, and... well, it went from there."

"How long were you dating before she brought you to meet us?" I feel the need, even though it's far too late, to fill in some of the blanks that have yawned in my mind for so long.

He shrugs. "A couple of weeks, maybe?"

That's *it*? No wonder he was nervous. No wonder we were.

"Anyway..." he says, and it feels like the end of the conversation. Henry is still asleep on Tom's chest, and outside it is dark. Andrew will be home soon, a prospect I dread. I know Elizabeth will have talked to him, whispered in his ear.

I'm very sorry to say, Andrew, that Diana's been at it again. She's such a disappointment to you. I really don't know how you stand it...

All sentiments I've heard before, at various times and places. When she came over years ago, when I was still in the fog of grief from losing my mother. She'd visited unexpectedly, and yes, I'd been a little out of it. I can admit that, but I hated how she went right to Andrew, after sending me up to bed like I was a naughty child.

I'd crept downstairs when I'd heard her querulous voice, my whole body cringing in shame at the way she spoke about me to my own husband.

And then, Andrew's reply, toneless and firm: *Thank you, Elizabeth, I'll take care of it.*

Which he did, by booking me in to see a therapist and taking away my Xanax. It was easy enough to get another prescription, but I kept myself from it for six months, which was something, at least.

But I don't want to return to that depressing cycle now.

"I should go change," I tell Tom as I uncurl myself from the sofa. "Clean myself up a little." I try to give him the kind of wry smile he gave me, but I don't think I manage it.

"Okay." He gestures to Henry, still asleep on his chest. "I guess I'm parked here for a while."

"He'll probably need feeding soon—"

"I gave him a bottle about an hour ago, before you woke up," Tom tells me. "And burped him, too."

"You did?" I can't keep the surprise out of my voice, and he smiles.

"Yeah, I know I'm still crap at this, but I'm not totally useless."

"You're not useless at all," I tell him firmly. He has learned so much so quickly, I am both impressed and envious, especially because I still feel fairly useless myself.

Slowly, I head upstairs, my feet dragging, my head still feeling fuzzy. I dread facing Andrew and trying to give him an explanation, an apology. He'll be quiet, tense, his disappointment like a palpable miasma in the air. I've felt it so many times before, and the worst part is, I know I can't even blame him.

As quickly as I can, I shower, brush my teeth and dry my hair before changing into a pair of loose linen trousers and a silk top. I want to look like the wife Andrew expects and needs me to be, even if inside I still feel like a jumble of broken parts.

I'm just putting on a pair of pearl earrings when Andrew comes into the bedroom. He looks haggard, his face gray and drawn, his shoulders, usually thrown back, slightly slumped. He had to run interference with all our friends and relatives, I realize, while I was completely checked out. Guilt needles me at the thought.

He stops in the doorway to gaze at me for a moment, saying nothing, and I still, my fingers on the clasp of my earring. Neither of us speaks for a long moment as we hold each other's weary, wary gazes, and then I break first.

"I'm sorry." The words come fast, like I can't wait to get them out of my mouth.

Andrew lets out a long, low sigh as he shrugs off his jacket, drops it onto the bed. "It was a hard day."

His resigned understanding only makes me feel worse.

"Did Elizabeth speak to you?" I force myself to ask, even though there is no part of me that wants to have this conversation.

He nods briefly, his gaze averted. "Yes."

I bite my lip, hating how miserable I feel, like a child who has messed up *again* and would rather their parent yell than look so very disappointed. Andrew often chooses anger to mask his own sorrow or fear, but with me he's only, always been disappointed. Sometimes I *wish* he would have raged or shouted at me. I think I might have felt stronger then. I would have come back swinging, argued with him, fought it out, maybe even felt like I'd gained some ground, or at least that we'd battled as equals.

But you can't argue with disappointment. You can only feel lesser, weaker, cringing helplessly beneath it.

I take a deep breath, let it out slowly. I decide not to apologize again, because it only makes me feel worse. "I spoke to Tom," I say instead. "He... brought me home."

"That was good of him," Andrew replies tonelessly. He takes off his tie and tosses it on top of his jacket before he begins to unbutton his shirt.

"I think we might have misjudged him, Andrew," I venture. "He's had a hard childhood. His dad left when he was a teenager, and he ended up in foster care because his mother wasn't—"

"So he was selling you his sob story," Andrew cuts in cynically as he gives a disparaging shake of his head. He clearly thinks I've fallen for a line.

"No, he wasn't!" I protest. "Far from it. I could tell he didn't want me to feel sorry for him. I was asking questions, that's all, and he was answering them..." I falter and fall silent, because I sense something from Andrew that is even worse than disappointment. It seems almost like despair.

Slowly, he takes off his shirt, drops it into the laundry pile, and then pulls on a polo, running a hand through his thick, silvered hair as he shakes his head wearily. "What do you want from Tom, Diana?" he asks finally, his voice grave. "Do you want him to live with us forever, in some kind of blended family?" He doesn't wait for me to answer. "Or is it that you just feel guilty for the way we treated him before?" He pauses, his voice getting even graver as he continues, "Or is what's really going on here that you're afraid that you can't manage Henry on your own? Because if that's the case, we'll hire more help. A full-time nanny, like I suggested." He pauses. "It helped before."

I flinch at what feels like an indictment, decades old. "I just want to give him a chance," I say quietly. "He's Henry's father, after all."

"He's a convicted *felon*," Andrew responds flatly. "And he's given me no real indication that he wants to be a part of his son's life. As far as I'm concerned, the only reason he's here is to see what he can get out of us. And the fact that he wasn't willing to take my offer of a very reasonable, very *generous* stipend suggests that we can't trust him an inch."

"But he's learning," I protest, even though I know Andrew has made some fair points. "He's so much better with Henry, and I think he really does want to try..." Or is this just about me being afraid to try? I wonder. I still feel so uncertain.

Andrew sighs and then walks over to me, placing his hands on my shoulders as he gazes down at me, his expression turning tender and yet also resigned. "I know this is hard for you," he says quietly. "Losing Sophie, of course, it's unimaginable, but also taking care of Henry." He pauses. "It brings up hard memories... for both of us."

I blink and look down, unable to bear the weight of his compassion as well as the fact of my own failure.

"But we can get through this, Diana," he continues. "We'll hire help like I said. You don't have to do it on your own. I talked to the lawyer again, and she said having some childcare help wouldn't hurt our case. It shows we're well-resourced and prepared to do whatever it takes."

"But Andrew... if it came to a custody battle..." My voice is dry and papery as I force myself to ask the question I haven't even wanted to think about. "What if... my history comes up?"

Andrew frowns as he gives a little shake of his head. "How would it? Tom doesn't know anything about all that."

"A lawyer could find out. There are records... And today..." I trail off, not wanting to put it into words.

Andrew sighs as he gently squeezes my shoulders. "We'll cross that bridge when we come to it. But in the meantime... please don't trust Tom, Diana. I know it's tempting, both because you're a trusting person and you're doubting yourself. But he's not a good person, no matter how he seems to you sometimes, and I do not want my grandson raised by him."

Andrew sounds so absolutely certain, and for a second it gives me uneasy pause. Does he know something I don't know?

"Is there something you're not telling me?" I ask cautiously. What he is saying is at odds with the man I saw and smiled with downstairs, the man who helped me when I was so vulnerable.

Andrew frowns and drops his hands from my shoulders. "What more do you even think there should be?" he asks, a touch of irritation to his voice. "He was in prison, he stole from us, he was high on drugs when we met him. He's refused a generous payment in order to undoubtedly try for more. He's only interested in Henry when it suits him, and he's come back from wherever he goes smelling of alcohol and cigarettes. What," he demands, "about his behavior suggests that he could be a good father to our grandchild?"

I think of Tom sprawled in the chair opposite me, his hand on Henry's back, his face touched with both sadness and humor. "I don't know," I whisper. "I just want to give him a chance."

Because Tom might have made a lot of mistakes, but so have I. And if my husband won't give our son-in-law a second chance, why should I trust that he will keep giving me one?

If Andrew gives up on Tom, maybe one day I'll be out of chances too.

TEN

As ever, when I have a setback—that's what Andrew has called them, over the years—I wake up early the next morning, determined to turn over a new leaf and be the woman I want to be, the wife my husband needs.

I spend several hours in the garden, deadheading more daffodils and weeding the flower beds to pristine stretches of soft brown mulch, all before Henry is even awake.

When I come inside, both he and Tom are still asleep. Mia has gone, Andrew already left for work. The house is quiet, and I let myself enjoy the momentary peace as I brew a fresh pot of coffee. Carmen won't be in for another hour, a silent, somewhat sullen presence who works around me and makes me feel guilty for employing her at all—another sign I can't cope, even though every woman of my acquaintance has help, and often a lot more than I do.

As my therapist informed me after my mother died, I'm far from the only middle-aged woman in Old Greenwich who has some kind of prescription on endless refill and a lot of household help.

I didn't go back to her after that offhand remark. I think she was trying to make me feel better, but it only made me feel worse, like I was a caricature, the depressed and doped-up housewife with too much time and money on her hands. And maybe I *am* that—I can be honest with myself, mostly—but I'm also *more* than that. At least, I've always wanted to be.

As I take my coffee to the patio, pulling my cardigan around my shoulders as the brisk morning breeze buffets me, the waves of the Sound ruffled in white below a pale blue sky, I sift through the memories of yesterday in my mind. Tom's unexpected kindness. Andrew's painful understanding. The sense that he might be holding something back. Jennifer Stanton's gossipy admission that her daughter knew about Sophie and Tom's marriage troubles.

Can that really be true? Did Andrew know about them, too? It wouldn't be the first time he's kept something from me for what he deems my own good. When Sophie failed her driving exam; when a stock he'd invested in crashed and we lost hundreds of thousands of dollars; when my mother had called to tell me the chemo wasn't working. Each time he kept silent as a way to protect me, or so he said, but it just made me feel more useless when I found out eventually, anyway.

Is that what's happening now? But if Andrew really felt Tom was some kind of danger—first to our daughter and then to us and our grandson—why on earth would he let him live in our house, and be alone with me? I know he wouldn't, so something else has to be going on.

For a second, I think of asking Sophie, and then I let out a trembling, tear-edged laugh as I realize the utter hopeless futility of such a thought. Of course I can't ask Sophie. I can never ask my daughter anything again. I'll never see her tilt her head as she considers her answer, give me that teasing smile of hers, or a quick, good-natured eyeroll. I'd even take one of her irritated huffs, the sideways glare, right now. Anything, to have her back.

I reach for my phone, flicking through our old text messages until I can get to one that she actually responded to, but it's been so long, those old messages have been deleted, which feels like another loss about the other far greater ones. All I have are my unanswered messages to her, one after the other, a damning line of pleading texts.

I go to my voicemails, which I never listen to since the only calls I get are marketing or spam, but maybe Sophie left me a message years ago that I kept, something innocuous about whether she can come over for dinner or if I can call the hair salon to make her an appointment, something I would have kept because I never delete my voicemails. I never even check them. Right now, I just want to hear her voice.

I scroll through, looking for her number, only for everything in me to still. There *is* a voicemail from my daughter, but it's from eight months ago, when she wasn't speaking to me, and I've never listened to it before. How could I have possibly missed this?

My breath catches as I swipe to listen to it and, with trembling fingers, hold my phone to my ear.

"Mom?" Sophie's voice is shaky and full of tears, and my stomach drops at the sound. "I know I've been crap about being in touch, but I've read all your text messages, and I've missed you so much..." Her voice wobbles as she trails off, and I close my eyes against the hot press of tears.

Oh, Sophie. Sophie.

"But I need you now," she continues, her voice choking. "Mom, I think I made a big mistake. A really big mistake. I need you..." She trails off on another sob, and then the line goes dead.

For a second, I can't breathe. Can't think. I can't even see, my vision blurring as I stare sightlessly in front of me, my hand going slack as I lower the phone from my ear. Eight months ago, my daughter needed me. She called me in desperation, and I *didn't even listen to the voicemail.* How could I have failed her so utterly, *again?*

And what had been going on, that she felt she'd made a mistake and needed my help?

I put down my phone and take a deep breath, forcing myself to stay calm when all I want to do is panic, scream, *shriek* with fear, of something that has already happened.

It's too late, I realize numbly. Whatever happened, whatever it was that made my beloved daughter think she'd made a terrible mistake, and that she needed me... it's already happened. She's dead, and she died without her own mother having ever helped her or even known that she needed help. Even worse, she died thinking I ignored that message, that I didn't care enough to call back.

For a few more seconds, I simply stare into space. I have no idea what to do now, what this new knowledge means for me, for Andrew, for this life we're trying to make with our son-in-law and grandson. Was the mistake she was talking about *Tom?* Ideas and images rollick through my mind—shouting matches, sudden bruises, my daughter crouching in a closet, scared and alone, the phone pressed to her ear...

I take another breath and force such dreadful thoughts back. They're the stuff of nightmares and made-for-TV movies, not my life. Not my daughter's life.

But my daughter is dead. It's her son I need to consider. To care for. I may have let my daughter down, but I still have my grandson to save.

Abruptly, I go upstairs, tiptoe down the hall, and slip into the nursery.

Henry is asleep in his crib, swaddled in a soft blue blanket and lying on his back. His tiny rosebud mouth is puckered, and in his sleep he makes little sucking noises that make me think he is dreaming of milk.

Gazing down at this precious little boy, I feel a sudden, intense rush of love that sweeps all my self-doubt away, turns it into an irrelevance, a useless nonentity. How could I have been so stupidly self-absorbed as to believe I was not equipped to care for this baby? To let myself languish and even revel in my own weakness, like I had that selfish luxury?

Once more, I am filled with shame, but this is a *cleansing* shame, a healing one. For the sake of this child, I need to be strong. I will be.

Even though he's still asleep, I gently scoop him up into my arms, simply because I need to hold him. To keep him safe. I breathe in his baby scent and press a kiss to his downy head, my eyes closed, my heart bursting with good intentions.

"I will take care of you," I whisper.

"What are you doing?"

The sound of Tom's sleep-filled and slightly surly voice from the kitchen doorway has me startling so much I nearly drop Henry, and he wakes with a startled cry.

"Tom..." My voice is hoarse. "Sorry, you surprised me." Gently I cradle Henry to me, his head nestled against my chest as I pat his back, and with a snuffle, he drifts back into sleep.

I force myself to look up and smile at Tom; he is dressed only in a pair of loose pajama pants, his chest bare, his tattoos on full display. I catch sight of the tattered butterfly in front of the gaping-mouthed skull on his breastbone, just like the drawing Sophie once showed me, and I look away quickly.

"Is everything okay?" Tom asks in an even voice that makes me think he knows I am nervous. And I *am* nervous... because despite how he took care of me yesterday, I don't know this man. I don't know what his marriage to my daughter was like, and if she was asking for help because she was scared of her husband.

"Everything's fine," I say, a little too brightly. "I think I'll go make Henry his bottle."

Tom frowns, like he wants to say something more, but I head out of the nursery, taking Henry with me, before he can.

Downstairs, I put Henry in his bouncy seat while I make his bottle. My mind is racing, racing, trying to think of some kind of solution. How can I find out what Sophie meant, and if in fact Tom is a danger?

She could have been talking about anything, I tell myself. Sophie did have a tendency to impulsive behavior and overreaction over the smallest things—a friend's sharp word, an unanswered text. She might have called me in such a moment and then forgotten about it the next day.

But what if she didn't? What if it was something serious?

It torments me that I have no idea what was going on in my daughter's life for a year and a half. Her random high school friend knew more than *me*, her mother. Yet how can I find out anything now?

I reach for my phone as an idea takes hold. I dial the number for Bergdorf Goodman's offices, although it's too early and no one answers. I leave a message, asking someone to call me back as I have a question about Sophie West—I stumble over her last name—and then I end the call, feeling far from satisfied. Would someone from her work know what was going on in her life? I have no idea, but it seems like a lot of people might have known more than I do.

Henry has fallen back asleep in his seat, and so I reach for my phone again and listen to the voicemail once more. It doesn't sound any better on repeat. If anything, it sounds worse.

"Mom, I need you now... I think I made a mistake. A really big mistake..."

I close my eyes as I listen to my little girl's broken voice.

"What's going on?"

My eyes fly open, and I stare at Tom, who is now dressed in

faded jeans and a T-shirt, his feet stuffed into unlaced work boots. He is glowering at me, his feet set wide in what feels like an aggressive stance, his eyebrows drawn together in a scowl.

"Was that a message from *Sophie*?" he demands incredulously. Clearly the message was loud enough for him to recognize her voice.

I open my mouth to say—what? My mind is a blank, and my heart is skittering with sudden fear. Once again, I am forced to face the fact that I have no idea what this man is capable of. By his own admission, his track record is terrible, and here I am alone with him, his eyes flashing anger, his face dark with suspicion.

I realize I have no good answer, and so I give him the truth. I swipe to listen to Sophie's voicemail again, this time on speaker.

"Mom, I know I've been crap about being in touch, but I've read all your text messages, and I've really missed you…" Her voice, wobbling with emotion and choked with tears, fills the kitchen. "But I need you now. I think I've made mistake. A really big mistake… I need you…"

The message ends, and the kitchen is plunged into a terrible silence. Tom is staring straight at me, his arms folded across his chest, his jaw bunched. I realize, bizarrely, I don't feel afraid anymore. I feel determined.

"She sent that eight months ago," I tell him. "I didn't listen to it. I didn't even *see* it." I have to take a breath to steady myself. "What was she talking about, Tom? What big mistake did she make?"

The silence feels electric, pulsing between us. From his seat, Henry snuffles in his sleep.

"Seems like you've already made up your mind about what it is," Tom says flatly.

"You don't care to enlighten me?" I ask, my voice rising. "Set the record straight?"

"Why should I?"

I shake my head slowly. "You're here on our *sufferance*," I tell him, and I can see instantly that this was the wrong thing to say, and in any case, I didn't really mean it. His eyes flash darkly with anger, and he settles more firmly into his stance, like he's spoiling for a fight. I force myself to continue. "All I'm saying is, I think you could at least be honest with us. Do you know what that call was about?" I wait for a reply, but he doesn't say anything, and so I press, "Was it about you? Were you and Sophie having marriage problems?"

Tom shifts back on his heels, his chin jutting out. "What does it matter now? She's dead."

I jerk back, startled by how cold he sounds. "You know why it matters!" I snap, and nod toward Henry. I don't know if I'm being phenomenally stupid or brave, maybe both, but I need to have the truth. The what-ifs will torture me otherwise.

"So you'll use one voicemail message to take away my son?" Tom surmises scornfully. He must see my look of guilty surprise because he gives a brusque nod. "You think I don't know that's what you and Andrew are planning? Why you even agreed to have me here in the first place? Andrew wanted to cut a deal, give me some kind of payoff... do you think I'm *stupid*?" he demands while I simply gape. "You've both been watching me, waiting me to do something wrong and then take it to your lawyers." He shakes his head, dropping his arms, his expression firming. "Well, that's not happening."

"Tom, I just want to know the truth," I say. I try to keep my voice even, but it trembles.

"The truth?" Tom repeats with a hard laugh. "How about this truth, that the only addict around here is *you*, and if you think you're in a better position to take care of *my* baby, you've got another thing coming."

Before I can react—and I can't, because I am reeling from what he's just said—he strides over to Henry and yanks him out of his bouncy seat. It takes me a few seconds—far too long—to realize what he is doing.

"Tom—" I begin, but he's already striding toward the back door, the baby in his arms. *"Don't!"* I cry as he flings it open and then storms out with his son.

I run to the door, sprinting out onto the driveway, but Tom and my grandson have already gone.

ELEVEN

I run all the way down the driveway, just in time to see Tom disappearing around the corner of the street, his son in his arms. Where on earth does he think he's going, with no car, no spare clothes, *nothing*? Henry needs his diaper changed *and* his bottle. In just a few minutes, Tom is going to have a very hungry and unhappy baby on his hands.

He'll come back, I tell myself, *when he realizes how ridiculous he's being*. He can't go far, anyway; the train station is over two miles away.

I walk back into the house, telling myself this was just a silly argument, and in a few minutes Tom will slip sheepishly back into the house, Henry looking disgruntled and wanting his bottle, and we'll pretend this never happened.

As soon as I have that thought, though, I know I can't take the risk. I grab my car keys and head to the garage. There's only one main road from here to the train station, Sound Beach Avenue, and Tom has to be on it.

But a few minutes later, as I cruise down the avenue, I only see a few joggers and power walkers, as well as a mother with a toddler in one of those high-tech strollers on Monster Truck type wheels.

No Tom. No Henry.

I drive through the whole neighborhood between our gated community and the train station—down every tree-lined avenue and pleasant street, looking for his rugged form heading down one of the sidewalks, a baby in his arms, but he's nowhere to be found.

Desperate now, I drive in the other direction to Greenwich Point Beach, even though it's over two miles from our house, but there are just the usual joggers and walkers along the wide sidewalk heading to the Sound, everyone enjoying a beautiful spring while I sit here, hunched over the steering wheel, my stomach seething with anxiety and fear.

Tom has disappeared—and so has our grandson.

A jagged little cry escapes me, and I press my lips together as I resolutely turn back toward home. Maybe he's already there, I think with a wild lurch of hope, and I missed him while I was cruising the side streets.

But when I get back to the house, the only person there is Carmen. She's getting bottles of cleaning spray from under the sink, putting each one down on the counter with a clunk.

"Carmen," I ask breathlessly, my car keys still clenched in my hand, "have you seen Tom? And Henry?"

"You *lost* them?" she asks, sounding unsympathetic, and I bite my lip hard enough to draw blood.

"No, they just went for a walk, but... I was hoping they'd be back by now."

Carmen looks unimpressed. "No," she says shortly. "I haven't seen them."

I deflate, everything in me going flat. I'll have to call Andrew. I'll have to confess everything—the voicemail, my ill-thought-out confrontation with Tom, how he stormed out of the house with our grandchild.

Upstairs in my room, I sink onto the bed as his number rings. It almost always switches to voicemail, as Andrew has never liked taking personal calls at work, but this time he answers it after just a couple of rings.

"Diana?" Already his voice is sharp with concern.

"Andrew..." I take a shuddering breath. "Tom is gone."

"*Gone—*"

"With Henry."

Andrew's breath hisses between his teeth. "What happened?"

Briefly, my voice and insides both leaden, I explain the events of the morning, although I don't mention the voicemail. I don't want to have to admit I missed such an important message, and so I simply say we argued. "I'm sorry," I finish wretchedly. "I shouldn't have gotten cross, but I just..." I realize I don't know how to finish that sentence. What did I hope to gain from confronting Tom the way I did? A sense of my own strength, maybe, the feeling that I was finally taking control. I wasn't thinking through how such a pathetic power play might affect Henry.

"I'll have to call the police," Andrew states. It's clearly not a matter for debate, but the prospect fills me with panic.

"Will they do anything?" I ask in feeble protest. "Tom is entitled to take his son where he likes—"

"The department owes me a favor," Andrew cuts me off. "We gave a big donation to their fundraiser last year. They'll at least send a car around the neighborhood—"

"And if they don't find him?" I whisper. What if, in his anger, Tom has done something to Henry? What if he's *left* him somewhere, a vulnerable baby, barely ten days old, all alone? He could be hurt or kidnapped, *killed...*

"Then I'll hire a detective," Andrew says with decision, before his voice subsides into a weary shudder, at a loss in a way

I haven't seen him before. "Diana, I don't know what else I can do."

"I'm sorry," I say again.

Andrew doesn't reply.

The next few hours pass with torturous slowness. I call Tom several times—he gave me his number when he first moved in—and then Sophie, just in case he still has her phone. Both lines switch to voicemail right away. They've been turned off, which scares me. I really have no idea where Tom is, or what he might be doing.

Andrew calls back to tersely inform me that the police did a sweep of the neighborhood and didn't see anything. How could Tom have disappeared so quickly? I wonder again and again. Despite Andrew's best efforts, insisting that Tom wasn't in a fit mental state to care for Henry, the police aren't willing to do anything more—no scan of CCTV footage, no checking train tickets or times, or whatever else they could do to track Tom's movements. Our son-in-law is gone, along with our grandson.

And it's *my* fault.

The guilt gnaws at me like a corrosive acid as Andrew hires a private detective, who comes to the house to search through Tom's belongings for any clues, but he brought nothing, save for a suitcase of shabby clothes, a few toiletries, and, somewhat jarringly, a red-covered Bible, the kind you'd seen in a hotel room, given by the Gideons.

By the time the detective leaves, it is late afternoon, Carmen has gone home, and Tom and Henry have been missing for eight hours, which feels like an unfathomable amount of time. Has Henry been changed? Fed? I hate to imagine him struggling, crying himself hoarse...

Andrew came back late this morning, and then went out

again, to search for Tom and talk to the police again, as desperate as I am to do something, anything.

Alone in the house, I am at a loss as to what to do. Outside, sunlight is pouring over the placid sweep of the Sound like liquid gold, turning everything to Technicolor. Now that the daffodils have had their day, the tulips are coming out, their slender green stems swaying in the evening breeze, their pink heads nodding. It's a beautiful evening, the kind that might have Andrew and I eat out on the terrace, watching the sun set and enjoying a silence that is more companionable than usual.

Instead I stand alone at the bottom of the lawn, the wind whipping my cardigan around me, as I stare at the sea and wonder if I'll ever see my grandson again. How can I get him back? How can I reach Tom?

I slip my phone out of my cardigan pocket and, feeling the futility of it all, dial Tom's number yet again. I've called him sixteen times since he left this morning, and every single time the call has switched to voicemail immediately.

This time it does too, and with a sigh I am about to slide my phone into my pocket when it rings. I glance at the screen, willing it to be Tom calling me back, but it's a number I don't recognize.

"Hello?" I ask with cautious eagerness. Maybe Tom is calling me from someone else's phone.

"Diana Lawrence? This is Kathy Steele, from Bergdorf Goodman. You were calling about Sophie? I was so sorry to hear about her death. Please accept my condolences." The woman's voice is smooth and assured but also brisk, with just the right amount of compassionate regret.

"Thank you..." With everything that has happened, I forgot I called the department store's office this morning. "I was just wondering..." I clear my throat. What on earth could this woman tell me about my daughter, or why she was so unhappy?

"If Sophie was doing well in her job?" I ask, painfully conscious of how I'm revealing my own ignorance. "It's just that, since her death, we've had some questions about what was going on in her life before she died..."

Kathy Steele is silent for several seconds. "I'm afraid I can't really speak to the last few months," she says, and her tone is still professional, but now slightly cool. "I thought you might have known, but Sophie was removed from her position here at Bergdorf Goodman about eight months ago."

"*What...*" The single syllable comes out in a shocked breath. It must have happened around the same time as the phone call; was that why she'd called? But if it had nothing to do with Tom, why did he leave the way he did? "Why was she fired?" I ask.

Kathy lets out a small sigh. "She'd become very erratic in her behavior. Missing work, skipping meetings... we gave her several warnings, but in the end we simply had to let her go. We have a high standard of professionalism here, and although we wanted to cut her some slack, we just couldn't." Her tone is final. "I thought you might have known," she says again. "Bill told Andrew he was having to let her go."

Andrew *knew*?

I have no response to that. Bill, an old golf buddy of Andrew's, hired Sophie as a favor. I understand why he would have told Andrew he was firing her... but why didn't Andrew tell me? Whether it was to protect me or not, it wasn't his right. And it begs the question... what else has he not been telling me?

"Thank you," I whisper, and I end the call. It feels like there is nothing more to say, even if I am still swimming in ignorance. There is so much I don't know, but bleakly I wonder if it even matters. Sophie is dead. Knowing how unhappy she was eight months ago doesn't change that. Nothing will bring her back.

And as for bringing *Henry* back... what can I do now but hope and pray?

Just then, my phone rings again. I turn it over, my heart leaping in my chest when I see who it is.

"*Tom!*" His name is a cry.

"Diana... I'm sorry." His voice is slurred, the words barely understandable.

"Tom, it's okay," I say quickly. I am filled with equal parts relief and terror. He sounds drunk, or worse. "Where are you?" I ask. "Where's Henry? Is he okay? Let me come find you. Help you—" The words spill from my lips, a desperate torrent. "Tom —" I fall silent, because while Tom has not replied, I can still hear him.

He's crying.

"Tom?" I say again, more quietly. My fingers ache from clutching the phone so hard. "Please, tell me where you are."

I hear the jagged sounds of his sobs, his breath hitching, his throat clogged. He tries to speak, but the words are garbled, impossible to understand.

"Tom, please." I gentle my voice, my throat aching with unshed tears of my own. "Is Henry..."

"He's here. He's okay."

Thank God.

Briefly, I close my eyes, offer a prayer of gratitude. "Tell me where you are," I say again. "I'll come find you. Tom, it's okay. It's going to be okay. I'll get you, and we can come back here and talk everything out."

"I don't want you to take him away from me," he says on another sob, and a breath rushes out of me.

"Tom, we won't. I promise, okay?" I know it's not a promise I can make, not if Andrew has anything to do with it, but I mean it. "We'll talk this through. Figure something out that works for everyone. Whatever it is. We can all make allowances..." In my fear, I am babbling, desperate to get him to agree. "Please, Tom, tell me where you are. For Henry's sake, and also your own. You don't sound well, and I want to help you, I really do—"

"I'm at a friend's house in Baychester," Tom says in a garbled rush. "On St Lawrence Avenue."

I suck in a hard breath. "What number—"

He gives it to me on another sob. "Please, can you come on your own? No police, and not Andrew—"

"I'll come on my own," I say, another rash promise.

"I'm sorry," Tom whispers, and then he ends the call.

I stand there for a moment, my phone clutched to my chest, my eyes closed. I know where he is. I can find Henry.

And I can't tell Andrew.

If I do, I know he'll insist on coming, maybe even along with the police. He'll want Tom arrested, or at least cautioned, maybe investigated for neglect or endangerment of a child... accusations that once could have been leveled against me.

I can't do that to Tom. No matter what happened that I don't know about, and all that I do, he deserves a chance to explain himself. To choose differently.

We all do.

Andrew might have been keeping secrets from me, but now I'm the one keeping them from him. But when I return with Tom and Henry, I tell myself, he'll understand. He'll have to.

Resolutely, I turn back to the house. I get my purse, some cash just in case, and the car keys. Then I pack a diaper bag with fresh clothes, diapers, and several bottles. As I sling it over my shoulder, I consider leaving a note for Andrew, but then I decide that explaining later will be easier. At least, that's how it feels right now.

I glance around the kitchen, pristine and empty, and regret wars with hope as I remember Sophie seated at the breakfast bar, regaling me with her latest drama, or practicing her pirouettes as a six-year-old ballerina, blond pigtails flying out. I think of when I held her as a baby, rocking her by the greenish light of the stove clock, aching with fatigue and despair. I think about how I once walked out of this very room without looking back, and how much it cost me.

I am redeeming all that history now, I tell myself. Tonight. And then I head outside, closing the door behind me, to go to Baychester to find my grandson.

TWELVE

The address Tom gave me in Baychester is a shabby-looking duplex, the front porch holding a sofa with its stuffing exploding out of it and a couple of broken folding chairs, trash littering the sidewalk in front. The whole place is dark, but there is rap music blasting out of the basement, and I am filled with trepidation as I pull my car up to the curb and let out a shaky breath. This is far from the kind of neighborhood I usually frequent, and my shiny BMW SUV is hideously out of place.

Andrew has called three times and texted me twice, and now, with the car parked, I finally text him back.

I think I know where they are. Be back soon.

It's a message that I know will fill him with both fury and fear, but I can't explain everything now. I can't let Andrew swoop in and make things worse than they already are.

Slowly, my heart beating hard, the diaper bag slung over my shoulder, I get out of the car, clicking my key fob to lock it, and walk up to the front door. I knock once, timidly at first and then more firmly, but there's no reply and so, after a few seconds of hesitation, I try the door. It opens into a living room that is empty, the coffee table covered with old pizza boxes and crumpled beer cans, a cloying smell of cannabis in the air. I take a step in, and then another. My hands are slippery, my heart pounding all the harder.

All I can hear is the bass beat coming from the basement, and so I walk to the back of the house. The door to the basement is in the kitchen, which is just as messy as the living room, with a rancid smell of trash adding to the unpleasant mix of odors. I hate the thought of Henry being in a place like this, and I pray he really is okay like Tom said.

The music throbs in my ears as I walk down the rickety stairs to a basement that feels like a dark, dank cave. The smell of cannabis and beer and sweat is so thick, I can taste it in mouth. There are only a few people in the room—a guy clearly stoned out of his mind sprawled on the sofa, another one lying on the floor, looking half-dead, and... Tom. He's in an armchair in the corner of the room, his head thrown back, his body loose-limbed, half a dozen crumpled beer cans scattered around him. Not one person notices me as I step into the room, looking around wildly for Henry, but I can't see him in the darkness.

Dear heaven, is a defenseless little baby in this hellhole?

As I come closer, Tom's eyes flutter open and he gazes at me blearily.

"Diana..." His voice is sleepy and slurred, and his eyes flutter closed.

"Where is Henry, Tom?" My voice is too sharp, almost angry, but I tell myself it's better than showing my fear.

Tom seems to get smaller, folding into himself, his head hanging low. "He's upstairs," he mumbles.

I run upstairs, throwing one door open after the other. In the final bedroom, a tiny square of space, I find him in the middle of a double bed, still wrapped in the blue blanket from this morning. A sob escapes me as I scoop him up into my arms, and his eyes flutter open; he looks too dazed and exhausted to summon a cry. Has he been fed? Changed? Ten hours is a distressing amount of time for a baby not to be cared for.

I draw him to my chest, pressing a kiss to his sweat-soaked head. I need to change and feed him, but I don't want to do it in this dirty place.

"I did give him a bottle," Tom says, and I look up to see him leaning against the doorway, still looking like he's half off his head. "And I changed his diaper," he adds in a slurred voice. "I bought some stuff at CVS. But that was a while ago..." He trails off as he slides down the doorway to the floor, drawing his knees up and dropping his head into his hands.

I want to be angry, to be high on self-righteous fury, but I know that I, of all people, cannot point fingers right now.

"Let's get out of here, Tom," I say quietly. "We can talk somewhere else."

He shakes his head, his fingers digging hard into his skull. "I messed up," he mumbles, his head still bowed. "I messed up so much."

"Tom..." I want to leave as quickly as we can, but already I am realizing that might not be possible, not with Tom the way he is right now. I put Henry down on the bed and get out fresh clothes and a diaper. "You did mess up," I state matter-of-factly. "And thank God nothing truly bad happened to Henry or you. But... we can get past this. If you want to."

Tom just shakes his head, and I focus on changing Henry. His diaper is full, his poor bottom red and chafed. I slather on diaper cream and then slip on a fresh onesie and sleepsuit. As I do up the buttons, he starts to cry—a thin, weak sound. Tom hasn't moved.

I take the bottle I'd made earlier out of the bag and perch on the bed, Henry in the crook of my arm, and begin to feed him. He gobbles down the formula quickly, greedy and desperate for milk. For a few minutes, I simply sit there, gazing down at my grandson's sweet face, watching him drink. *Thank God he seems okay*, I think with a wave of relief. This all could have been so much worse.

I glance back at Tom, who is still sitting on the floor, his head in his hands. If Andrew were here, I'm pretty sure he'd tell me to leave him where he is, take Henry and let Tom sort himself out, if he can.

But I don't want to do that. I *can't*, because I know what it's like to mess up as a parent. To feel like you can't cope another second. To fail. And I don't want Tom to have the regrets I still struggle with.

"Tom," I say gently. "I want to help you. But I can't if you don't talk to me."

A shudder escapes him and slowly he lifts his head. "I don't know what to tell you," he says in a low voice.

"What was Sophie talking about, on that voicemail?" I'm not sure if it's the right question to ask right now, but it feels like the root of it all. "And why did it make you walk out this morning the way you did?"

"Because..." He lowers his head again, as if in defeat. "Because I didn't want you to find out."

My stomach turns over and my heart skips a beat. I press Henry to me, glad he is safe in my arms. "Find out *what*?"

Tom lifts his head to stare straight at me, his expression so terribly bleak. "Sophie made that call because we had a big fight when I found out she was pregnant," he confesses in a low voice. "I... I wanted her to have an abortion."

I flinch, I can't help it, and Tom nods in resigned understanding.

"I know. I shouldn't have asked her. I'm sorry. And she freaked out about it, told me I was a monster for even suggesting it, but..." He blows out a breath. "Things were really hard. Sophie..." Another pause as he trails off, his gaze unfocused. "*She* was hard," he says quietly, and I flinch again.

What does he mean, my daughter was *hard*?

And yet I think I know exactly what he means.

"She was all over the place, emotionally," he continues in a low, defeated voice, his gaze unfocused. "I didn't know how to handle it. I loved her, but... she'd go from crying to raging to telling me how much she loved me. I never knew what to expect. And then she lost her job... I didn't even know she'd been skipping work. And we couldn't afford an apartment, never mind a baby, on just my pay. I didn't know what to do. I knew we couldn't afford a baby, we couldn't afford anything... and Sophie just didn't seem to understand that."

He blinks me into focus, his expression turning resolute, his face haggard. "I shouldn't have walked out today. I wasn't thinking. I know I'm not a good dad and I don't know how to be one but..." He gazes at Henry, still tucked in my arms, drinking his bottle. "I want to try, and I was afraid you won't let me. That you wouldn't let me, if you knew about all that... I know you guys have all the money and power. You could get a lawyer and sue for custody, and you'd win, and maybe you *should* win, but... I want to *try*." He scrubs his face with his hands, hard enough that it looks like it might hurt, and then drops them to gaze at me in mute appeal.

I want to try. The words echo through me, a whisper of my own thoughts when I wasn't far off where Tom is now. Is there anything more we can do as parents than want to try?

"And I want to help you do that," I tell Tom with sudden, desperate honesty. "Please, let us help you. Come back home and let us help you be the dad I know you want to be." And I can be the grandmother I want to be, interested and involved, without all the doubts that dogged me before. "We can do this, Tom," I say, my voice rising with determined stridency. "We can do this together."

Hope flickers across his face and then dies. "What about Andrew?"

I take a deep breath. Andrew, we both know, is the obstacle in this scenario. "I'll talk to him," I promise. "We both can—"

"He wants me out of the picture," Tom says flatly. "I know he does." He sighs, passing his hand over his head. "Hell, I'd want that too, if I were him."

"You are Henry's *father*, Tom," I remind him firmly. "Nothing can change that."

"Yeah, and I don't want to be a crap parent like both of mine ended up being. I don't want Henry to go through that."

"All parents are crap parents," I tell him, and then almost smile at his look of astonishment. "I was," I admit. "When Sophie was first born, I couldn't cope at all. I got seriously depressed and ended up..." I pause, wondering if it's wise to confess this to Tom. If it *does* come to a custody battle, he could certainly use this against me.

And then I realize that telling him commits me to making sure that it doesn't.

"I walked out on her," I say quietly. Tears of shame prick my eyes, and I blink them back as I gaze down at Henry. He's fallen asleep, the bottle half-finished, his lips slack on the nipple, although he continues to make little sucking noises in his sleep. His golden lashes fan his plump cheeks and right now he is the most beautiful thing I have ever seen.

"She was just six weeks old," I continue. "She'd been crying and fussing and I just snapped. I changed her diaper, I swaddled her, I put her in her crib, and then I walked out of the house. I didn't tell anyone, and Andrew was at work. I drove to the beach and just sat on the sand, for I don't know how long. Hours." I pause. "They only found her when our landscaper stopped by and heard her cries. He rang the doorbell and when there was no answer, he called the police." A sigh escapes me. "If he'd just called Andrew... but I think he was worried something violent had happened. Of course, social services had to get involved then, so I know what that's like..."

Tom stares at me, his mouth slightly agape, as if he can't believe what he's hearing. I feel a stirring of uneasy regret, wondering if I should have been smarter than to hand him what is essentially a grenade he can lob at any moment, but then I remind myself that I want to show him I trust him.

I trust him with Henry, and I trust him with this.

I just hope I don't live to regret it.

THIRTEEN

By the time I pull onto our street, it is nine o'clock at night. Tom is slumped in the passenger seat, and Henry in his car seat in the back, both of them asleep. After my confession, Tom clambered wearily to his feet.

"I'll go back," he said, his voice resigned, and I gathered up Henry and his things, grateful to be escaping that desperate place.

But I'm still afraid of what the future holds, and how I'll explain this all to Andrew.

As I come up to our drive, my heart sinks and my stomach swirls with dread, because the blue and red lights of a police car are flashing in the driveway.

Tom stirs and then lets out a groan as he sees the police car.

"I knew it," he says dully.

"Andrew was just worried," I tell him quickly. I'd texted him again when we'd got to the car, telling Andrew I had both Tom and Henry. There was no need for him to get the police involved, but obviously he disagreed, and the realization gives me a little spike of anger. Couldn't he have trusted me... for *once?*

I pull up in our drive, next to the police car. I get out slowly, taking my time to get Henry, leaving him in the car seat since he's still asleep. Tom hovers by me, still looking worse for wear, which won't help *either* of our causes.

Steeling my spine, I head inside. Andrew is at the kitchen table with two police officers who look a little bored as well as annoyed; I imagine the police of Old Greenwich get a lot of call-outs by entitled people who expect them to do their bidding.

Andrew jumps up from the table when he sees me. "Diana, thank God, you're back!" He comes toward me and pulls me into a quick, hard hug before stepping back, his eyes narrowed in a glare aimed at Tom. "I don't know what excuse you think you possibly have—" he begins.

"Andrew, *don't*." I set down the car seat and turn to the officers. "This is a purely domestic issue and we're in no need of your support, but thank you for coming out," I say firmly.

The older officer, grizzled and weary-looking, glances between me and Tom. "Ma'am, we had reason to believe you might have been in a coercive situation..." He looks meaningfully at Tom, who is still seeming like he needs to sleep it off.

"No, I was not," I say in the same firm voice. "My husband misunderstood the situation. Everything is absolutely fine, and there's no reason for anyone else to get involved, as we're all back safe and sound, as you can clearly see." I keep his gaze, although inside everything in me quails. This is bringing up too many memories I've buried deep inside, from that horrible day when I left Sophie alone. The police came, and social services were called, a report made. I felt like a criminal, the very worst kind, the mother who abandons her child. Does anyone have compassion for that kind of woman?

I do not want to be made to feel that way now, and I don't want Tom to feel it, either.

"Really, we're fine," I say firmly.

To my annoyance, the cop glances at Andrew, as if for confirmation, and my husband waves his hand in reluctant agreement.

"My wife is right," he says stiffly. "Thank you for your service."

The other policeman rises, and then Andrew escorts the two of them out to the car.

I turn to Tom. "Why don't you take a shower?" I suggest gently. "Clean yourself up? We can talk later." I touch his arm in a gesture of reassurance. "Nothing's going to be done or decided anytime soon, okay?"

He glances at me uncertainly, and then slowly nods. By the time Andrew returns, he's already upstairs.

The atmosphere is thick with tension as Andrew closes the door behind him. I wait, my hands resting on the back of a kitchen chair, my heart fluttering inside my chest like a trapped bird. I've been here before, but it was different back then, I tell myself.

It's different now. I am. Telling Tom the truth of my struggles, and helping him with my own, has strengthened something inside me. I have more determination now than I think I ever have before, and it feels good.

"Why didn't you call me?" Andrew asks, and he sounds only sad. "Why didn't you tell me what was going on?"

"I didn't want you bringing in the police," I reply steadily. "Which you did."

"Because I was *scared*, Diana!" His voice rises before he falls silent, shaking his head, whether in condemnation or confusion I can't tell. "Aren't we in this together?"

"I want to be, Andrew." I take a breath. "Of course I do. But..." I pause and then resolutely plunge ahead with the truth. "I feel like you're keeping things from me."

He stares at me, looking incredulous. "*I'm* keeping things from *you*?"

"Yes," I reply firmly, even though I know he has a point. I'm the one who has been keeping secrets today. "You knew Sophie had lost her job," I state, "and you never told me."

He shakes his head slowly, seeming bewildered by my statement. "Diana, that was *months* ago—"

"*Still.*" I silence him with a single word, my voice coming out stronger than it has in years, maybe even decades. For far too long I've been so weak, always apologizing, always afraid, mired in the guilt of a single moment twenty-four years ago, and all the mistakes I made after, all *because* of that guilt. It's defined me for too long, and I want to be different now. I want to shed the past like an old skin, let it flake away, and for the first time I feel like maybe I *can*. Tom's own weakness has, perversely, made me strong. I wasn't able to be strong for myself, but maybe I can for someone else. For Tom, and also for Henry. "You should have told me," I tell Andrew. "When it happened. Instead I found out from some stranger at Bergdorf Goodman."

He frowns, confused. "How did you?"

"I called the office, because I wanted to know what had been going on in her life," I tell him. "And they told me she'd been fired *eight months* ago, and that you knew about it."

He sighs heavily, his chin dropping toward his chest, his arms hanging loosely by his sides in a posture of defeated resignation. "Yes," he admits. "I knew."

I try to keep my voice level as I ask, "Why didn't you tell me?"

He lifts his head, and once again I only see sadness in his eyes, hear it in his voice. "You know why."

"Because you didn't think I could handle it," I force myself to say, my voice stiff. "You don't trust me. Even after all these years—"

"It's not about *trust,* Diana," Andrew says, his voice rising. "It's about knowing what you can handle... and what you can't."

I flinch at that. "You've never thought I could handle

anything!" I sound like Sophie, throwing out accusations to hide my own pain. "If you'd just trusted me—"

"Diana, I've been trying to *help* you, "Andrew exclaims, and now he sounds both astonished and aggrieved. "By not giving you more than you can bear. And as for Henry..." He glances at our grandson, still asleep in his car seat. "We can hire a nanny—"

"I don't want to hire a nanny," I cut him off. "Not again. I know I've doubted myself, Andrew, but I don't need you doubting me, too. And Tom doesn't need that, either, which is why I went to get him tonight." It's time to bring it back to the present, because the past is simply too painful to address. "He feels bad enough, and he's *trying*. Instead of fighting him, we should be *supporting* him. Helping him to be a good father, because he wants to be one. He told me that tonight."

Andrew shakes his head, his lip curling. "And you believe him?"

"I do. He's overcome a lot. His childhood—"

"Yes, I know," Andrew cuts me off with another shake of his head. "His dad walked out when he was a teenager, and his mother isn't involved. He was in foster care from the age of fourteen. Plenty of people have had similar."

"I didn't know you knew all of that," I say. I told him some of it before, but Andrew speaks like it's all old news.

"When he and Sophie eloped," he admits, 'I hired a private investigator to look into him. I wanted to know what we were dealing with," he says simply.

"And you didn't think to tell me any of that, either?" I shake my head slowly. "All this time, you've been treating me like a *child*—"

"Would it have helped?" Andrew demands. "Knowing he has some sob story he can trot out when it suits him—"

"Actually, yes." My voice is hard, strong. "Having a little empathy for him would have helped a lot, but *you* decided I didn't need to know. How many other things have you decided I didn't need to know? How can I trust *you*, Andrew?" The words ring out, rising in condemnation, and Andrew seems to deflate right before me, his shoulders slumping, his face looking even more haggard. He's become so used to me being passive, *pathetic*, he doesn't know how to deal with me now.

"Diana..." His voice is pleading. "I was just trying to help. I didn't want you to worry..."

"But I was worrying anyway!" I burst out. "Of course I was! We hadn't seen our daughter in a year and a half—" I stop abruptly, because something about Andrew's expression, the caginess of it, makes me say slowly, "You saw her. Didn't you? I can tell by the way you look right now, like you're guilty." My voice rises again, a jagged cry. "When did you see her?" I demand on a gasp.

"When she was fired," he admits heavily, his shoulders slumping further. "They told me they were going to let her go and I went over to the office on her last day, waited for her to come out. She was..." He blows out a breath. "Not herself. At least, not the way I remembered her, the way I want to remember her. She must have been pregnant then, although I didn't know it, and... she was furious with me. Refused to talk to me. Tried to *hit* me, even." He sounds incredulous, as if he still can't believe it all these months later. "I asked her to come home, *begged* her even, and she wouldn't listen at all. Said we didn't care, didn't even answer her messages, wasn't there when she needed us..." He lets out a broken cry and I flinch, his words falling like hammer blows. "*What* messages?" he demands. "She never once contacted me, and I know if she'd reached out to you..." He stops, and I know he can see the same caginess on my face that I saw on his, along with the guilt. Always the guilt. "Diana...?" he asks quietly, a touch of something almost like menace to his tone.

"She left me a voicemail," I admit in a whisper. "I didn't see it until today. I don't know how I missed it..." I trail off, abject, apologetic, my brief blaze of fury now completely quenched. How could I have possibly missed such an important message? How could I have let myself, lost in my own sadness?

Andrew doesn't say anything, but I see the judgment in his face. I feel it in the very air. If I wasn't so hopeless, spending far too many afternoons asleep on the sofa after too many Xanax, maybe I would have seen that message. I know that's what he's thinking.

It's what I'm thinking.

"Tom told me what it was about," I tell him, and now I sound stiff with affront, like I'm offended rather than filled with wretched guilt. "They'd had an argument about the baby. He didn't feel they could afford to have a child, and Sophie was determined—"

"But if she was already pregnant..." Andrew begins, and then falls silent as the realization kicks in.

I nod, confirmation of his unvoiced suspicion. "He wanted her to get... an abortion." Andrew's lips firm and his eyes spark. "We might not agree with it, Andrew, but it's understandable, and especially because you weren't the only person Sophie lashed out at. She fought with Tom too, and he found it really difficult."

"This is our *daughter* we're talking about," he says icily.

"I know, and I love her—loved her—with every breath in my body." The words come painfully, each one like a wound opening, bleeding out. "But she *was* challenging, Andrew. I think we can both admit that now. Her moods, her insecurities, her anxieties... it was hard. She was so young, and maybe she would have grown out of it all eventually, but... we did our best." Even if my best felt like so very little. "Let's help Tom do his best, too," I say quietly. "At least give him a chance. Doesn't he deserve one?"

Andrew is silent for a long moment. "When you found him

today," he says at last, "was he drunk? High? With Henry there?"

"He'd had a few beers," I allow. "And obviously it was very irresponsible, which he accepts. But should we judge his parenting by one unfortunate episode when he was upset? Cause it to color everything afterward?"

My words hang in the air, heavy with import, because we both know I'm not just talking about Tom. I'm talking about myself. I've spent *decades* trying to atone for the day I walked out of the house and left Sophie alone. I tried to do everything right—hand-sewed Halloween costumes, sung her to sleep every night for years. I went to every tennis match, every doctor's appointment, became an expert on eating disorders and anxiety attacks, researched endless therapies and medications, was her relentlessly cheerful cheerleader even when she was angry and impossible and I felt exhausted and despairing myself.

Still the scales never balanced, not in my eyes, and not in my husband's either. I want them to balance for Tom. I want to help him be and feel like a good parent, because I never did.

Andrew doesn't answer, and I hold his gaze as a silent conversation unspools between us, of acknowledgment and accusation, sorrow and regret. There are no answers in that conversation, no resolutions. Just an understanding of all that has passed.

"All right," Andrew finally says. "We'll give him a chance, although I don't even know what that means, because that's basically what we've been doing all along—"

"No lawyers," I tell him. "No working on a custody agreement on the side. No waiting in judgment for him to put a foot wrong, because that's how he's felt—"

"And now I'm responsible for his *feelings*?" Andrew asks, his tone sharpening, before, impatient and defeated, he shrugs his assent. "Fine. I'll do my best. You can't ask more than that."

"No," I agree quietly. "None of us can."

In the ensuing silence, Henry stirs, begins to snuffle and fuss. Quickly, I unbuckle him from his car seat, bring him to my chest, my arms recognizing the warm weight of him now.

"He's probably hungry," I murmur. "I'll change and feed him."

I walk away without waiting for a reply. I don't need Andrew's permission. I don't even need his approval. After twenty-seven years, maybe I'm finally learning to live without either.

Tonight marks a new chapter not just for Tom, but for me. In helping him redeem himself, I can redeem my own past, if not in Andrew's mind, then at least in my own. I've been mired by my own guilt and regret for far too long. It's time to take control.

Determination fires through me as I head upstairs. Everything, I tell myself, is going to be different now.

I'll make sure of it.

FOURTEEN

I wake the next morning, still hopeful and determined, but wondering how it's all going to work.

After our confrontation, Andrew disappeared to his study and Tom came back downstairs, showered and dressed and looking much better, if rather cautious, which was understandable. He gave Henry his bottle while I made us grilled cheese sandwiches, the silence in the kitchen feeling surprisingly companionable, and then Andrew joined us for a meal that felt stilted and strained, but at least it was progress, of a kind. We were sitting together, having dinner. I tried to give Tom an encouraging smile, but he wasn't looking anyone in the eye, his focus was on the food in front of him, which he wasn't even eating.

It was going to take time, I told myself, to figure out a way forward, how we could *be* with one another, when our history was so fractured and fragile. And if I thought about the future too much, my mind started to blur with something approaching panic. How would this actually work? In six months, a year, two years... what would that look like?

After dinner, with Henry asleep in his bouncy seat, Tom

disappeared to his room while I cleared the dishes and Andrew sat at the table, brooding.

"I don't see how this is going to work," Andrew said in a low voice. He nodded toward the door Tom had just gone through. "He's like a teenager, just sloping off on his own. Do you really want to be this responsible for him, making sure he takes care of his own son? It'll be exhausting, Diana, and I think you—"

"He needs time," I replied swiftly, cutting off any further diatribe, or, worse, insinuation that I couldn't handle whatever was coming toward us. I focused on stacking plates in the dishwasher, one after the other, finding something soothing in the rhythm. "We all do," I added, with more pointedness than I usually let into my voice. I did not want Andrew to derail whatever it was I was trying to build, and I wasn't even sure what that was yet.

Andrew was silent for a moment, and in his seat, Henry started to fuss. He went over and slid him out of the bouncy seat, cradling him in the crook of his arm, and something in me both ached and melted to see my husband, his face suffused with tenderness, looking so lovingly at our grandson.

Somehow, over the twenty-seven difficult years of our marriage, Andrew and I had lost sight of each other. He just became someone I had to please, or maybe only appease, rather than someone to love and share life with, a joint adventure to embark on, hand in hand.

The shared looks and jokes of our early years had morphed into a painful negotiation where what was unsaid was so much more damaging than what was. But now, looking at him look at our grandson, I am reminded of what we once had, like a faint echo, the whisper of something I can barely remember wanting, much less having.

Is it even possible to get that back again? I really didn't know the answer.

Andrew gazed down at Henry, cradled in the crook of his

arm. A sigh escaped him, long and low and weary. "What are you thinking, Diana?" he finally asked. "Are we just going to let him live with us forever? The son we never had?"

He spoke sarcastically, and the wistful thoughts I'd been having vanished like so much vapor. Andrew's question was particularly pointed, because I knew I *was* feeling maternal toward Tom. Maybe it was the loss of Sophie, or maybe it was because I understood how overwhelmed you could feel when you were faced with a newborn, but ever since I'd gone into that pit of a basement and seen how despairing Tom had been... I'd felt protective toward Henry *and* Tom. And I didn't want to let either of them go.

"Not forever," I allowed, speaking evenly, like I had a plan, and I knew exactly how to enact it. I wish I did. "But maybe for a few months, or, if it's going well, even years." I glanced at Andrew, pitching both my tone and my gaze somewhere between level and defiant. "Why shouldn't we help him, Andrew?" I challenged. "He's our son-in-law, and if we support him, we can only be helping Henry. And staying in his life. Better that than Tom taking off with Henry—"

"*Again*," Andrew put in pointedly, and I sighed.

"People do strange things when they reach a breaking point," I stated quietly, and the silence pooled between us, spread out to cover the whole room, like a heavy, suffocating blanket whose weight I recognized all too well. I'd been hidden and bowed beneath it for over twenty years.

I waited for Andrew to say something else—either about Tom or the ancient history of my postnatal depression and the mistakes I made during that painful time, I didn't know which—but he didn't say anything, and that, I realized, was exactly what I expected. So much of our marital life had been defined by silence.

And so, predictably, Andrew just shook his head, seeming wearier than ever, and I tried for something like a smile.

"Let's just take it one day at a time," I told him. It was meant to be an encouragement, but he scowled.

"And hope that Tom isn't going to take off again with Henry, *or* the family silver while we do?" he replied tartly as he rose from his chair. He put Henry back in his bouncy seat, shaking his head, emanating weary disapproval. "All I can say is," he told me, "that I hope we don't live to regret this."

"So do I," I answered quietly.

Andrew walked out of the kitchen without replying. The conversation, I reflected, had felt deeply unsatisfying. We hadn't made any progress, or had any real honesty, but at least, I told myself, we hadn't gone backward.

I finished cleaning up the kitchen and then took Henry upstairs for a change and his last bottle before bed. I paused by Tom's door, wondering if I should ask him to do it himself, but then I decided not to. It had been a long enough day as it was, and Tom needed his sleep.

I slipped into the nursery by myself, murmuring nonsense to Henry as I changed his diaper, tickled his tummy, my mind and body settling into old, timeworn routines, both comforting and painful in their familiarity. I felt as if I could almost see the ghost of myself, of Sophie, in this room—tears sliding silently down my cheeks, Sophie screaming in distress.

On the changing table, Henry let out a gurgle of delight, and it made me both want to laugh and weep. If Sophie had been an easier baby, if my mother hadn't died weeks before... would I have been able to cope? Would everything in my life have been so different?

Because the truth was it had been so unbelievably, unbearably hard. Those first few weeks... my body torn open and throbbing from the emergency caesarean, Sophie screaming all the time, the endless ache of missing my mother, longing for her common sense and comfort, for her to walk me through all those tricky moments and reassure me that I wasn't crazy, I'd get through it, we all would...

I settled into the glider, the same one I used with Sophie, Henry tucked into the crook of my arm as I gave him his bottle and he took it eagerly. Outside, the sky was velvety black, pinpricked with stars. An owl hooted, and in the distance I could hear the comforting whoosh of the waves lapping the shore. I closed my eyes, so grateful for this child in my arms, and yet also aching with sadness for the daughter I would never see again. I wondered whether sorrow and happiness can even exist without the other. For me, they are forever intertwined.

I don't know how long I sat there, rocking Henry as he drank his bottle, but eventually his mouth went slack and I draped him over my shoulder, smiling when the burp came, a gentle pulse before his tiny body softened into sleep. I settled him into his crib and then went to bed alone; Andrew was still downstairs, and I suspected he would be for a good while. We'd made progress today, but maybe not enough. And yet, I told myself, I would choose to be content. It felt like we were finally on the right track, and I wanted to trust that.

To believe in it.

The next morning when I roll over to check the time, I am jolted to see that it's past eight in the morning. Andrew has already gone to work, and Henry must be awake, even though I didn't hear him cry in the night.

Feeling a mix of unease and hope, I shower quickly, dress and head downstairs. Tom is in the kitchen, Henry in his bouncy seat, and the smell of fresh coffee scents the air. This feels like a good start, but also a fragile one. I still can't imagine, at least not completely, a future where Andrew, Tom, and I are all working harmoniously together, for the sake of the child that binds us all.

"Coffee?" Tom asks and then ducks his head. "I mean, obviously you can get your own... I don't mean to be presumptuous, helping myself..."

"No, it's fine. It's good." I slide onto a stool at the island. "Thank you."

He pours me a cup and adds a generous splash of milk and a teaspoon of sugar, which is just how I like it. I didn't think he'd noticed.

After he passes me the mug, Tom places his hands flat on the marble counter, like he's bracing himself. "I want to thank you," he says, "for giving me another chance."

"And I should thank you for taking it," I reply warmly. "That's not always easy."

The smile he gives me is lopsided. "I'm not sure Andrew is glad that I did."

"He has his reservations," I admit as I take a sip of coffee. "But he'll come around, Tom, especially if you really do what you say you want to, and what I believe you *want* to do, and try to be a good father to Henry." I glance at my grandson, nestled in his seat, bright-eyed and placid, seeming at the moment like he poses no problem whatsoever. "Did you get up with him this morning?" I ask Tom.

Tom grimaces and hunches his shoulders. "I wanted to, I really did, but I was so tired, I didn't hear him crying. Honestly..."

I still, my mug halfway to my lips. "Did Mia stay longer?"

"No, Andrew got up with him." I stare at him in surprise, and he nods in uneasy confirmation. "He changed him and gave him his bottle. By the time I woke up, he was needing to get ready for work, and I took over, but..."

I can tell Tom wishes he'd been more on the ball, just as I do. I'm glad Andrew is taking an interest in his grandson, of course I am, but I can't help but wonder if even that is an indictment. After all my grand statements last night, I couldn't even be trusted to wake up with the baby, and neither could Tom.

"I'm sorry," Tom says, as if reading my mind. "I should have—"

"It's okay. We can take turns with this, Tom. It's a lot for one person, especially when you're grieving."

"But you're grieving, too," he replies quietly, and I nod, not trusting myself to speak for a few seconds. Yes, I am grieving, and I will be for a long time. But meanwhile we have a baby to consider, to care for, and to love. That needs to be my focus.

"We need to make an appointment with the pediatrician," I tell Tom, all brisk practicality now. "We should have done it a few days ago, but I'm sure the doctor will understand. She was Sophie's, back when..." I stop, start again. "And maybe we can get a few more things for him?" I suggest. "Some sleepsuits and onesies, maybe? They grow so fast at this age." I glance at Henry, who, at not quite two weeks old, is already looking bigger, his cheeks rounding out, dimples in his elbows.

"Okay," Tom says, and I smile at the thought, my spirits lifting. It will be so much easier, so much better, if we are in this together, working toward a common goal. I am mentally planning a shopping trip, imagining the little blue bibs and booties I am going to pick out, when I sense something serious from Tom. His hands are flat on the table, his head bowed.

"I feel like I need to come clean with a few things," he says in a low voice. "About, you know, my past."

"You don't have to..." I begin half-heartedly, because I can already tell that he feels he does, and while I am curious, I am also apprehensive. I don't want any new knowledge to disrupt the fragile equilibrium we are still trying to find. Even so, registering Tom's determined expression, I fall silent and summon a smile. "But okay," I say, trying for a tone that is appropriately serious yet also upbeat.

"I wasn't a drug dealer," he states. "I want to say that

upfront, because I know that's what you thought and it's what I was sent down for, but... all I ever did was deliver the stuff. I was a courier, which is bad enough, I know, but I never dealt and I *never* used."

I am silent, absorbing this information, although the particulars of the drug world are beyond me. Still, it *is* bad enough, but it's certainly a lot better than what we'd thought, when I suspect both Andrew and I envisioned Tom as some kind of kingpin. "Why did you get convicted of dealing?" I ask, keeping my voice gentle. I don't doubt him, at least I don't think I do, but I want to understand.

Tom sighs. "It was a stitch-up by the dealer." He holds up one hand, palm facing me. "I know how that sounds, and it's why I never bothered setting the record straight before. I didn't think you'd believe me, because hardly anyone ever does. You get convicted of dealing, you must be a dealer." He pauses, his face contorting for a painful second. "The only person who ever believed me was Sophie."

I think back to that evening when Sophie told me about Tom for the first time. *People have let him down in so many ways. His life's been really unfair...*

I'd mentally scoffed at such excuses, been concerned far more for my daughter, but now the words come back to me, an indictment of my own judgment. "I'm glad she did," I tell Tom. He so clearly needed someone to.

"Anyway," he resumes, stoically determined to keep going, "I just don't want you to think I was into all that stuff, because I really wasn't." He blows out a breath. "I mean, I *was,* as a way to make money, but..." He lets out a shaky laugh as he passes his hand over his eyes. "I'm not making this much better, am I?"

"No, you are," I assure him. "I'm glad you told me." I pause. "But why didn't you tell us all this before?"

Tom grimaces. "I hate it when people assume the worst of me. I've seen it so many times ever since I went into foster care.

It's like they think foster kid equals screwup. If someone is the problem, it was always going to be me. So... I guess I did what I could to make sure it *was* me. Which doesn't make any sense, but sometimes it felt better than trying and having everyone believe the worst anyway."

"Oh, Tom." My heart aches with sympathy for him. I can understand his reasoning, at least in part. Can I honestly say we would have believed Tom if he'd come to us with these explanations on the night we met him? The truth is, we probably wouldn't have. I think of what Tom said to me before, that we are our own worst enemies. Perhaps some perverse part of him felt better when he was controlling the narrative, even if it was a bad one.

"And Andrew?" he asks tentatively. "Do you think he'll believe me now?"

I can already imagine Andrew's tart response. *You really fell for that line?* He has been unimpressed by everything we've learned about Tom so far, including the hardships he's suffered as a teenager. I can't believe that anything Tom has told me now would make much difference. "I don't know," I am compelled to admit. "It might take him some time, but I hope so. Eventually."

Tom nods slowly, resigned but accepting. "Okay," he says. "I guess that's fair."

He is, I realize, extending more grace to Andrew than my husband has ever shown him, but I appreciate we all came into this with attitudes that meant it was impossible for it to work. My apprehension, Andrew's horrified shock, Tom's ingrained distrust. So often people say if you're just honest everything will work out, but they don't acknowledge just how hard, and even impossible, that honesty can be. How painful.

"I really do want to do better now," Tom tells me earnestly. "I mean that."

"I know." I straighten, give him a brisk smile. "So why don't you start by calling the pediatrician and booking an appointment for Henry?"

Tom looks startled, as well as a little apprehensive, as if he didn't expect me to put his well-meaning words into practice right away. I know every step of this journey is going to be hard for him, but I also know I can help. *I* can be the person for him that I didn't have anyone to be for me.

Back when I was pregnant with Sophie, my mom had planned to come for her birth, stay for a couple of weeks to see us settled in our new family unit. Instead, I'd attended her funeral just two weeks before Sophie was born. They blur together in my mind, life and death tangled up, just as they are now, with Henry and Sophie, and give me a unique understanding into what Tom must be going through.

Because I, of all people, can understand how confusing it can feel, how joy turns to sadness and back again, and then both feel like guilt. I want to help him navigate that maelstrom, to be the father he wants to be, even when it's hard. To give him the opportunity as well as the confidence, neither of which I ever had.

"Okay," Tom says, and I smile, relieved, even ebullient.

"I'll just find the number."

Over the next few weeks, we find a pattern—halting, tenuous, at times feeling unfamiliar and jarring, like dance steps we didn't know but are trying to learn. We take Henry to the pediatrician, the same one Sophie went to, a briskly kind woman who is now nearing retirement. I've always appreciated her no-nonsense manner, especially in the aftermath of my postnatal depression when Sophie was so small, and she is no different now, which is a relief, even if being back at a pediatrician's office brings back all sorts of memories—Sophie as a baby, when I felt so overwhelmed; later, when she was a teenager, and we needed referrals to eating disorder specialists. And the years in between that seem so sweet now, when we were all managing and nothing was really wrong.

As I go into the examining room with Tom, who is carrying Henry in his car seat, she gives me a hug and then exclaims how Henry looks so much like Sophie, even though I can't see it. Not yet, anyway. I am grateful for the sympathy, but even more so when she gets to work, treating us just like any other family, Henry like any other baby, because that's what Tom and I both need, to be treated as if we are normal. Maybe if we're treated that way, we'll start to feel it. Because as much as we attempt to stumble forward into something good, things can still feel strange and hard.

I run into an old tennis friend of Sophie's in King's Market, and have to stammer through my explanation of her death when she asks how she is. The poor girl is horrified, and so am I, and we both scuttle away from each other, desperately relieved the conversation is over. I wonder how many times I will have to tell people my daughter is dead.

And yet the ever-present, ever-pressing knowledge that Sophie is gone is tempered by the existence of her son—and her husband. I never expected to find an affinity with Tom, to see something of myself in him, but I do. And getting to know Tom feels just as precious as coming to know my grandson.

One sunny spring day, we stroll into the center of Old Greenwich, Tom pushing Henry in his stroller, to have lunch at Sweet Pea's Café. I pass a few people I know, only to nod to, which is a relief because I really don't want to have conversations. I'm existing in something of a bubble, and I like it that way.

As we settle into our seats, Henry dozing in his car seat on the floor between us, I see the tattooed letters on Tom's knuckles flash past as he opens his menu. I've become so used to them, I hardly see them anymore, but now I am compelled to ask,

"What is the meaning of the words on your knuckles, Tom? Hold Fast?"

He tenses, looking embarrassed, and then shrugs. "When I was.... When I was in prison, there was a chaplain. A Catholic guy. He was really nice to me, had a lot of time, you know, for just shooting the breeze. Had a lot of patience when I was pretty angry about everything. And he kept saying that..." He ducks his head, seeming even more embarrassed. "He kept saying to hold fast, because God was holding fast to me. I don't know if I believe all that stuff, but... it helped, to think that maybe I wasn't as alone as I thought I was, you know? That someone was holding onto me."

It's such a wistful statement, and it fills me with equal parts hope and grief. If things had gone differently that night we met him, maybe *we* could have held fast. We could have helped Tom as well as Sophie, and even if it didn't change the course of Sophie's life, or the fact of her death, it would have made for a very different year and a half.

I know there's no point to such thoughts now, as they only lead to regret, but they strengthen my determination to be different... with Tom, with Andrew, even with myself. "I'm glad you had someone like that in your life," I tell him. "Did he give you the Bible?" Tom's eyes narrow, and too late I realize what I revealed.

"Yeah," he answers slowly, "But how did you know about that? Did you go through my stuff?"

Compelled to honesty, and with little choice anyway, I nod, offering a shamefaced and contrite smile. "When you'd gone off with Henry... we were just looking for clues as to where you might have gone, that's all. I didn't want to be nosy, but..."

Tom is still and silent for a moment, and then he sighs. "I guess that's fair," he said.

"How did you get to the Bronx?" I ask, like it's a matter of curiosity, nothing more, and, in truth, I want it to be. Surely it doesn't matter how he did now, because we've moved past that point. "I looked all over for you," I continue, "and it was as if you'd disappeared..." I trail off at the uncomfortable, even guilty look on Tom's face, and realization trickles coldly through me. "You must have had some help," I say slowly, feeling my way through the words, the idea. "A ride to the station?"

I recall my frantic fear that morning, how I'd run out and then driven down all the streets of Old Greenwich, scouring every sidewalk for Tom and Henry. How when I'd come back, Carmen had been quietly, sullenly, getting out cleaning sprays.

"It was Carmen, wasn't it?" I say. Even before Tom nods, I know. I feel a deep, leaden disappointment, as well as a hot flare of outrage. Why would she betray us that way? She must have realized Tom was running away—no stroller, no diaper bag, *nothing*. She must have known we would have been beside ourselves with worry. And she *did* know, when I came back and asked her. When I was worried all day, and certainly when the police came. All that time, she remained silent.

"She was just being nice," Tom says. "Please, don't blame her."

I nod slowly, acting as if I am accepting, when the truth is I don't know what I feel. I know if I tell Andrew what she did, he would fire her in a heartbeat. And I realize I don't want that, but I want to understand why she did what she did. Carmen has been with us for twenty years, since Sophie was small. Would she really work against us in that way? Because right now, that's how it feels.

"It's okay," I tell Tom. I turn to the menu, trying to sort through my jumbled thoughts. "Now, what do you think looks good?"

. . .

We keep the conversation innocuous for the rest of the afternoon, and it isn't until we get home, and Tom is upstairs changing Henry's diaper, that I realize I have to say something to Carmen. Once upon a time, I might have existed in a haze of ignorance, or even feigned ignorance, because it felt easier, and I couldn't face confronting anyone about anything.

But those days are gone. I want to be different, to make different and stronger choices, and that means asking my housekeeper why she drove my son-in-law to the train station when he was so clearly running away with my grandson... and doing my best to understand her answer.

"Carmen." I find her in the family room across from the kitchen, a yawning room with a cathedral ceiling, two L-shaped leather sofas and a large flatscreen TV that Andrew and I haven't used since it's been just the two of us at home. I can't remember the last time I was even in this room, yet Carmen dusts and vacuums it religiously. Now I am wondering why.

She glances up from the coffee table she's polishing, already suspicious, as soon as I say her name. "Yes, Mrs. Lawrence?"

I swallow dryly, my courage already seeping away. "I realized..." My voice is small, tentative. "It came to my attention," I start again, realizing belatedly that I am sounding like a schoolteacher, "that you drove Tom to the train station, when he had taken Henry." I pause, waiting for her reaction. The only one I get is that her lips tighten and she gives a tiny, jerky nod. "Why?" I ask, and now I sound plaintive.

"Why?" she repeats, her mouth puckering further. "Because he asked."

"Yes, but... you must have realized it was a volatile situation," I say carefully. "That him storming out of our house with a baby in his arms wasn't... the best way to go about things. And," I add, my voice rising, "why didn't you tell me you helped him? All day you saw me being frantic, having no idea where he was and I asked you..." I trail off, more hurt than angry now.

What have I ever done to make my housekeeper deceive me in such a way?

Carmen folds her arms, her expression stony. "And if I had said something," she asks, "what would you have done? What would Mr. Lawrence have done?"

"We needed to know—"

"You would have *fired* me," she says flatly. "Maybe you will still fire me." She shrugs and then reaches for the rag she'd dropped when I first started in with my questions. She goes back to polishing the coffee table, her head bent, like the conversation is over.

"Still," I persist. I feel like I have already lost control of the conversation. "I don't understand why you did it."

Carmen is silent for a long moment, her resolute gaze on the now-gleaming coffee table. I wait, sensing there is something more from her, wondering what it is.

"Because," she finally bursts out. "I have a son like Tom. Not," she practically spits, "that you have *ever* asked."

I stare at her blankly, trying to make the connection between these two statements.

"A son like Tom," I finally repeat. "In what way?"

"He is a good boy, but he has been in trouble. He tries." She glares at me. "It is people like *you* who don't give him a chance."

People like me?

"Carmen," I protest, "I've never even met your son—"

"Exactly," she retorts. "You never met, never know, never even ask. I work for you *twenty years* and never once you ask."

I gaze at her, silent, a blush of shame rising to my cheeks. Have I really never asked about Carmen's family? I was always so self-conscious with her, feeling like she disapproved of me somehow, wanting her favor without even trying to get to know her. And meanwhile, I acknowledge, she was witness to all my trials and tragedies—the challenge and pain of Sophie's eating disorder, the many fights and tears of her stormy teenaged years, the way I retreated into myself when she went to college. More than once, Carmen left a bottle of water by the sofa when I had fallen asleep from too many Xanax. She was there the night we first met Tom, cleaning in the kitchen as our domestic tragedy unfolded.

And all this time, I never once asked her about her own family. To come to my own defense, I did give her a generous gift card for her birthday, an extra week's pay at Christmas. When she arrives in the morning, I always ask how she is, and her answer is always that she is fine.

But it's never gone beyond that. It never even occurred to me that it should.

"What is your son's name?" I ask now, and she stares at me as tears come into her eyes that she blinks away.

"Jorge," she says.

"And how he is doing?" I ask. "He's had some hard times, you said, but how is he now?"

She sniffs. "He is okay. He works in a nursing home." She sniffs again before admitting, "He went to jail for stealing. He was very stupid, but he knows better now."

"That's good," I say quietly. "And I'm sorry I've never asked before. I never even thought to ask, and maybe that's worse, but..." I pause, trying to figure out a way to explain that isn't just making excuses. "For so many years," I tell Carmen, "I've felt so... helpless. Lost. I didn't know how to be a mother, and I'd lost my own, and Andrew's world wasn't mine and it all felt so overwhelming, and then Sophie was so challenging in so many ways..."

I trail off because they all sound like excuses, and yet I mean them. They are what kept me from being the person, the mother, I wanted to be, and maybe they *shouldn't* have, but they did.

"I wish I'd been better," I whisper. "In so many ways."

Carmen sighs and then, to my surprise, she comes over and

puts her arms around me. I don't think we've ever touched before, and the feel of her soft, motherly arms around me breaks something inside, and I start to cry.

"Poor *bambina*," she murmurs soothingly, like a mother to her child. "Poor little *bambina*."

And that's how I feel—like a child in need of comfort, even though I'm a grown woman with a grandchild of her own. Once, I would have been ashamed to feel and be seen as so weak, but now I am only grateful for Carmen's comfort—and her understanding.

With a sniff, I step back and wipe my cheeks. "Thank you," I say, and she smiles.

The next few weeks pass in a pleasant haze; spring has truly arrived, and the garden is awash in blooms. I spend every moment I can out there, pruning, planting, weeding, and simply enjoying the beauty all around me. The tulips have given way to irises and azaleas and rhododendrons, huge bushes bright with blossoms that line the path to the rocky beach.

Sometimes I take Henry outside, lay him on a picnic blanket, letting him kick his bare legs as he gazes up at a blue, blue sky and gurgles with happiness. Sometimes Tom comes too, so we sit on either side of his son, simply enjoying the day and the peace it brings.

We've taken to dividing the childcare pretty evenly; Tom gets up in the mornings and gives Henry his first bottle of the day, and then I take over so he can go for a run, shower and dress, and sometimes look for work. I'm not pushing him on that front, but I can tell Tom wants to feel useful, and I want him to, too.

In the afternoons, Tom puts Henry down for his nap, and we rock him in the evenings, his fussiest time, before putting him down for the night. He's sleeping six hours at a stretch now, and so, somewhat recklessly, I tell Mia we don't need her services anymore. I want to believe we can manage, and I want Tom to, as well. And we *do* manage, taking turns getting up with Henry, taking naps when we need to. Carmen helps too, offering to watch Henry when he's happy in his baby seat, or rock him when he fusses. Since our heartfelt conversation, she's been so much friendlier, and so have I. Maybe that is the difference.

All in all, I realize it's so much easier when you don't feel so alone.

And where is Andrew in all this? On the periphery, in the shadows, and often at work. He comes home after dinner most nights and closets himself in his study after a mumbled hello. To be fair, he engages with Henry a little, giving him a smile and sometimes a quick cuddle before he disappears into his study, but it feels perfunctory, and he never meets my or Tom's eye while he does it.

We barely speak, moving in our separate orbits, and on some level, I think we both prefer it that way. Just like with Sophie, I suspect Andrew is angry with me for choosing Tom over him, and I am too tired, or maybe too annoyed myself, to attempt to coax him out of his stubbornness. It's not particularly healthy or wholesome, for us to splinter into separate lives, and after three weeks, when Henry is six weeks old, I decide it needs to stop.

It's a gorgeous spring afternoon in late May, the air balmy, the sea cerulean, and I text Andrew that I've bought steaks, and it would be great if he could barbecue. It's a small enough suggestion, and yet after the silence and tension of the last few weeks, it feels like a lot. He texts back that he was planning to work late, and I text back one word.

Please.

He agrees.

I do my best to make everything pleasant and welcoming. I

marinate the steaks and open a bottle of wine and make sure Henry is bathed and fed. When Andrew arrives, Tom and I are in the kitchen; he is tossing a salad and I am getting out the plates.

I turn to my husband with a determined smile. "Hey," I greet him. "I'm glad you're back. Join us."

Andrew's gaze moves from me to Tom and back again. For a second, I think he's going to refuse and my hope to turn us into a family simply by sharing a meal suddenly seems silly and pathetic. Did I really think it would be that easy?

"Okay," Andrew says, and while he still sounds guarded, he doesn't seem angry. "Let me just go change first."

As he leaves the kitchen, I give Tom an encouraging smile, which he uncertainly returns. These are small steps, but they still feel like progress, and I am determined to hold onto that.

When Andrew returns, dressed in his usual weekend wear of a polo shirt and khakis, he seems a little more relaxed, if slightly stiff. He nods at Tom and then crouches down to the bouncy seat, where Henry is kicking his legs, and gently chucks him under his chin.

"How are you, my little man?" Andrew asks.

In response, Henry gives him a wide, drooly, open-mouthed grin that has Andrew exclaiming, "He smiled at me! He actually smiled." He sounds incredulous.

I laugh. "Yes, he's just started smiling. Doesn't it feel amazing?"

Andrew shakes his head in wonder. "Yes, truly amazing," he murmurs.

For a few seconds, it feels as if we are suspended in a bubble of contentment, and all the things that have divided us disappear in the light of a single smile. Outside, the sun is shining as it starts to sink beneath the Sound, and despite the ever-present grief I feel for my daughter, I also feel hope—deep, fierce, true.

This can work. *We* can work.

We are still all smiling when the doorbell rings. Startled, the bubble bursts; Andrew straightens, Tom shifts his feet, and I put down the plates I was holding.

"I'll get it," I say.

I hurry to the door, hoping it's nothing—a delivery, maybe, or a neighbor letting us know they're going away for a week—rather than something that might disrupt the fragile bond we've only just started to form.

But when I open the door, it's neither. A stranger is standing there, a woman around my age and yet so different, her blonde, silver-streaked hair pulled back into a messy bun, the lines of her face seeming only to add to her sense of competence and strength. She's wearing worn cargo pants in army green and a fitted grey T-shirt, and her body is both wiry and muscular; she looks like she could be in the army. A duffel bag is at her feet.

"Yes...?" I greet her hesitantly.

"I'm looking for my son," she tells me in a firm, no-nonsense kind of voice. "Tom West."

PART TWO

FIFTEEN

AUDREY

I probably shouldn't be here. I'm still jet-lagged, having come direct from the airport, after a grueling eleven-hour flight from Santiago, and before that a twelve-hour trip in a truck from Antofagasta in southern Chile. I'm hungry and aching and gritty-eyed with fatigue, and this woman is already turning up her nose at me.

She's exactly what I'd expect for Sophie's mother—I'm assuming that's who she is—with her coiffed hair and her neutral silk and linen separates, discreet diamond studs in her ears, pearls at her throat. Everything about her screams moneyed privilege. She's the woman who chose to reject her daughter rather than accept her son-in-law. That's all I know about her. It's all I need to know.

"Is he here?" I ask when she still hasn't spoken.

"Yes... yes." Her voice is faint, and one hand hovers by her throat, fingering her pearls. "I'm sorry... we weren't... we weren't... expecting you."

"I know."

Tom doesn't even know I was coming back to the States.

Our last communication was over a year ago, before Sophie was even pregnant. I only heard about what had happened through my brother-in-law, with whom Tom has some sporadic contact. That's the kind of mother I am and have been, not that I'm telling Mrs. Perfect here anything about that.

"Is he here?" I ask again, and this time I let myself sound pointed. She doesn't need to leave me standing on the doorstep like some vagrant.

"Yes... yes, he is." She still looks dazed. "I'm sorry, please do come in. I'm Diana Lawrence."

I heft my duffel bag onto one shoulder as I step into the soaring foyer, with its floor of checkered marble and a diamond-pane skylight high above, creating a fractaled pattern of light on the floor, tiny gleaming squares that I step onto while Diana Lawrence just stares at me.

"Audrey West," I tell her, and she nods jerkily as a silence tautens between us. After several tense seconds, I raise my eyebrows in inquiry, and she flushes.

"Sorry," she murmurs, gesturing for me to follow her. "Come through. You can leave your... bag... here."

I imagine what her *bag* must look like—matching designer suitcases in monogrammed leather, no doubt.

I drop my duffel bag onto the floor with a thud and then follow her into a kitchen that is at least twice as big as the apartment I shared with two others back in Antofagasta. A marble island the size of a swimming pool takes center stage, and Tom, my son, is standing at one end of it.

His mouth drops opens as he catches sight of me, and I force a smile, although I already know how fraught this moment is going to be, and I would rather it wasn't witnessed by two privileged strangers, even if they're my son's in-laws.

Diana's husband, silver-haired and distinguished in a moneyed way, the silver and gold link of a Rolex on one muscular wrist, is standing on the other side of the island, by a baby seat that holds my grandson. Not that Tom had even told me I had one. And not that I can blame him.

"What are you doing here?" he asks, and I feel the mood in the room imperceptibly shift, from dazed suspicion to a swelling, self-righteous indignation. Andrew draws himself up, shoulders back, chest out, and Diana moves protectively toward Henry. Clearly I'm a threat, now that they know Tom isn't thrilled to see me.

"I'm here because I wanted to see you," I tell Tom. "And meet my grandson."

Tom shakes his head slowly. "How did you even know I was here?"

"Uncle Jack." Jack, my husband Matt's older brother, a mining engineer in Perth, Australia, who has never been close enough to matter, but still tried to take an interest in my son, to his own credit, as well as my shame.

Tom shakes his head again. "I don't know what to say," he admits, and I force another smile, rueful this time, because I don't know, either. Maybe I shouldn't have come, but that's been the choice I've made too many times already, and this time I wanted to be different. I wanted Tom to be, too, but right now he looks as guarded and wary as he ever has. He doesn't want to see me, that much is clear. He never has.

"I'm sorry it's such a surprise," I tell him. "I would have texted, but..." I hesitate, grappling for an excuse. I *should* have texted, but I was afraid if I did, Tom would refuse to see me. A visit by stealth felt like the only option, but I am certainly questioning that now, as three hostile strangers all stare at me, because, yes, my son is a stranger to me. I've tried for him not to be, but I've never gotten far. "I wanted to see you," I say again. "And my grandson."

"Weren't you in Africa or something?" Tom asks, and I hear a sullen note creep into his voice, one I am well familiar with.

"South America. Chile." I glance at Diana and then her husband, trying to make this moment a little less awkward. "I'm sorry for dropping in unannounced—"

"Not at all," Diana says quickly. She looks shaken as well as nervous, and I wonder what exactly she's scared of. Does she think I'm going to swoop in and steal her grandson? Hardly likely when Tom is barely speaking to me. "We were just about to eat," she continues stiltedly. "Would you like to stay for dinner?" She asks the question as if it costs her something.

I should say no. I *would* say no, usually, but right now I don't want to. I told myself I was going to be different, and the only way to be different is to make different choices.

"That's very kind," I tell her, injecting a warmth into my voice I don't actually feel. I glance at Tom, who has folded his arms across his chest in a way I remember, a way that is basically telling me to butt out. "Thank you," I tell Diana. "Thank you so much."

I don't know if I've made the right decision, but I'm here to see my grandson and reconcile with my son, and I can't do that if I bow out at the very first hurdle. And since Tom himself would accuse me of doing that before, I don't want to do it again and give him any more reason to resent me.

"Andrew?" Diana asks, her eyebrows raised, her voice sounding both strained and musical. "Do you want to get the steaks out of the fridge?" She turns to me, her smile taut at its edges. "Audrey, would you like a drink?"

I glance again at Tom, who is still glowering. "A glass of water would be fine, thank you," I say.

Already I am doubting myself, whether I should have come like this, unannounced and unwanted. Yet what choice did I have? Tom wouldn't have seen me anyway. The last time I saw him was through Sophie; the time before that was when he was in prison and had no choice. I can't remember the last time he actively sought me out or even agreed to see me on his own terms. So maybe, I acknowledge, this *isn't* the change I want it to be. Maybe everything is staying exactly, depressingly the same.

Andrew, who must be Sophie's father, disappears outside with the plate of steaks, and Diana hands me a crystal tumbler of ice-cold filtered water from a jug in the fridge. *Even their water is fancy*, I think as I murmur my thanks and take a sip.

How can I compete with these people? Because already that's what it feels like I'm doing. What I have to do, if I want to have a place in my son's life—and my grandson's.

"So, Audrey," Diana says, playing the perfect hostess, "how long were you in—South America, was it?"

"Chile," I confirm with a nod. "Antofagasta, in the *campamentos*." She gives me a blank, questioning look and I clarify, "The tent cities around one of the lithium mines in the Atacama salt flats."

"Oh, I see."

She clearly doesn't. She can't even begin to imagine what life is like for someone living in the tent cities made of cardboard and corrugated iron, eking a living out of the lithium mines, with no access to medical care, sanitation, or even clean water. The thought that hundreds of thousands of people are living like that while this woman stands in her palatial kitchen, in her even more palatial house, eyebrows elegantly raised in query, can infuriate me if I let it, but I try not to. I know such self-righteous anger doesn't serve any good purpose, certainly not today.

And then, as I'm standing there, I suddenly remember that Diana Lawrence's daughter died just a few weeks ago, and I am filled with an acid rush of guilt.

"I'm so sorry for your loss," I tell her. I turn to my son. "And you too, Tom. For Sophie..." I trail off, because I feel like I shouldn't have mentioned it. Diana Lawrence has drawn back in seeming offense, and Tom is scowling even more.

"Thank you," Diana says after a moment, her voice stiff.

"She was a lovely person," I say. The sentiment sounds trite, but I do mean it. Sophie seemed like a vivacious, positive person. When I'd met her, I'd hoped she would be good for Tom. Soften his rough edges, make him less bitter.

Diana stares at me, her expression now turning cool. "I didn't realize you met her," she remarks. She does not sound pleased that I did.

"I only met her once," I explain, almost like an apology. "I was visiting about a year ago, and she reached out." I glance again at Tom, who hasn't changed his stance. "I appreciated the effort she made."

My son's jaw bunches. "She didn't realize what you were like," he says, and it feels like the temperature in the room drops by at least twenty degrees.

"Why don't we go outside?" Diana suggests, a little desperately. "The weather's been so beautiful…"

She trails off as Tom and I simply stare at each other, a standoff, as ever. As usual, I break first.

"I'd love to be introduced to my grandson," I say with a crooked smile. "Uncle Jack said his name is Henry…?"

"Yeah." Tom unclenches his jaw as he nods toward his son in his bouncy seat. Henry is in a sleepsuit of soft blue fleece. He has a tuft of blond hair and deep blue eyes, a rosebud mouth and plump pink cheeks. One hand is up by his face, tiny fingers bunched into a fist that keeps missing his mouth. My grandson. Does he look like Tom as a baby? I think he might, at least a little bit.

"He's almost found his hands," Diana says with a wobbly laugh. "He's been trying for days. He's so close."

For some reason, this innocuous statement causes a hot flare of jealousy to sear through me. This woman has witnessed my grandson's development day by day, has been there for every milestone—his first smile, as well as his first tears—while I wasn't even informed of his birth. I know I have no one to blame but myself. No matter how long and hard I've tried, some things can't be absolved. I *know* that, but I keep trying to fight against it. Maybe it's futile, but I can't stop now, not when I've come all this way, left everything behind, and have nothing else left.

"Shall we go out to the patio…?" Diana suggests uncertainly.

Tom scoops Henry from his seat, cradling him with an ease that I know had to have been learned, and it fills me with a longing, as well as a pride I have no right to feel, because I had absolutely no part in it.

Silently, I follow Diana and Tom outside to the enormous garden, banks of bright rhododendrons and azaleas framing an endless expanse of velvety green lawn that rolls right down to the sky-blue sea. A terrace overlooks it all, with deep sofas and a table that seats twelve, as well as a massive barbecue and a full bar.

Andrew is grilling steaks. He turns as we step through the sliding glass doors, his eyes narrowing as he catches sight of me. I feel even more like a persona non grata, public enemy number one. *Nobody* wants me here.

"So, Audrey," Diana says, in a valiant attempt to maintain social niceties, "how long are you in the States for?"

"Not long, I'm sure," Tom interjects in a hard voice. "She never is."

I blink, absorbing that barb, and then reply to Diana, "I'm not sure, actually. A few months, maybe?" Or longer, depending on how things turn out.

"And where are you staying?" Diana asks. "Do you have a base…?" She sounds out of her depth, like she doesn't know how people like me even exist.

"I'm renting a place in Stamford." I found a studio apartment in a big, blank building near the train station, but I haven't even stepped inside yet, and in any case, I won't be able to afford it for more than a month, maybe two. After that, I don't know what I'll do. In some secret part of myself, I am hoping that Tom might move in with me; he can work, and I'll take care of the baby. It's not what I once would have dreamed about, and at the moment it certainly feels far-fetched, but it's still my secret hope, barely voiced even to myself.

"And where will you go next?" Diana asks. Her voice is friendly, but I am getting the definite sense that she wants me gone, and these questions are her way of urging me onward.

"I don't have any firm plans at the moment," I tell her. "Right now, I'd just like to get to know my grandson." I turn to Tom. "May I hold him?"

For a second, I think he isn't going to give him to me, and part of me wouldn't even blame him. I have been far from the world's best mother. Truth be told, I haven't even been a mediocre mother. Since Tom was eight years old, I've barely been a mother at all, and when he was fourteen, I absented myself from his life completely, at his request. It's hard to come back from that, but I keep trying, if sporadically so.

After several long, uncomfortable moments, Tom finally hands Henry over. I lurch forward, my arms outstretched, feeling awkward and inexpert until he places him in my arms. Then I instinctively remember what to do, my hand cradling his head, my arms drawing him toward my chest, a warm, solid bundle.

Diana watches me silently, her lips pursed.

I gaze down at his tiny face, his blond eyelashes fanning his plump cheeks every time he blinks. "He looks so much like you when you were tiny," I tell Tom on a broken laugh. "I'll have to show you a photo."

"He has Andrew's nose," Diana states, her tone almost querulous.

I decide not to reply. As I hold this precious child in my arms, I am realizing two things. First, that I will do whatever it takes to stay in his—and my son's—life. And second, that I'm almost certain Diana Lawrence will do whatever she can to stop me.

SIXTEEN

AUDREY

The morning after I showed up on the Lawrences' doorstep, I am getting ready to meet Tom for breakfast. I'm pretty sure this isn't the victory it first felt like, because I'm afraid he only agreed so he can take the opportunity to tell me to butt out of his life.

The dinner at the Lawrences' last night never abated in its awkwardness. If anything, it only grew worse. Andrew brought the steaks over, and Diana fetched wine and salad, and Tom put Henry back in his bouncy seat while we all ate, struggling to make even the most innocuous conversation. Every question felt loaded, every comment barbed. It was clear that Tom had told the Lawrences *something* about me, and it wasn't complimentary.

"So Tom told us you've been living abroad for many years," Diana remarked, her hostessy tone not quite hiding her hostility. "Do you prefer it to America?"

"Do I prefer the rest of the world to America?" I replied, an edge to my voice. "No, not necessarily, but there are certainly a lot of places where people are suffering and need help."

I have always resented both Tom and my husband Matt's

attitudes that my charitable work was somehow selfish. That helping people elsewhere wasn't as important or necessary as being with my family. And I would have believed that, of *course* I would have, if I hadn't seen for myself just how little they needed me.

"Well, it all sounds very *worthy*," Diana remarked in a tone that suggested it wasn't.

All this time, Tom barely said a word. When Henry started to fuss, he muttered that he'd change him and give him a bottle, and nearly half an hour passed before he returned on his own, having put Henry to bed in his crib. I was starting to feel pretty unwelcome by that point, and so I decided to make my farewells.

"Maybe we could have breakfast tomorrow?" I suggested to Tom as I was leaving. It was clear he wasn't going to see me to the door, and so I had to make the request in front of Diana and Andrew, both of whom were frowning, seeming as if they couldn't wait to have me gone. "I can come into Old Greenwich, I'm right by the train station." I sounded like I was begging, which I was, and everyone knew it.

For a second, Tom didn't respond, and I braced myself for another rejection. I'd traveled over five thousand miles to be here, and he couldn't even meet me for half an hour? It frustrated me, because a person can play the penitent for only so long. At some point, I need my son to try, too. We've both made mistakes, after all.

"Fine," he said in a surly tone which I did my best to ignore.

"Nine o'clock?" I asked, and he nodded.

Now I stare at my gaunt face in the mirror. My blond hair, liberally streaked with silver, is up in its usual messy bun. I'm fifty-four, and although I am athletic and fit from my work, I fear I look older, lines of care carved deep into my face, my brown eyes, the same color as Tom's, always looking tired, like they've seen too much, which, of course, they have.

With a sigh, I turn away from my reflection. I can't let myself regret the choices I made, even if I'm so very sorry for some of their consequences. It's a nuance I've never been able to explain to Tom, at least so that he'll understand and accept.

As I walk to the Stamford Diner where Tom agreed to meet me, I wonder what I'm even hoping to get out of this conversation. For Tom to let me into some part of his life? I don't even know how that would work. I have very little savings, no job, no car, and no *life* here. Working overseas for as long as I have means I no longer have any friends back in America, and my parents died years ago. I have no siblings, no support work, nothing.

Starting over isn't going to be easy. I don't even know if it's possible. And yet what other choice do I have? Tom—and Henry—are all that I have now. I have to do whatever I can to be part of their lives, something I know Tom won't understand or believe, and yet it's true.

I'm just opening the door to the diner when Tom pulls into the parking lot in a huge, white BMW SUV. He strides out of the massive car with a slight swagger that annoys me, although I try not to let it show in my face. Is he enjoying all the perks of living with Sophie's parents? How did that even happen, when, according to what I've gathered from Sophie, they completely rejected him nearly two years ago?

"Nice ride," I say. I swear I didn't mean to sound snide, but it comes out that way.

Tom scowls. "The Lawrences have been really kind to me," he says stiffly, and I can't keep from replying.

"It certainly looks like it." I want to take the words back as soon I say them, but I can't. Tom's scowl turns to a full-on glare. This is not the start I wanted to our time together. "I'm sorry," I say quickly. "I didn't mean that."

"Yeah, right." Tom shakes his head. "You never change."

You never let me. This time, I bite the words back.

"Tom, please. Let's... let's go inside and order some breakfast. And then we can talk."

"I'm not sure there's anything to talk about," Tom replies ominously, but at least he starts heading into the diner. Maybe a plate of bacon and eggs and some strong, hot coffee will help us both. I certainly hope so.

Once we're seated in a vinyl booth with tall, laminated menus, having ordered cups of coffee, the silence stretches between us, like a heavy weight. I struggle to think of something to say that won't set him off again, and nothing comes to mind.

"I really am sorry about Sophie," I finally say, because surely that can't be said too many times. "Uncle Jack told me she died in childbirth—?"

"Septic shock from her C-section scar." Tom's tone is brief. "It was quick."

I shake my head slowly. "I can't even imagine."

"No."

We fall back into silence; it feels like tipping into a well.

"And the Lawrences stepped up, I guess?" I ask, trying for a conciliatory tone. "I know they weren't very supportive before, but I'm glad they seem to be now."

"I'm not sure they really are," Tom replies, surprising me with his candor. "At least Andrew. He's pretty suspicious of me still, and I don't know that I can even blame him." He sighs, scrubbing his hands over his face. "It hasn't been easy."

"No," I say quietly. "Managing grief *and* a newborn as well as difficult relationships... I'm sorry, Tom. I... I wish I'd been here, so I could have helped."

He drops his hands from his face to stare at me. "You've *never* been here."

And here we are, back to the same old argument, a broken record played over and over again, with Tom never tiring of the tune.

"I've tried," I tell him quietly. "I know I haven't been great, far from it, but I *have* tried." Worried I sound too plaintive, I do my best to moderate my tone. "And I'm here now."

"Yeah, why?" He lifts his chin, sounding belligerent. "Because you waited awhile, but then you always do—"

"*Once*, Tom." I cut across him, my voice as sharp as a blade. "I waited once."

"Yeah, well, it was kind of important," he mutters.

The waitress comes to fill up our coffee cups, and I murmur my thanks before we both fall back into a miserable silence. Will there ever, I wonder, be a way to get past this? It's been twelve years, and we still haven't managed it. Maybe we never will. Maybe, I reflect glumly, I shouldn't have come.

But what else could I have done?

"Diana Lawrence seems like she likes you," I say as brightly as I can. "And I'm sure she enjoys having Henry around."

He hunches one shoulder, just like he used to as a little boy. "Yeah, kind of…"

"What do you mean, kind of?" She seemed pretty protective to me.

"Babies are hard work," he replies. "Especially for someone her age. I mean, I do some, but… I don't know." He frowns, seeming unhappy. "The whole setup is kind of weird. Sometimes I feel it works, and other times it doesn't." He stops abruptly, drumming his fingers on the laminate tabletop, looking like he wished he hadn't said so much.

"How long are you planning on staying with them?" I ask carefully. I know Tom worked in construction when he was with Sophie, but it doesn't seem like he's working now, and the truth is, there's far too much I don't know about my son's life. My attempts to learn more are almost always rebuffed, even as I recognize they're not nearly enough.

I'm his *mother*. I should never stop trying, no matter how much I'm rejected, no matter how much it hurts. I tell myself that, but I don't always follow my own advice.

"I don't know," Tom replies. "I need to get a job, save some money." He moves restlessly in his seat. "But childcare is so damned expensive, and anyway, I think Diana would be willing to help with all that." He pauses. "I just don't know how many strings would be attached."

I nod in understanding. The Lawrences don't seem like the type of people who offer anything for free. "What kind of strings do you mean?"

He shrugs. "I don't know. Sometimes I can't shake the feeling that they really just want me out of there, so they can keep Henry for themselves."

I stiffen instinctively. "They have no right to—"

"Maybe they do," Tom says in a low voice. "What do I know about raising a kid?" His tone suggests that I might be to blame for his ignorance, because what do *I* know about raising a kid? I wasn't around for a lot of it.

"What does anyone know, when they first start out?" I tell my son. "You're handed your baby, and it feels like a cross between a precious Ming vase and a stick of dynamite." That, fortunately, raises a very small smile. "It's terrifying and wonderful all at once, and sometimes you want to hunker down and sometimes you want to run away. That's *normal,* Tom. You learn on the job. Every parent does."

He stares at me for a moment, and for a few brief, wonderful seconds I think we're getting somewhere, and then he lets out a huff of hard laughter as he shakes his head. "I can't believe I'm listening to *your* parenting advice."

I try not to take offense at that, even though I stayed at home with him for the first three years of his life, took him to school every day until he was seven. I could have won prizes for being a good mom until I decided I had to do something more with my life or die trying. That's a decision that incurs a *lot* of judgment— from the children who feel neglected, the husbands who do the same and no one cares, the world that sees a mother who doesn't absolutely *love* being a mother as someone unnatural and even evil.

The waitress returns to take our orders, and after she leaves, I struggle to fill the silence.

"I'd like to help you," I finally say. "However I can. I'd like to get to know Henry, and you too, for that matter, now that I'm back."

"For how long?" Tom challenges, his chin thrusting forward once again. "A couple of weeks until your next job? Where are you going this time? Asia? Africa? Somewhere where other people *need* you?"

I flinch, I can't help it. This isn't the first time these kinds of accusations have been hurled at me, and yet every time they hurt. "Actually, I don't have anything lined up," I say quietly. "So I can be here for as long as you need me."

"I don't *need* you," he flashes back, and I take a sip of coffee to keep from saying something I'll regret. And the truth is, I may not have another job lined up, but I'd like one. I don't know who I am without my job. I have no idea how to be. Crisis Action may have forced me into a temporary retirement, but I'm not ready for it to be permanent... not that I want to explain all that to Tom just now.

"So why did you come back?" he asks. "Was it just because you heard about Sophie?" He pauses, his eyes narrowing. "You don't have cancer or something, do you?"

I almost laugh at that. In some ways, it would be easier if I did have some dreaded disease. Maybe I'd get a little more empathy, anyway. "No, I'm not sick," I tell him. "When Uncle Jack told me what happened, I wanted to be here." Which isn't the *entire* truth, but it's enough for Tom, at least right now. He'd take the whole truth and twist it, make it sound like I was being selfish. Again.

He frowns, his hands flat on the table. "So you just dropped everything and came back here?"

"Pretty much." I try to smile, aware that there is an element of deceit in my reply, but I know Tom will use the truth as an excuse to walk away from me.

He shakes his head slowly. "I don't know how you can help."

"I can help with Henry," I offer. "I'm renting an apartment if staying with the Lawrences stops working out. Obviously, it's not nearly as nice, but it's here, Tom, and there are definitely no strings attached."

His frown deepens as he gazes down at the table. "Andrew Lawrence offered me money," he admits in a low voice. "Some kind of stipend, for giving up access to Henry's trust fund."

"Henry has a trust fund?" I realize I should not be surprised.

"It was Sophie's, and it goes automatically to him. I could be the guardian of it—I *should* be, as his dad—but the Lawrences don't want that. So he said he'd give me a couple of grand a month to let him be in control of it." He pauses. "I refused, but now I'm thinking of taking it. That's a lot of money, for me."

"But if you should have control of it by right..." I hate the thought of how high-handed Andrew Lawrence is being, assuming Tom would squander his son's inheritance just because he can. What does that say about how he views my son, and his role in his own son's life? "And if the Lawrences control Henry's trust fund," I add, thinking it through, "they'll most likely try to control his life, too... Do you want them that involved, Tom? Deciding where he goes to school, who his friends are? What kind of *person* he is?" I can picture my grandson already, with his popped collar and leather loafers, swinging a golf club in one hand.

"He'd have a better chance in life than I did," Tom replies in a low voice. "Should I refuse him that, just because I don't like it?"

I stay silent, imagining how the Lawrences might control

Henry, and through him, Tom. I picture them subtly but surely edging him out of his own son's life. In their moneyed, gentrified world, Tom will always feel like an outsider. Eventually, he will choose to be one, until one day he'll be as absent from his own son's life as I was from mine… or even more so, because it won't be by choice.

"Maybe you should talk to a lawyer?" I tell him.

"Lawyers are expensive—"

"There is free legal aid, and I have some money saved." Not much, and probably not enough, but maybe this is a way I can help. A way Tom will let me. "It's worth a try, Tom. Don't give your rights away as a parent. Not yet."

His mouth twists. "Oh, maybe should I wait until he's seven or so and then just walk away?"

Anger flares through me, although I try to keep it from my voice, my face. "You know it wasn't like that."

"It felt like it, from my end," he retorts, always ready to rehash this familiar fight.

"You and your dad were very happy together, and I came back every three months for six weeks," I say in a low, insistent voice. There are only so many cheap shots I can take. "I didn't *abandon* you, Tom."

"Yeah, not then," Tom agrees. "You waited a couple of years for that."

Just then, the waitress comes with our meals—bacon and eggs for Tom, a bowl of oatmeal for me. I stare down at it, my appetite vanished. I'm so tired of having to accept these accusations, over and over again. It feels like being punched when I'm already laid out on the floor.

"I know you don't want to forgive me for that," I finally say. "And I understand it, at least in part. But there were other factors, Tom, as you know."

"Yeah, those poor orphans in Tajikistan who mattered more to you than I did—"

"And your father, who walked out first," I am goaded into replying. "Yet you never seem to be angry with him."

"Because he's *dead!*" Tom's voice rises to a cry that has the diners near us glancing our way, curious as well as condemning. We're making a scene.

"I know, and I'm sorry." My anger is gone in an instant, replaced by a deep, unshakeable sorrow. "I'm so sorry, for so much of it," I say. "I wish you could believe that."

Tom lowers his head, his shoulders bowed. For a few moments, he doesn't speak, and I wait, both tense and grief-stricken, having no idea how he might respond, but knowing I'll need to deal with it, whatever it is.

"I know," he finally says, lifting his head, his voice heavy. "I actually do know that." A huff of grateful amazement escapes me, and he cracks a wry smile. "Surprise."

I laugh then, and Tom's smile stays, and whatever hits us next, it feels like something good might have happened here. For the first time since my son was fourteen years old, I feel like I reached him. *Just.*

And for the first time in years, I am daring to be hopeful for the future we can have… together.

SEVENTEEN
DIANA

I gaze down at Henry lying in his crib, his hands flung up by his face, his whole body softened in sleep. It took two hours to get him down, and I feel wrung out and a little shaky by it all, as well as relieved. I love this child with a ferocity that sometimes scares me, but looking after a newborn can be such very hard work.

Especially when so much in my life feels fragile.

It's been a week since Audrey West exploded into our lives. That's what it felt like, as if a grenade had been hurled into our happiness, leaving nothing but shattered fragments. I think of the moment before the buzz of the doorbell, when Andrew was smiling with wonder and Tom looked shyly pleased and I had so much hope. For a moment, no more, everything felt possible, the happy ending we'd never had finally within reach...

And then Audrey walked in, and everything spun into different and unwelcome directions. For the last week, Tom has been going out to see Audrey every day. He might have said they were estranged, but they certainly don't feel so now. Sometimes he takes Henry, which provides its own kind of break but makes me burn with envy—and fear. What if Tom decides to take Henry and live with Audrey? His *mother*. The words keep searing themselves into my brain, reminding me that I am nothing more than a poor substitute. Yes, we can offer Tom certain material benefits, but the last thing I want to do is hold him ransom to those, or make him feel there are strings attached to our generosity.

And yet that's exactly what Andrew wants to do.

"Why shouldn't we make it clear that if we're going to provide for Tom and his son, we have certain expectations?" he asked yesterday morning, while I was loading the dishwasher and he was about to head off to work. Tom had gone out again, leaving me with Henry, who was in his bouncy seat, having just had his bottle. "We're not being unreasonable here," Andrew continued. "And we're not a hotel or a babysitting service. We've been very generous in many obvious ways." He nodded meaningfully toward the driveway; Tom was driving our BMW SUV like it was his own. I'd offered it, but I realized belatedly that I hadn't expected him to accept it with such alacrity. "Tom needs to know that," he finished firmly. "He needs to understand what's at stake here."

"He hasn't seen his mother in a year," I reminded him. "He's certainly entitled to spend some time with her." And I was glad their relationship seemed to be getting stronger. Of course I was, because it would be cruel not to be.

"He is, naturally," Andrew agreed in a steely voice. "I'm not saying he isn't. But we need *parameters*, Diana. We need to know where this is going, in the long term. Maybe I should talk to Tom—"

"*No.*" I spoke quickly, not wanting Andrew to launch into another diatribe about managing Sophie's trust fund or a potential custody agreement. Not yet, anyway, when everything still felt fragile. "We're still gaining Tom's trust, Andrew. We need to remember that, before we move in with some ultimatum."

"And he needs to gain our trust," Andrew fired back. "I'll be honest, he hasn't done all that much to do so, all things considered—"

"That's not fair," I felt compelled to point out. "I know he's had some wobbles, but..." I paused before admitting, "I have, too. And for the last few weeks, he's been very helpful—"

Andrew pressed his lips together, already disapproving. "Has he even looked for a job—"

"I think he's *tried*," I protested, although I wasn't convinced he'd tried very hard. I'd mentioned it a few times, but Tom had said it wasn't really the time for hiring, which seemed like an excuse. Still, Tom had certainly been involved in Henry's care, and I'd enjoyed seeing him grow in confidence with his son. If we'd had a few more weeks or months without interference, I feel like we would have really gotten somewhere.

If only Audrey hadn't showed up, I think, not for the first time, and then feel guilty for such an uncharitable thought.

"And Henry is still so young," I tell Andrew. "We need to give Tom some time and space, to grieve, as well as get used to being a father."

"On our dime," Andrew replied with a shake of his head, disapproval turning to dismissiveness. "There's only so much generosity you can show before you start to feel like a chump. It would be better for all of us if we had a frank discussion to determine just exactly where we are. Asking for a firm custody arrangement benefits everyone."

"And what would that arrangement look like?" I asked desperately. I was afraid of scaring Tom away, but I was also still worried about having the complete care of a very young baby. I'd come a long way in confidence, just like Tom, but I still doubted myself sometimes. "What would you even suggest?" I asked. "We take full custody of Henry—"

"Why not?" Andrew blustered. "He'd have a better life with us, you can't deny that, and sometimes I think Tom feels that, too."

"If he does, it's our fault," I told Andrew. "Because we make him feel like he doesn't belong here."

"Diana," Andrew said, his tone turning almost gentle, "he doesn't."

For a second, I could only stare. "Andrew, Tom is Henry's *father*."

Andrew sighed, his shoulders slumping a little, the certainty draining out of him. "I know," he said as he reached for his briefcase. The words sounded like defeat. "I know."

Now I gaze down at Henry, finally asleep, thankfully, and start to tiptoe out of the nursery, taking every step so very carefully because lately he has startled awake at the smallest sound. My hand is just on the doorknob when he gives a little whimper. I still, my heart beating hard, and Henry subsides back into sleep. Slowly I open the door, not too wide in case it creaks. I am just slipping through when my hip nudges the knob and the door emits a small, protesting creak. I hold my breath, and...

Henry lets out a thin wail of distress. I wait, hoping he might still settle down, but it's no good. He's crying in earnest now, snuffles and sobs, and I stride back to the crib and snatch him out, making him cry harder before I bring him to my chest and pat his back.

"S*ssh, sssh*..." I say wearily, feeling as if I am on autopilot. It will probably take another two hours to go through the whole process again, and I'm aching with tiredness myself. We never should have given up the night nurse. For the last week, Henry's nights have been so broken that even between Tom, Andrew, and I sharing the load, I'm exhausted. And, in truth, I'm the one who gets up with him the most.

I rock and sway, trying everything I can think of to get him to settle, but he just keeps crying, each newborn warble louder than the last, his face red with distress and fury.

I feel my nerves start to fray. It's moments like this one that I remember so well and now dread. Moments I'm afraid I *still* can't handle.

"S*ssh*..." I say again, my voice breaking.

"Diana, let me take him."

I turn to see Andrew in the doorway. It's the middle of the day, and he doesn't usually come home early from work. He puts down his briefcase and then walks toward me, holding his arms out. I hand Henry over, wordless with surprise.

Andrew drapes him over his shoulder, murmuring to him as he rocks back and forth like an expert, and his cries quieten, which is both a relief and an annoyance. Why couldn't he stop crying for me?

"What are you doing home?" I ask, keeping my voice low for the baby's sake.

"I thought it might be nice to spend some time with you and Henry," he replies, and I sense something guarded in his tone that makes me stiffen.

"Are you checking up on me?" I demand sharply, and he turns, his eyebrows raised, his expression flummoxed.

"*Checking up* on you? I'm trying to offer some support."

"Funny you never thought to do that when Sophie was small," I reply tartly, before I can think better of it. We so rarely talk about those dark days, preferring to draw a curtain across it all.

Andrew stares at me for a long moment, his brows now drawn together in perplexity. "Diana, what are you talking about?" he asks, and now I'm the one to stare.

"What do you mean what am I talking about?" I ask, still striving to keep my voice to a whisper. "You were never around when Sophie was a baby. I know you were busy with work, as you've said before, but you never once got up at night, never gave her a bottle, never rocked her like you're rocking Henry now..." I trail off because Andrew is shaking his head, a slow, resolute back and forth.

"I know I could have done more," he says, "maybe a lot more, all things considered, but never...? That's just not true."

I stare at him, amazed that he's rewriting history that has shaped us both for so long. Andrew was busy and uninvolved, I was exhausted and overwhelmed. I cracked, and then at his behest, a nanny swooped in, and I have spent every moment since trying to make up for it all and failing. We never talk about any of it, but that doesn't change what happened.

"I gave Sophie a bottle most nights at eleven," Andrew continues steadily, "before she went down. And I gave her a bath every night, when I got home from work."

"*What?*" I stare at him incredulously. My memory of those first few weeks and months is a blur of fatigue and grief, an endless march of days of exhaustion and loneliness. Andrew isn't anywhere in them, except when he breezed in, fresh from the 7:05 train, after Sophie was in bed.

"I even had a bath song," he says with a small, wry smile, although his eyes are shadowed with concern. "Bathtime for Soph-a-lofa," he sings in an offkey warble. "Bathtime for Soph-a-lofa-loo."

Those silly words strike a distant chord deep inside me, like the chime of a faraway bell, and for a second I can see it—Andrew with his shirtsleeves rolled up, utterly intent on Sophie sitting in the little plastic baby bath, a yellow rubber ducky floating in the water even though she was too little to play with it.

"Don't you remember?" he asks, and now, and *only* now, I do. At least I start to, and it completely floors me.

"I..." I shake my head and then walk slowly to the glider, sinking down onto the seat.

Andrew continues to rock Henry, who has fallen back

asleep, his mouth in a perfect o, his cheeks so plump they droop down like an old man's. Our little old man.

My heart squeezes with both love and confusion. How could I have forgotten so much, if that's really what I did? Did I just remember the pain and confusion and fear, rather than the good parts?

Another memory falls into my mind, as if dropping out of the sky. Andrew asleep in this very glider, his head thrown back, Sophie cradled in his arms.

How can this be? I can't tell if I'm making up what I so often wished for, or am remembering things that actually happened. I know my therapist told me once that our memories are funny things, and our minds often have a negativity bias, so the hard and painful things stay with us, while the good aspects drift away, as ephemeral as if they never happened at all.

And judging from the way Andrew is looking at me, with a mixture of confusion and concern, I think that is what happened to me. I just didn't realize it because we never dared talk about it before.

I didn't.

"I didn't remember," I whisper hoarsely, a confession. "Those first few months... they're a complete blank in some ways. I didn't remember you doing anything for Sophie, just how... how *alone* I felt, all the time." I swallow, a gulping sound.

"I know you did, and I'm so sorry you felt that way," Andrew says quietly. "I know it was hard, harder than I can imagine, especially after your mother's death, and I *should* have been more supportive, but... please don't think I didn't try, at least, even if my trying wasn't nearly enough."

"I don't think that now," I say honestly, and I can tell from Andrew's sorrowful expression that he knows I *did* think that, for far too many years. I stare vacantly ahead, trying to recalibrate my memory of those years, and even of our entire marriage. How many other faulty memories do I have, lost in the haze of my unhappiness that I let swallow me whole?

"I know I haven't always been a good husband," Andrew says stiltedly, the words coming painfully. "I work too hard, and I disengage when I'm..." He pauses, his throat working before admitting in a low voice, "When I'm afraid. When Sophie started to struggle with her eating disorder, when I saw how obsessive she was about so many things... I didn't know how to handle that. I left it all to you, and I shouldn't have."

I shake my head, an instinctive denial. "It was hard—"

"It's always been hard," he agreed. "*Sophie* was hard. We both loved her, I know we did, so much, but she was hard... and it was harder when we weren't working together. I know that was my fault sometimes. I didn't know how to handle things, and so I shut down. Or got angry, like I did with Sophie." For a second, his face crumples. "I've regretted how harsh I was, when she first showed up with Tom. I think I was just so *shocked*. I thought she was just trying to get a rise out of us, the way she sometimes did, like when she dyed her hair green and got a belly-button piercing. Do you remember?"

I sigh, a ghost of grief filtering through me. "Yes."

"And I honestly believed that she'd come to her senses, when she saw how upset we were about it. I never dreamed she'd double down and run off with him."

"I know," I whisper. I've always suspected as much, anyway, but Andrew has never admitted so much before. Never been willing to. It makes me wish we'd spoken honestly earlier, *years* earlier, but even as that thought flashes through my mind, I know we couldn't have. I don't think either of us had that kind of honesty or courage within us to confess how ill-equipped we both felt for the challenges we'd faced.

I'm amazed we have that courage now, and the truth is, maybe we *don't*, we just have the willingness to try. Just like with Tom, maybe that can be enough.

"I'm sorry," Andrew whispers brokenly. "If I hadn't been so harsh with her, maybe—"

"You can't torture yourself with those kinds of what-ifs," I tell him firmly. "Neither of us can. It serves no purpose now."

He nods slowly and we both subside into silence, dazed by the revelations we've both shared. I wonder what they mean for us now, if Andrew and I can be more of a united front, now that we've spoken so honestly. If this can change things for the better.

Andrew presses a kiss to the top of Henry's head. "I think he's asleep," he whispers. "Shall I try to put him down?"

I think of the two hours I spent trying to do just that. "If you can."

"Are you saying it might take a while?" Andrew asks, a teasing note to his voice that I haven't heard in years.

"It might," I agree with a small smile. I rise from the glider. "You can sit and rock him for a little bit. That helps."

"Okay."

I offer another smile and then slip out of the room, still feeling so disoriented from our conversation, from the shift in perception, in memory, in what I thought my marriage was. Can a single conversation change anything, never mind everything?

I am still considering the question as I come into the kitchen, stopping suddenly when I see Tom come through the door. He tosses the keys in the ceramic bowl by the door, stilling when he sees me, his expression turning as guarded as it was when we first knew him.

It hurts me, that look on his face, because I really believed we'd moved past all that. Moved past all the tension and suspicion and hostility, but right now it feels as if we haven't, as if it's grown worse, and I realize I am just as afraid to lose *Tom* as I am Henry. I thought we'd created a bond, had helped each other, but since Audrey arrived, it feels like we are only moving backward.

"Hi, Tom," I say, trying my best to keep my voice bright, even though I fear the note rings false. "How are you? Were you with your mother?"

"Yeah." He slouches into the kitchen, his hands jammed in the pockets of his jeans, looking like he doesn't want to say anything more.

"How is she?" I ask, my voice rising from bright to a little manic. "Is she settling in well? She's in Stamford, isn't she?"

"Yeah, she's got an apartment near the train station."

"I'm glad you guys are getting along, because I know you said you weren't all that close before." If I'm hoping the unsubtle reminder of how much he's shared with me in the past might make him remember that we once felt close, I am disappointed. Tom's expression only closes up all the more.

"Yeah, well, we're doing okay now," he says, and while I know I should be glad they seem to have reconciled, I only feel uneasy. "I was thinking of having Henry over at her place for a bit," he adds. "A couple of days, maybe. Give you guys a break for a little while."

"Oh?" My voice rises and wobbles. "Is her apartment suitable for a baby?" I know he's brought Henry over there for a few hours at a time, but several nights? What next?

He frowns and then shrugs. "She's got one of those portable cribs, I think."

You think? I am not ready to trust my grandson to his father and grandmother in some apartment in the city, not like this, and yet I also know I have no choice. Tom has every right to take Henry to stay with his own mother. He doesn't need to ask my permission.

"I'd love to have her over here for dinner," I say suddenly. I think about Andrew once saying we need to keep our enemies closer. I don't want to think of Audrey as my enemy, but right now that's what she feels like. Until she came, Tom felt like my friend. "Is she very busy? Maybe Friday night?"

Tom looks unenthused by my suggestion, which worries me all the more. Why has he seemed so hostile ever since Audrey came into our lives? What is she whispering in his ear?

"I guess..." he says reluctantly.

"And then, if you like, you could bring Henry back to your mother's place after." I don't want that, but I feel like it will shorten the time Henry is away—and give me some sense of control over the situation. "And maybe we could all meet up for breakfast in the morning."

I know Tom isn't fooled by my suggestions, that he realizes I'm trying to limit the whole interaction.

And, in truth, I don't know what I'm hoping to achieve by inviting Audrey over. Maybe I just want a chance to get to know her better, to find some sympathy with her, or, more likely, to assess her motives. Because I am realizing more and more that, just as Andrew said, this situation can't stand. I can't take care of Henry day after day, learning to love him, while never knowing if one day Tom might simply disappear with him. I couldn't survive that kind of uncertainty and heartache, and neither, I believe, could Andrew.

His demanding clarity on a custody agreement isn't, I suspect, the clawing for control I assumed it was. It's a heartrending attempt not to be hurt, and for *me* not to be hurt.

And most of all, for *Henry* not to be hurt.

It's as if my mind is a kaleidoscope that has been turned to a whole new swirl of colors, a new pattern of thoughts. Everything looks different.

But what that can possibly mean for the future and the child we all love, I have no idea.

As Tom walks out of the room without another word, I'm afraid it's nothing good.

EIGHTEEN

AUDREY

I stand on the doorstep of the Lawrences' palace of a house, determined not to feel uneasy or out of place. I'm not sure why they invited me, or what they hope to gain, but I remain as suspicious of them now as I have from the moment I walked into their house nearly two weeks ago. They want something, I'm sure of it, and I'm pretty sure it isn't me or my son.

The last few weeks with Tom have been both good and fraught. I'm glad and grateful that he's willing to spend time with me after so many years of silence, but it hasn't been easy, or sometimes even particularly pleasant. Every so often, a sneering remark of his slips out, a shot across the bow that reminds me of just how much he feels I failed him. It leaves me on edge, especially when I'm trying to help him, which I *am*, even though I can't afford it.

After contacting Connecticut Legal Services and waiting on the phone for over an hour to talk to a real person, I discovered that Tom wouldn't be able to talk to one of their pro bono lawyers for at least a month.

"A *month*!" I exclaimed. "But the cases you're dealing with must be urgent—"

"Exactly," the woman replied tiredly. "We're working as fast as we can, but we have a serious backlist. A month is the best we can do."

I didn't want to wait a whole month, not when I feared that the Lawrences might take some kind of action against Tom. And while I tried to tell myself I had no real reason to think that they *would*, it felt as if all the signs were pointing to it.

There was the fact that they hadn't so much as spoken to Tom or their own daughter in the year and a half before her death. Tom told me Sophie had been on a stipend that her parents had cut off the very *evening* they'd met him. On the same night, they'd also terminated the lease on the apartment they'd been renting for her. All within their rights, I suppose, but it pointed to a kind of coercive control that I strongly suspected they were already exhibiting toward Tom—and, more importantly, toward Henry, especially when Tom explained again how Andrew Lawrence had urged him to sign over his guardianship of Henry's trust fund, and, it seemed, more or less bow out of his life.

Getting some information about Tom's legal rights felt like an important and necessary protection. And so I called a local lawyer I'd looked up online, a woman, who agreed to meet with us to discuss Tom's case. She charged two hundred and fifty dollars an hour, money that neither of us really had, not that I'd told that to Tom. I put it on my credit card and figured I would pay it back when I was working again. *If* I was working again.

"Of course, the guardianship of the trust would naturally go to Tom," the lawyer told us, "in most reasonable cases." Her tone was both brisk and ominous, suggesting that Tom's case was not reasonable. "His criminal record, I'm afraid, will count against him. If any suggestion could be made he might abuse the guardianship or use the money for himself, or that his wife had not been happy in the marriage or intending to leave him, his position becomes weaker." She paused, looking between us.

"I'm not saying it's impossible, but I'd strongly suggest you find a way to work this out amenably." She gave us a sympathetic and rueful smile, her expression still shrewd. "So many cases of family law could avoid the drama and expense of a courtroom battle if people were just willing to talk to one another."

"That's not something I've heard a lawyer say before," I joked feebly, and her smile dropped as she straightened in her chair.

"If you'd like me to take on this case," she stated, "then I would require a three-thousand-dollar retainer."

That was money we really didn't have, and I was pretty sure she knew it.

"Maybe it's better this way?" Tom said when we were back at my apartment—a tiny studio in an anonymous corporate block whose only concessions to homeliness were a kettle and an iron, a microwave and a minifridge. It was inhabited by depressed commuters and divorced dads. The other day, I saw a little girl, no more than twelve years old, hovering outside the apartment next to mine, looking as if she were afraid to knock. A few seconds later, the door was thrown open by a defeated-looking dad who widened his smile, clearly desperate to see his daughter.

"Honey!"

She'd hugged him dutifully but without enthusiasm, and my heart had ached at the sight. I didn't want that kind of existence for Tom. It was what *I* had had with him, after I'd chosen to go back to work, throwing myself into disaster relief areas, grateful to escape the unending drudgery of school lunches and spelling tests, and yet knowing I was missing out on so much more.

I'd told myself I had the best of both worlds, meaningful work *and* quality family time, but the six weeks when I came home never truly worked for any of us. Matt was resentful of the time I'd been away, and let me know it at every opportunity, and Tom never seemed to know what to do with me. Or, if I'm honest, maybe I didn't know what to do with him. Either way, it always felt like a guilty relief when I went back to wherever it felt like people *really* needed me.

"Better what way?" I asked Tom as I went to fill the kettle. "For the Lawrences to control Henry's future? Because if they have control of that money, you know that's what they'll do. They'll decide every aspect of his life."

I could already picture Andrew Lawrence setting Henry up for a private prep school, giving him his college tie, steering him toward investment banking and golfing and God only knew what else. If that was the way it went, Tom would be slowly but surely edged out of his own's son life... just as I'd felt I was.

"Yeah, I know they will." Tom slumped onto the sofa, his head bent as he dragged his hands across his stubbly buzz cut. "And maybe that *is* better. What future do I really have? A job in construction if I can get one? I was fired from the last one, so I can't even get a reference. Who's going to hire me?"

That was the first I'd heard he'd been fired. "Why were you fired?" I asked, making sure to keep my voice gentle, and a sigh escaped him, heavy and low.

"I missed too many days because of Sophie. She was pretty miserable at the end of her pregnancy, said she couldn't stay home alone because she might *do* something. It scared me."

"Do something?" I repeated questioningly, and Tom grimaced.

"You know... to herself."

I stared at him, shocked by the admission. I remembered Sophie as a bubbly, fun, lighthearted girl, and one who had made the effort to reach out to me—but maybe that had been some kind of act, put on for my benefit, the one time I saw her? Or maybe she'd careened between effusiveness and despair, caught between two emotions just as she was between two worlds—the one she'd grown up in, and the one she inhabited with my son.

"Oh, Tom," I said softly. "I'm so sorry."

He shrugged, hunching into himself. "I still loved her, you know. And maybe... maybe I wasn't good enough for her."

"You were—"

"She said once she only married me to make her father mad. I think it was probably true. I mean, we're so different. I'm an ex-con." He stared up at me, his face so full of bleakness it made my heart twist within me, with both guilt and pity.

"You made a mistake," I said quietly. When I'd heard that Tom had been arrested for drug dealing, I'd been in Kenya. I hadn't seen him in two years, at his request, but I came home right away for his hearing, stayed throughout the trial, and visited him in prison until he refused to see me. All too little, too late. As always.

"And if the Lawrences find out that," he continued doggedly, "which they might, because, you know, Sophie had friends she saw. She might have told them stuff about me. Us." Slowly, he shook his head. "I don't think I have a case."

"You're Henry's father," I reminded him fiercely. "Of course you have a case."

"Just being related to someone biologically doesn't mean much though in the end, does it?"

I stilled then, because I knew he wasn't talking about him and Henry. He was talking about him and me. Slowly, I lowered myself onto the sofa next to him.

"Tom," I said quietly, "I know that you might not believe me, but I have *always* loved you."

He gave a little shake of his head, as if to deny the words, the sentiment, and I didn't know whether to go on. After a few seconds of silence, I decided to.

"I know it seems like I chose work over you, when I went back," I said slowly. "And maybe I *did*, in a way. I can admit that. But my work with Crisis Action..." A sigh escaped me as I thought back over my years of work, the intense satisfaction and sense of purpose I'd gained from it. To go without that had felt like going without a vital part of myself. "It was so much a part of me," I told Tom. "Too much of a part of me, probably." I thought of why I had to leave, and whether I'd be allowed back, and I knew that was true, but I loved it so much. I'd always loved it so much—feeling like I was doing important work, work that nobody else could do. Seeing how I made a difference. The energy and adrenalin, the purpose and the validation, so different from a life of suburban drudgery. "It just..." I closed my eyes. "It gave me meaning. I felt needed in a way that I didn't when I was packing your school lunches and making sure you had a shower. Dad felt like the one who was your real buddy, the one you did things with, who you turned to with anything important."

He stayed silent, so I had no idea what he thought about my confession, or how selfish it sounded. Mothers, I knew, weren't meant to feel that way, and if they did, they certainly weren't meant to admit to it. But when he'd grown out of babyhood, Tom had always been closer to Matt, which had made my husband's disappearance the true tragedy of our situation.

Six weeks after he walked out, Matt was found in a hotel, dead of an overdose. By that point, Tom was in foster care, with the kind of two-kids-and-a-dog family that made me feel like I couldn't offer him anything, and he'd applied to social services to stay with them until he reached majority. Matt's death made him double down on all of that, and a month after the decision, I was back at work, this time in Haiti, my busyness feeling like a relief.

"I know I was close to Dad," Tom finally said in a low voice. "But you were important, too."

"I know." I let out a breath, a gust of regret. No matter how I felt at the time, distance has given me some painful perspective.

"I think I realized that later," I told my son. "That doing those things, simply being there, was more important than I'd ever thought or felt it was. But by that time..." I couldn't finish the sentence. By that time, my son was in foster care, my husband was dead, and I had escaped to a place where it felt like people both needed and appreciated me a lot more than anyone back home had.

And even before that, in the last months, and even years, before it all went wrong, my marriage had been breaking down, my husband trying to hide his depression, so much so that I had no idea he was in danger of walking out on our son, much less killing himself. When social services called me, Tom had been alone for a whole week before being taken into care.

I was assured he was safe and well with a family, and so I took two days—two days I thought wouldn't matter so much in the grand scheme of things—to arrange my replacement, make sure the disaster relief we were providing to refugees from an earthquake could continue. In retrospect, I suppose I thought I was more important than I really was. And in light of the broken families and destroyed homes I was witnessing after an unimaginable earthquake, it was hard to put the problems of my personal life into perspective. But, in truth, I think I was afraid of going home and facing the mess I'd left behind—a missing husband, an angry son.

But those two days cost me more than I could have ever imagined.

I blink the memories away as I press the doorbell of the Lawrences' house and listen to the cathedral-sounding chimes echo within. I don't know why Diana invited me to dinner. I suppose, in a normal world, we are related by marriage and so should get to know one another, observe all the social niceties. But, of course, none of this is normal.

"Audrey." She opens the door with a wide smile that makes me think of a crack in a plate. She's dressed as immaculately as ever—cream linen pants and a floaty top in a slightly darker shade. Her hair is in its usual smooth bob, a few slender gold bangles sliding down one wrist. I glance down at my own outfit—gray cargo pants and a fitted black T-shirt. I don't have any other clothes besides the ones I wear for work, utilitarian and hard-wearing, and I feel both out of place and defiant about it. I don't want to fit into their moneyed world, but I'm afraid of what it might cost me—as well as Tom and Henry.

"Come in, come in," Diana says, and I step inside, just as I did two weeks ago, already sensing that I am not welcome.

Her heels click across the marble as she leads the way to the kitchen. "We're all in here. I don't know why we have a dining room that seats sixteen, when we always seem to eat in the kitchen." She lets out a little trill of laughter while I silently grit my teeth. Is tonight just going to be reminder after reminder of how much more they can give my grandson than I can?

Tom is in the kitchen, drinking a beer, which worries me a little. It looks like he's started early. He seems tense, and I wonder what has happened, because it feels like something has.

"Where's Henry?" I ask, and my voice comes out sharper than I meant it to.

"Andrew is settling him," Diana explains smoothly. "He's been so fussy lately—the pediatrician says he might be teething, although it seems a little early... Anyway, we thought Tom could use a break."

I glance at Tom, whose face is stonily expressionless, and I wonder if I am reading too much into that light remark. Is Diana implying that my son can't handle being a father? Are they making their case for custody even now? I feel a tension in the room that I don't think has to do just with me, and it worries me.

"Would you like a drink, Audrey?" Diana asks, her hand poised over an open bottle of white wine chilling in a silver bucket.

"Just water, thanks."

"I'd love to hear about your work," Diana remarks as she gets me my water, just as she once did before. "It sounds so interesting. You must truly love it. Is it hard to leave the project you're working on? Are you always dying to go back?" She smiles at me expectantly, eyebrows raised.

I know what she's doing. She's trying to edge me out, as well as drive a wedge between me and Tom. Remind us both of how I've not been a good or present mother in the past, and I certainly can't be one now, because any minute I'll be on a plane out of here.

"It can be," I reply evenly. "But I'm very glad to be here to support Tom and get to know Henry, and I certainly intend to stay for quite a while."

It's as if I've lobbed a grenade into the room and it's there, pulsing between us, about to go off. Diana's mouth tightens as she pours herself a glass of wine.

"Of course," she murmurs.

An uncomfortable and awkward silence is punctuated a few minutes later by the arrival of Andrew, looking jovial and determined, and *not* holding a baby.

"Where's Henry?" I ask, and again I sound sharp. I feel like this is a setup, like the Lawrences have called me here for a reason, and it's one I'm not going to like.

"We hired a babysitter for the evening," Andrew tells me in a smooth, self-assured tone. "I was just getting her settled with him. Henry's been a bit fussy lately, and we didn't want to be having to get up from the table every few minutes to see to him. I thought it could give us all a chance to talk."

The words are laden with import, and I tense all the more, because I'm pretty sure my suspicions were right. This *is* a setup.

I glance at Tom, who flicks his gaze away from me. What is going on?

"I thought," Andrew continues in the same, slightly smarmy tone, "that we could have a chat about the future. Expectations of what that would look like... and what would be best for Henry, in the long term."

So here it comes. I turn to Diana, to see how she is taking this, but she is looking away as she sips her wine. I get the sense that she's not entirely comfortable with whatever is coming next, but she's willing to go along with it.

"And what do you think that would look like, Andrew?" I ask in a voice that I pitch both pleasant and steely. I have always found confrontation better than waiting for the boom to drop. It was one of the reasons my marriage floundered; Matt preferred passive-aggressive innuendoes and loaded silences rather than simply thrashing it out. My attempts to do so made him retreat all the further, another reason why escaping to a place where everything felt straightforward, if challenging, was so appealing.

"Well, that's a good question, Audrey." I can tell Andrew is slightly surprised by my confrontational tone, but he recovers his composure quickly. "Obviously, Diana and I are well placed to give Henry a comfortable and stable home life, one that offers a great deal of opportunity for him, in quite a few significant ways."

"Andrew..." Diana murmurs and then falls silent. Again I wonder if she is not as on board with this plan as her husband is.

"And let me guess," I say, not bothering to hide my hostility. "Tom and I aren't?"

Again, Andrew seems discomfited by my plain speaking. "Well, I'm not saying that, not exactly, but you have to admit there are some challenges there."

I fold my arms as I stare him down. "Such as?"

I've pushed too hard, and now Andrew looks annoyed. "Do I have to spell it out?" he asks, an edge entering his voice. "Tom is a convicted felon—"

"Who has served his time," I remind him evenly.

"And you don't even live in this country—"

"I do now."

He raises his eyebrows. "You've been absent from your son's life for over *ten years*. Are you telling me you're never going back to your job overseas that mattered so much that you left your son over it?"

For a second, I can't speak. I hate that he has formed a judgment about me, based on whatever limited information he has gleaned from Tom. And I hate that Tom has told him enough to form that judgment, that there is enough truth in it all for them both to have done so.

"That remains to be seen," I reply coolly. "Not that it's any business of yours—"

"Actually, it *is* my business, because Henry is my grandson," Andrew cuts me off. "So, naturally, I'm concerned that his father has the support he needs, especially if he's not going to take the support we're offering."

I draw a steadying breath and then glance at Tom who has been silent this whole time, his gaze lowered as he sips his beer. I set my untouched glass carefully on the counter, trying to both organize my thoughts and keep my cool. "And what support are you offering?" I ask finally.

"Tom might have told you, but we're willing to give him a monthly stipend, if he signs the guardianship of Henry's trust over to us. That trust was set up by my mother, and so you can appreciate we have some concerns regarding how it is administered."

I let my lip curl. "You think Tom will run off with your money?" I sneer.

"I'm trying to be reasonable," Andrew says in a tone that suggests I am the one who is not.

"You're trying to be rude and controlling," I correct. "And edge Tom out of his son's life. Say he signs over the guardianship, and you give him the stipend. What then?"

Andrew pauses, glancing at Diana seemingly to see if he has backup. She is pale, her fingers clenched around the stem of her now-empty wineglass, her gaze lowered. "Well..." he finally says slowly, "naturally we would expect Tom to find some sort of honest work—"

"*Honest!*" I scoff, furious at the way my son is being treated. "You mean you don't want him falling back into his criminal ways?"

"Naturally we don't," Andrew replies icily.

I take a step toward him, balling my fists. "Do you even know how he ended up in prison?" I demand. "Because I do, since I was there every day of his trial. He was *set up* by a drug dealer who was a moneyed jackass, just like you."

"I really think—" Andrew begins, his face flushing, but I steamroll right over him.

"Yeah, I know what you think. You think Tom was a crack dealer in the 'hood, running drugs for gangs and snorting coke on the side, like something you once saw on *The Wire*. When what really happened is he became friendly with a preppy college dropout, the kind of guy who doesn't yet have access to his trust fund but really wants some cold, hard cash, and Tom got duped into delivering drugs for him." I hold up a hand to forestall any of Andrew's blustering objections.

"I'm not saying it was smart," I go on. "But this kid had parents like you, parents who like to arrange everything to protect their little darling no matter what he's done, and so Tom was given *three years*, while the rich kid got a slap on the wrist." I break off, breathing hard, while Andrew simply stares at me and Diana goes even paler, her hand trembling so much she has to set down her wineglass on the counter, which she does with enough force to crack the stem.

For a long, taut moment, no one speaks.

"Tom," Diana finally whispers. "Is that true?"

He shrugs, his gaze downcast. "I told you some of it before."

"I know, but..." She shakes her head slowly. "I didn't realize..."

"Didn't realize it was people like you who screwed him over before?" I fill in cynically. I'm so angry, I'm practically shaking.

"You can't tar us with the same brush," Andrew protests. "We're hardly the same—"

"Aren't you?" I cut across him. "Trying to arrange things so Tom looks like the bad guy here. I know how this goes. If he doesn't agree, you'll take him to court. Force the issue and get custody of Henry at the same time. Because while Tom is out doing his *honest work*, where is his son?"

Again there is a ringing—and damning—silence.

"Tom hasn't given us any real indication that he's interested in caring for his son—" Andrew finally states, like it's an incontrovertible fact.

"That's not really true," Diana protests in a whisper.

"Isn't it?" Andrew retorts, glaring at me. "He disappears for hours at a time, is happy to let my wife handle the nights, barely knows how to give him a bottle..."

"I do know how," Tom says in a low voice. He's still staring at the floor, his jaw bunched, his shoulders tensed. "I've been trying."

"Not hard enough," Andrew states crisply. "Not for a judge."

"*Andrew*." Diana shakes her head, looking near tears. "We're going about this all wrong. I didn't... I didn't want things to become so acrimonious. I thought we could figure out a way to work things out, share the load..." She trails off unhappily and I wonder if she means any of it.

"How?" I ask her. "How would we *share the load*? Are you suggesting joint custody?"

"Maybe?" she whispers, her tone uncertain. Her gaze darts between Tom and me. "I don't know, we'd have to work it out..."

More vague nothings that hide the cold hard truth—she and her husband want to take Henry away from Tom.

For a second, I falter in my fury, as I consider why I am so angry. Tom *has* seemed ambivalent about taking care of Henry, but I'm pretty sure that's just his insecurity talking. But Andrew, as much as I hate to admit it, is right. He and Diana *are* in a much better place to take care of a baby than either Tom or me. Maybe what they're saying isn't that unreasonable, and what's making me so furious is my own painful history of being a mother who wasn't good enough, who was seen to fail, whom the social services agreed should not have custody of her own son, in accordance with his wishes.

This feels like a repeat of history, and this time I want to be on the right side of it, along with Tom. I'm not walking away from my grandchild, and I'm not letting Tom walk away from his son.

Even if it might be the best thing for him?

I ignore that treacherous little whisper as I stare down the Lawrences. Andrew gazes back with belligerent determination, while Diana looks away, reaching for the wine bottle to refill her glass with an unsteady hand.

"I think tempers are running a little high here," Andrew states in an authoritative, *I-know-best* manner. "Why don't we all have a drink and take a few minutes to calm down?"

"Diana's already had several," I retort before I can think better of it, and the temperature in the room chills several degrees as Andrew's eyes narrow and Diana pushes away her glass without taking a sip, looking shaken.

"I really think, Audrey," Andrew says, "we can keep this civil."

I take a deep breath, let it out. Taking potshots doesn't help anyone, least of all me. "Why," I ask Andrew, when I trust my voice to be level, "did you bring a judge into the conversation? *Are* you intending to sue for custody in court?"

The question lands with a thud and stays there, in the middle of the room, with no one answering or meeting anyone's gaze.

"Yeah," Tom says, finding his voice at last. "I'd like to know that, too. You've asked me what my plans are, but I'd like to know *yours*."

Another silence, this one stretching even tauter.

"Ideally," Andrew says at last, his tone resigned, "we'd like to come to an amenable arrangement that everyone is happy with. I have no desire to wind up in court."

"So you want to pressure Tom into giving up custody voluntarily," I state. On the plane to Haiti, having left Tom with his foster family, I'd felt like I'd done that too, even though it had been court-ordered. I should have tried harder. Fought harder, for my son.

"I'm not *pressuring anyone*," Andrew says testily. "I merely want to have a civilized discussion and come to a reasonable arrangement."

"Which is what I said with different words."

Andrew mutters under his breath and we stare at each other, neither of us willing to back down. Then Tom sets down his beer bottle with a clank, and we all turn.

"Screw it," he says. "Henry is my son. *Mine*." He glares at Andrew. "I know you can give him stuff I never can, but there are plenty of parents out there who still provide for their kid without having a BMW or a golf club membership. Henry doesn't *need* this. I don't, either."

While we all watch, mouths agape, Tom strides from the room.

"*Tom...*" Diana calls, her voice tremulous. She turns on her husband. "You shouldn't have been so harsh!" she cries. "You've scared him away!"

"I was *trying* to be reasonable," Andrew exclaims. "Diana, we both agreed that Tom wasn't pulling his weight..." He trails off, giving me an uncertain and angry glance, clearly not wanting to say anything more.

"This is *your* fault," Diana insists, and to my surprise I realize she's talking to me, her face now twisted with anger and even hatred as she points one shaking finger at my chest.

"Mine?" I practically gasp.

"Before you came," she spits, "Tom and I were getting along. I was helping him. He *liked* being here, he was learning..." Her voice breaks and she draws a shuddering breath. "And then you came, and started *whispering* things to him about us, and ever since he's been hostile and suspicious." She shakes her head, a violent back and forth. "Just because you failed him, doesn't mean we have to."

I jerk back, shocked by how much her accusation hurts. And then the realization slices through me—for Diana, at least, this battle is as much about Tom as it is Henry.

"He's my son," I tell her coldly, "not yours."

"Well, then maybe act like a mother for once!" she snaps before turning away, her hands up to her face.

I feel a flush of humiliation wash over my whole body as I struggle to think of a reply that isn't defensive, but I can't come up with one. And before anyone says anything more, Tom strides back into the kitchen. He has Henry in his arms, a diaper bag slung over one shoulder.

"Tom, *don't!*" Diana cries.

Tom jerks his head toward me. "Let's go."

As proud as I am of my son in this moment, I feel like I am tipping over into a future that feels incredibly tenuous. Can we really provide for a baby in my crappy little apartment? I don't have a car seat. I don't even have a *car*.

"Tom..." I begin, only to see Andrew give a smirking little smile, like he's read my thoughts and knows we've painted ourselves into a corner. I straighten, meeting his gaze with a cold look of my own, knowing I have to see this through. "Okay," I say. "Let's go."

Tom starts toward the door while Diana begins to cry, and Andrew blusters something about how they'll be talking to their lawyer. It feels surreal and somehow wrong, to just walk out of a house with a baby I barely know. I've spent very little time with Henry since I came back into my son's life; he has been, I realize now, more of a concept than an actual person, but I am certainly aware of him as a baby now as he begins to cry.

"Take the car seat," Diana insists through her tears. "For safety. It's in the car."

"I'll get it," Andrew says tersely, and it both humbles and shames me that they're thinking of Henry in this moment, so much so that they're willing to help us.

In silence, Andrew goes to the garage and gets the car seat out of the car. He comes back into the kitchen and hands it to me. I loop it over one arm while Henry continues to wail piteously, and Tom starts to look stressed.

"Please don't cut us out of his life," Andrew says quietly. "Whatever words have passed between us tonight."

I nod jerkily, because I don't want to be cruel, but as we walk out of the Lawrences' house with their only grandson, I feel as if I've committed a crime.

NINETEEN
AUDREY

Tom and I don't speak as we walk down the driveway in darkness while Henry wails. Everything about this feels wrong, but I don't want to think like that, much less voice it to my son.

"Should I call an Uber?" I ask, and wince at the shakiness of my voice. Henry's warbling cries pierce the still spring night.

"Did I do the right thing, Mom?" Tom asks, desperation in his voice as he turns to me, and for a second I am speechless because I can't remember the last time he called me *Mom*. It's enough to bring tears to my eyes, even—and especially—in this difficult situation.

"Yes, you did," I tell him, injecting a certainty to my tone that I don't yet feel, but I *will*. I'll make sure of it, for the sake of my son. "Henry is *your* son, Tom. He belongs with you."

"Yes, but..." Already Tom is looking like he might be regretting taking his big stand, and I am reminded of how young he is, how vulnerable, even if he tries to seem strong. "Diana was really nice to me," he mumbles as he ducks his head. "And even Andrew wasn't so bad. I think he's just the kind of guy who's used to being in charge, and I can understand that."

That's an understatement, I think but don't say.

"We're not cutting the Lawrences out of Henry's life entirely," I tell Tom firmly. "We're just showing them that they can't bully you. Now, let me call an Uber, we'll head back and get Henry settled, and then we can talk." I nod toward the diaper bag slung over his shoulder. "Do you have bottles and formula and diapers in that?"

"Some," Tom says, ducking his head. "Enough for one night."

"Okay." I let out a breath, trying to steady my nerves, even though Henry is still screaming.

A woman in a designer tracksuit, walking a bichon frise, gives us a dark look as she passes us on the other side of the street. I can't really blame her, as I know we must look an odd and uncomfortable sight, standing on this moneyed street corner with a crying baby and no vehicle as it's getting dark.

I focus on my phone, determined to bring some order to this chaotic moment. *We weren't crazy,* I tell myself, *to do what we did.* Even if right now it feels a little crazy. I take another breath, and then order the Uber, a sense of calm coming to me as I complete this simple act.

I've comforted mothers whose children have been buried alive; I've rebuilt homes and dug wells and provided emergency medical care, all with a cheerful, calm competency, my superpower. I can handle this moment, even if it's only as a mother that I've doubted myself.

I won't now.

"The Uber's coming in four minutes," I tell Tom, and he nods jerkily as he transfers Henry to his other arm, patting him awkwardly on the back as he continues to cry. "He was asleep when I went upstairs," he tells me. "I had to wake him up, and I don't think he liked it."

"What did the babysitter say when you did?" I ask, more out of curiosity than anything else.

Tom shrugs as he jiggles Henry against his shoulders. "She looked kind of scared, to be honest," he admits. "I was kind of... quick." He sighs unhappily as he glances down at his screaming son. "Maybe I shouldn't have done this."

"He's *your* son," I remind him for what feels like the umpteenth time. I'm starting to sound like a broken record, like it's the only line I can trot out, but it's *true*.

We don't talk for the next three minutes, which feel like the longest of my life. I'm half-expecting Andrew to come storming down the driveway, waving his phone and saying he's called his lawyer, or for a police car to come around the corner, siren wailing, lights flashing, to arrest us as potential kidnappers. *Something* to stop us, but no one does.

Then a black sedan comes around the corner and glides to a stop in front of us. Our Uber has arrived.

The next uncomfortable half-hour is a blur. We wrestle Henry into his car seat, and then the car seat into the Uber, and then spend a tense twenty minutes driving north to Stamford, while Henry screams all the way, and the Uber driver looks more and more unhappy that he agreed to pick us up.

By the time we get to my apartment, my nerves are frayed and what I want most is some peace and quiet and a stiff drink, neither of which is available. We make it up to my apartment, both of us heaving a sigh of relief as we get Henry inside. I am conscious that this building is not the kind that generally houses children. Thin walls and small spaces are not conducive to crying babies.

Fortunately, by the time we're inside, Henry's sobs have subsided to mere sniffles. He's exhausted himself, and his eyes flutter closed as Tom slumps onto the sofa.

"Good Lord." He lets out a shaky breath as he tries for a smile. "I'm exhausted."

"Yeah." I glance down at Henry, his tiny face softened in sleep. "Babies are hard work."

"Yeah." Tom is silent for a moment, his gaze distant. "Diana has been doing a lot of it," he admits in a low voice. "I mean, I *tried*, you know, and I changed him and gave him bottles and stuff... but the last few weeks, he's been really fussy and, I don't know, I just let her take over." He pauses, glancing up at me with the uncertainty of a small boy. "Maybe I shouldn't have?"

"It's understandable," I say as I sink onto a chair at the tiny table for two. I glance down at Henry again, grateful he's asleep. But for how long? I look around my tiny studio apartment, wondering how we will all fit in here. There's a portacrib in the closet, a double bed, and a sofa, so theoretically, we *can* fit... but it will be a squeeze, and it's certainly not sustainable. Besides which, neither Tom nor I am gainfully employed at the moment, and I'm not sure what our prospects are, if Tom has no reference and I...

Well, I don't like to think about what my future at Crisis Action might be. Meanwhile, I have enough money in the bank to see out the month, and that's all.

"Did you mean what you said?" Tom asks hesitantly. "About staying? Not going back to work, wherever it is you go?"

Wherever it is you go. I picture Tom as a little boy, being asked where his mommy is, and stumbling over the answer. *It begins with N. I think it's in Africa.* Once, that image would have given me a rush of pride, that my son knew the important work I was doing. But now it only makes me feel sad.

"I can't go back," I tell him on a gusty sigh. "I've been... suspended."

Tom stares at me for a moment, his mouth hanging open. "What?"

"A junior staff member filed a formal complaint. Apparently I was..." I make claw-like quotation marks with my fingers. "Emotionally abusive and uncomfortably intense."

"*What?*" Once more, Tom goggles. "How? I mean, why?"

I shrug, as if it doesn't matter, when the truth is it still both hurts and shames me, deeply. Thirty years I worked for Crisis Action, only to be scolded like a schoolgirl, after being tattled on *by* a schoolgirl, or at least a twenty-two-year-old intern. That's who I assume complained about me. They refused to tell me, but it wasn't that hard to figure out. Aimee Lowther made no secret of the fact that she thought I made her work too hard, was too harsh when telling her to get in gear, and didn't have a lot of time for her daily mental health crises.

I am aware, of course, that I could and should have been more sympathetic to a young, vulnerable woman. We were working in a difficult and devastated area, and before her internship Aimee had never been out of the United States. I could remember, distantly, feeling as overwhelmed as she must have, when I first started. But I don't think I whined about it as much as she did.

"I was seen as being too... demanding," I tell my son. "And harsh. And one of the younger employees complained."

"And you got suspended, just like that? After so many years working for them?" Tom sounds indignant on my behalf, which makes me smile, because it's both so unexpected and welcome.

"Basically," I tell him. "And I understand it, sort of. I'm the old guard. I'm used to just getting on with it, no complaints, and the newer employees need a gentler touch." I lean my head back against the sofa and close my eyes. "Times are changing, and I wasn't changing with them."

"Tell me about some of the places you went to," Tom says after a moment, and I open my eyes to stare at him in surprise. Not once, in all the years I've worked for Crisis Action, has my son asked me to tell him about the places I've been, the things I've done. I've offered the information sometimes, especially when he was small—playfully, hopefully, wanting him to take an interest and also to understand. Sometimes I fear it just pushed him further away.

"I was last in Chile," I begin hesitantly. "In the tent cities by the lithium mines, in the Atacama Desert. It's a pretty brutal place, one of the driest on earth, and the migrants who work in the mines aren't treated very well. I was helping to organize food and medical care to the most vulnerable there. Not a disaster zone, *per se*, but a place of incredible deprivation."

Tom is silent for a long moment, and I have no idea what he thinks about what I said, and really, who I *am*.

"I never really thought about what you were doing, when you went away," he finally remarks reflectively. "As a kid, I mean. I just focused on the fact that you weren't with me." He pauses. "That you chose not to be with me."

"Tom—"

"I know it wasn't exactly like that," he cuts across me quickly. "I know it was a lot more complicated. I'm just saying that's how it felt, sometimes."

"I understand that," I say quietly, and I do.

He sighs. "I'm sorry I was angry with you for so long. And when I was with the Taylors..." He trails off. "That wasn't even anger. I just wanted to be with a family that *felt* like a family."

"I understand that, too." The Taylors, the family that fostered him, ticked all the boxes. Dog. Picket fence. Station wagon. Family meals. Basketball in the driveway, baseball in the backyard. To Tom, who was used to living alone with his father in a two-bedroom apartment, it would have seemed like a fairy tale.

"Too bad they didn't treat me like family," Tom says, with a laugh that isn't really a laugh.

I frown. "What do you mean?"

His lips thin into a hard line as he explains, "Halfway through senior year they said I couldn't live with them anymore. I hadn't *done* anything. I'd toed every line I could think of, made sure to be helpful. I was getting good grades, applying to college. The guidance counselor thought I could get some decent financial aid, considering my situation. But then the mom got breast cancer, and suddenly I was too much. I had to go."

He sighs, his eyes closing. "I mean, I sort of understood it, but I also didn't. They derailed my life, just like *casually*. There were no other placements and so I had to go into one of those group homes, and those places are messed up." He gives a little shake of his head. "And I had to change high schools. My social worker tried to make a case for me to stay, but it was too far, and I couldn't get a ride, so..." He shrugs, dismissive of a decision that clearly cost him so much.

"Oh, Tom..." I am aghast. I thought he'd left the Taylors of his own volition; it was a time when he wasn't talking to me, and so I'd made assumptions. Wrong ones. "I wish..." I swallow hard. "I wish I'd known that. I would have come back."

Tom opens his eyes. "Would you have? Really?"

"*Yes*." I lean forward. "Yes, I would have," I say firmly. I am speaking the truth. "Just like I came back for your trial. I know it doesn't make any difference now, and maybe it makes it worse, to hear it like this, but I *would* have, Tom, I promise."

He stares at me for a long moment, and in the stark lines of his face, I see a hint of the little boy who never stood at the window to watch me go. Who chose not to—not because he didn't care, I am realizing now, but maybe because he cared too much.

"I believe you," he says at last. "But I guess none of that matters now, because..." He gestures to the space between us, the *baby* between us. "Here we are."

"Here we are," I agree heavily. Henry is still asleep, but he's going to wake up soon and we need to decide a way forward. How to make this work, and what we want to do about the Lawrences. "We don't need to decide anything tonight," I tell Tom as well as myself. "We can sleep on it and have a fresh perspective in the morning."

Tom nods slowly. "I want to go back to the Lawrences'," he says. "Just to talk. I don't want to cut them out completely."

"Okay." I have a feeling that if we give them an inch they'll take a hundred miles and then some, but I know Tom is right. They have as much of a bond with this baby as I do, maybe even more because their daughter is dead, whereas I am sitting here with my son, the past no longer a pulsing wound for both of us. For that, I am so grateful, and I know it wouldn't have happened without everything else that did. Right now, I can't regret any of my actions tonight, because it led to Tom and I finally reconciling.

But... we still need to decide what to do about this baby.

As if on cue, Henry stirs, his eyes fluttering open before he blinks sleepily. He looks angelic for about one second before his eyes widen, his face screws up, and he lets out a bleating cry.

Tom gives me a startled, questioning glance, clearly looking to me for guidance. Maybe Diana Lawrence did do most of it, I reflect as I haul myself up from the sofa.

"Why don't you get a bottle," I instruct my son, "and I'll change his diaper."

I unbuckle Henry from the car seat, lifting him out carefully, absorbing the warm weight of him that stirs something deep inside. As Tom gets out a bottle and a can of readymade formula, I sling the diaper bag over my shoulder and take Henry to the double bed and lay him down.

"Well, hello there, buddy," I murmur, tickling his tummy. He stops crying for a few seconds simply to stare at me, and my heart starts to melt. I unbutton the snaps on his sleepsuit and lift his little legs out. "Don't worry, food is coming," I tell him as I unsnap his onesie and roll it up over his tummy. His onesie and sleepsuit are both damp with sweat, and I decide to change both, carefully taking his little arms out of the sleeves and easing the onesie over his head.

"The bottle's just about ready," Tom says.

"Great. He's almost changed." I reach for a fresh onesie and sleepsuit and then turn back to my grandson. Then I suck in a hard breath as I stare down at his tiny body in horror.

"Oh Tom," I whisper.

What have you done?

TWENTY

DIANA

The aftermath of their leaving is like the devastation after a hurricane or a tornado; the landscape that was once so familiar to me now feels like a foreign place. It's eerily quiet, with the stillness that comes from total shock, and neither Andrew nor I speak.

They've gone. They've actually gone.

The words reverberate through me, the stark fact of Tom and Henry's absence slamming into me again and again, leaving me breathless and reeling. I turn to Andrew, open my mouth to say something but nothing comes out.

"They'll come back," I finally say, my voice faint and hoarse. "They will. They have to..."

Andrew simply stands there, shaking his head back and forth. His shoulders are slumped, his face gray with shock and pain. My heart aches for him, and yet within that rush of sympathy is a hot flare of anger that he pushed for this. Just like with Sophie, he drove them away. And once again, just like with Sophie, we might never get them back, no matter what I just said.

"I didn't..." Andrew begins, still shaking his head. "I didn't mean..." He stops and then walks over to the sofa, collapsing into it, his head falling into his hands. It isn't until I see his shoulders shake that I realize he is crying, silently, like he's been broken in half.

With another rush of sympathy, I walk over and sit next to him, putting my arm around him. He leans into me, his head on my shoulder, accepting my comfort in a way I'm not sure he ever has before.

"I'm sorry..." he mumbles through his tears. "I'm sorry, I'm sorry..."

"Oh, Andrew." I close my eyes. "I'm sorry, too. This is just as much my fault as it is yours."

If I'd been stronger...

Always, if only I'd been stronger. Back when Sophie was a baby, and when we met Tom, and even now. If I'd stood up to Andrew, if I'd insisted we reach out, if I hadn't been so weak and frightened...

"This isn't your fault, Diana," Andrew says as he straightens, wiping his eyes. "It's mine. I've been too stubborn all along." He shakes his head. "I should have tried to get to know Tom. I should have realized his story might be more complicated than we thought." A sigh escapes him, long and low and weary. "All we can do now is try to fix the future. I'll call him and apologize..." He sighs again. "He might just think I'm giving him lip service, but what else can I do? I want Henry back in our lives."

"I know. I do, too." And, I acknowledge, I want Tom back in our lives. Andrew might not have the same kind of bond I did with him, but I refuse to see working with Tom as no more than a means to an end. He needs our support, and I had felt, amazingly, like I had some to offer. I want to be able to give it, for us to all work together as I'd said, so haltingly, when we'd been having that awful confrontation.

Which makes me think of Audrey, and all my good will

about working together vanishes in an instant. I feel deep in my gut, in my bones, that Audrey is poisoning her son against us. If she hadn't come and stirred everything up, hurling accusations, making it all ugly, Tom would still be here... and so would Henry.

But I know there's no point thinking like that now, and so I swallow my bitterness and hug my husband again, and tell him things will look better in the morning. Andrew nods wearily in a way that suggests he doesn't believe me, but it's eight o'clock at night and there's nothing we can do now.

"I'll call the lawyer tomorrow," he says. "To discuss access arrangements."

It doesn't escape me that instead of asking our lawyer how we can get full custody as we once were planning, we're now going to have to plead to find a way to see our grandson at all. And it's our fault that it's come to this. It's mine.

"I'm going to check on some work stuff," Andrew says, and he trudges out of the kitchen, a defeated man finding solace in the one area of life he knows how to handle. I drift around the kitchen, taking out the casserole that has been simmering in the oven, putting the salad back in the fridge. So much food, but I'm not at all hungry now.

I glance at my glass of wine, and then the bottle still chilling in a bucket of melted ice, and then I pour both down the sink. I think of Audrey's snide comment, *Diana's already had several*, and my cheeks burn with shame. I've thrown out all my Xanax, I've been so *good*, but two glasses of wine and I feel like a sloppy drunk. I'm resentful that Audrey has made me feel that way and also annoyed with myself that I let her. That I didn't defend myself, *and* that I had that second glass of wine. Or, if I'm honest, even the first one.

I finish cleaning up the kitchen, wiping the already-clean counters just to have something to do. The house feels unnaturally quiet and empty, and I didn't appreciate quite how much looking after Henry defined both my days and nights, gave me a structure that scared and stabilized me in turns.

I miss him now. I miss his solid warmth, the way he snuggled into my neck, the sweet, sleepy smell of him. I even miss the way his snuffles turned into sobs, how his whole body would go rigid when he was really upset, and how I—*I*—could comfort him, in a way I never could with my own daughter.

A sound escapes me, something between a sigh and a sob, and I shake my head. Tom will come back tomorrow. We have a bond, whether Audrey realizes that or not, and it counts for something.

At least I'm praying that it does.

I head upstairs, resisting the urge to take something to help me sleep, and get ready for bed. I lie beneath the duvet, gritty-eyed and aching, unable to sleep, until Andrew comes up, well after midnight. He undresses quietly, folding his pants, resting his belt on top as he always does.

When he slides into bed, I am surprised by how he scoots over to me, tentatively, like a question, one hand resting on my arm. I roll over to face him and we wrap our arms around each other, holding each other silently, the only comfort we can find —and give.

The next morning, I wake early; I'm used to getting up with Henry and the morning feels empty and long as I make coffee and potter around the kitchen, feeling like I have nothing to do. I called Tom twice earlier this morning, but it switched off without even going to voicemail both times. I text him, feeling as futile as I did when I texted Sophie all those times before.

Hi Tom, please, let's talk.

I left it at that, hoping he'd respond, but by mid-morning there's still no reply.

Andrew has decided to work from home, and after breakfast he closets himself in his study to talk to the family lawyer about this wrinkle in our situation. I'm already afraid of what she might say.

Since Tom is his biological father and legal guardian, there's not much you can do. Grandparents don't actually have any right under law to see their grandchild.

A quick search on the internet told me as much, that grandparents have no legal rights in this kind of situation. I know Andrew said our case was different, with Tom's criminal history and the fact that Sophie is dead, but now I wonder if that is so much bluster. Already I can imagine how we might be portrayed in court, if it came to that—privileged, snobbish, grasping, coercive.

Which is how Audrey made me feel.

Andrew is still in his study, on the phone to the lawyer, when the doorbell rings, and my heart gives a lurch of hope as I practically run to answer it. I don't know why I'm thinking it will be Tom, when he has a key, but I *am*, so the sight of an unsmiling woman in a cheap pantsuit with a lanyard around her neck has me stilling.

"May I help..." I ask falteringly.

"Hello, I am Naomi Bryson from the Connecticut Department of Children and Families." She holds out her lanyard for me to inspect, but the words and photo on it swim blurrily before my startled gaze. "I'm here to discuss a report that's been made about Henry West."

I stare at her blankly. "A report?"

"May I come in?"

Instinctively, I do not want to let this woman into my home, but I know I have to. At least, I have to if I want to know what on earth she's talking about. Has something happened to Henry?

"Yes, of course," I murmur, and step aside.

"Is there somewhere we could sit down and chat?" the woman, this Naomi, asks. Her tone is kind but with an efficiency to it I don't like.

"Yes, come through to the kitchen."

I glance at the closed door of Andrew's study, wondering if I should get him, but I can hear his low voice on the phone and I decide it can wait. First, I'll find out what this woman wants—and what she knows.

"You said a report," I begin once we are both seated at the kitchen table. I keep my voice only mildly curious, like this isn't a matter of grave importance.

"Yes." The woman folds her hands on the table and gives me a stern yet sorrowful look that makes me tense. "A report was made yesterday that Henry West was seen to have bruises on his arms and torso."

For a second, I can only stare, the words not computing. "Bruises..." My voice is a whisper. "What do you mean? Who made the report?"

"I'm afraid I can't disclose that information," the social worker replies evenly, "but, as you might be aware, reporting of any physical or sexual abuse of a minor is mandated under Connecticut law."

I stare at her, feeling sick. Henry has *bruises*? How come I never saw them, when I changed his diaper, usually several times a day? Is this some sick ploy of Audrey's, I wonder with a surge of fearful fury, to gain custody? Is she trying to discredit us, casting aspersions of *abuse*?

"I never saw any bruises on my grandson," I tell Naomi Bryson with stiff dignity. "I'm not sure if you're aware, but last night my husband and I had an argument with our son-in-law and his mother regarding Henry's care. If one of them made this allegation, then I have a strong suspicion it could be spurious."

The effect of this prissily sanctimonious speech, which I was, for a brief moment, proud of, is to flatten Naomi's expression as she answers carefully, "No one is making any allegations, Mrs.... Lawrence, is it?"

"Yes."

"At this point, DCF is simply trying to establish the facts. Could I talk to you and your husband, as well as Henry's father? I believe Henry has been living with the three of you?"

"Yes." I swallow dryly. "But last night Tom—Henry's father —left with him, and I don't know where either of them is."

"Left?" Her eyebrows lift and her mouth purses. "After this... argument?"

I lift my chin an inch, not quite defiant, but almost. I will not let this woman make me feel like I've done something wrong. Not this time. "Yes."

"And could you tell me what this argument was about?"

"As I said before, it was about Henry's care." I want to go get Andrew, but I feel like it will make me look guiltier, as well as weak. What if there is a file on me that they can access, back from when Sophie was small? The thought is both humiliating and terrifying. "In particular with regard to a trust fund in my daughter's name, that passed to Henry upon her death," I explain, before adding with a sniffy sort of pointedness I can't keep myself from, "I don't know how much you know about our situation, but my daughter died the day after Henry was born, of septic shock." Saying it out loud still causes a flash of pain to blaze through me, and I have to look away for a moment.

"I'm very sorry to hear that." Naomi's voice is grave, but I still don't trust it, or her. "And Tom and Henry came to live with you at that point?"

I swallow, the sound unfortunately audible. "Yes."

"Do you have any way to be in touch with Tom?" she asks,

cocking her head, her calm, assessing sweeping coolly over me. "A phone number, perhaps? It would be helpful if we could speak with him, as well as see Henry."

"To check if he has bruises?" My voice comes out sharper than I meant it to, and I wish I could bite the words back. "I changed him last night," I explain in a more moderate tone, "and I didn't see any."

"That very well may be," Naomi replies, "but, as I'm sure you're aware, we have to take every mandated report we receive seriously, otherwise we wouldn't be doing our job." She smiles, slightly, as she gentles her tone. "But I understand that this might be both distressing and alarming for you, especially when you're still dealing with your own grief. Please believe me when I say we're here to help, not to make a situation more difficult."

It doesn't feel like that, I think but manage not to say.

"Why don't I get my husband?" I suggest. "He's working from home today, and I think he should be part of this conversation."

Naomi waves a hand in acceptance. "By all means," she says.

I rise stiffly from the table and walk to Andrew's study. I tap on the door and then open it; Andrew swivels in his chair to face me, the phone clamped to his ear. He points to the phone, and I shake my head.

"Andrew," I say in a whisper that I hope the lawyer on the call can't hear. "Someone from the Department of Children and Families is here. To talk about Henry."

Andrew stares at me in wordless shock before he quickly ends the call. "Social services?" he demands as he slips his phone into his pocket. "Has something happened?"

"Someone," I say, my voice numb with the shock that is still reverberating through me ever since Naomi Bryson told me why she was here, "has anonymously reported that they saw bruises on Henry."

Andrew's jaw drops. "*Bruises?*"

"Audrey must have reported it," I whisper. "To discredit us."

He frowns as he starts to shake his head. "You really think she would stoop that low?"

I shrug, unsure. Maybe I'm being too suspicious, but who else could it possibly be? "I changed him yesterday," I tell Andrew. "And I didn't see anything."

Andrew is silent for a moment, his gaze distant as he absorbs this news. "And this person is here now? Wanting to talk to us?"

"Yes, in the kitchen."

He nods slowly, firming his jaw. "All right, then."

In the kitchen, Andrew reverts to his charming businessman mode.

"Andrew Lawrence," he tells Naomi in a honeyed voice, stretching out one hand for her to shake. "I understand you're here in relation to our grandson?"

"Yes, Henry West." Naomi shakes his hand briefly before repeating what she's already told me, about the mandated report of bruises on Henry's arms and torso.

"And this report was made last night?" Andrew asks.

Naomi gives a short, brisk nod. "Yes."

Andrew shoots me a swift, significant glance, but I can't interpret it. If the report was made last night, surely it had to have been Audrey, after she and Tom left here?

"What I'd really like," Naomi says, "is to get in touch with Tom and have a chance to see Henry. Do you think that would be possible?"

She makes it sound as if we're hiding them in a cupboard upstairs.

"We'd certainly like that, too," Andrew replies. "But my son-in-law stormed out of here last night, after an argument regarding my daughter's trust fund." He sounds, I fear, a little pompous, and I don't think that will do us any favors.

"Yes," Naomi replies in a carefully expressionless voice. "Your wife told me as much."

A shiver of unease ripples down my spine. She doesn't sound as if she's on our side, and Andrew's attitude definitely isn't helping. And, I realize, I probably shouldn't have accused Audrey. Maybe she wasn't even the one who made the report.

Although if she didn't, then who did—and why? Henry didn't have bruises on his arms and torso the last time I checked. I picture myself changing his diaper yesterday afternoon, before I started dinner. I didn't actually take his arms out, I recall uncomfortably, or lift his onesie high enough to see his tummy. So, realistically, I might not have seen bruises... if there were any.

But there couldn't be bruises on our grandson, I tell myself. Who would have made them? *Tom?*

The prospect shivers through me. Should I have been keeping a closer eye on my son-in-law? At the beginning, I was worried *I* wouldn't feel safe with him, but why didn't I think more about Henry, and making sure *he* was safe?

"Do you think you could call Tom?" Naomi asks us. "And have him bring Henry back here? Then we could all have a chat together."

I glance at Andrew before saying uncertainly, "I called him this morning, but there was no reply. I can try again."

They both wait in silence as I do just that, letting the phone ring, loud enough for everyone to hear. Then, to my surprise, it's answered.

"Diana?" It's Audrey rather than Tom, her voice terse, almost angry.

"Audrey—"

"We're coming over," she says, and then disconnects the call.

Despite this assurance, I feel uneasier than ever. I turn to Naomi. "They're coming over now," I say, although I'm pretty sure she heard.

"Great." She smiles, thinly, and my unease deepens.

Because it has occurred to me, far too late, that if Henry has bruises, then Audrey and Tom will have seen them after they left here. And if Audrey sounded angry, insisting they're coming right over, I doubt she thinks Tom made them.

Which means she thinks I did.

TWENTY-ONE
AUDREY

When I first saw the bruises mottling my grandson's arms and tummy, my heart plummeted right to my toes, and I felt sick. He was so *tiny*, and it would take some force—some frustration—to make bruises that livid on such a little baby.

I glanced at Tom and saw him staring at his son's bruised body not just with horror, but with what I knew was guilt, and I felt even sicker.

"Tom..." I whispered, and then stopped because I didn't want to put my suspicions into words. I didn't want him to, either.

"I swear..." he began, and then he stopped, too. We both stared in silence at the purple marks on Henry's body and then he screwed up his face and started to cry, so I finished changing him without saying anything more.

We didn't speak about it as I gave Henry his bottle, and Tom got out the portacrib from the closet and set it up in front of the TV—the only space where it could fit. We had no sheets for it, so we spread a T-shirt of mine across the thin mattress, tucking in the corners as best as we could. All of it made me realize how unprepared we were to take care of a baby for more than a few hours. I'd checked the diaper bag and we'd be out of both formula and diapers by lunchtime tomorrow. We could buy more, of course, but everything about this situation felt temporary and unsustainable.

What we needed, I was realizing more and more, was to go back to the Lawrences and figure out a way forward that worked for all of us.

"Let's get some sleep," I told Tom once Henry was settled. I made up the sofa for him, my heart and body both aching with the knowledge of the bruises we still hadn't talked about. What would this mean? Had the Lawrences seen them? If so, why hadn't they mentioned them?

And if they *hadn't* seen them, was it a secret I really wanted to keep? I had a responsibility to Tom, but I also had one to Henry.

With my mind swirling with unhappy thoughts, I barely slept, but I wouldn't have slept anyway because Henry woke up nearly every hour, crying and fussing. Tom and I took turns walking the room with him, both of us blank-eyed with exhaustion. At one point, after Henry had been screaming nonstop and the neighbors were banging on the wall to get us to be quiet, I thrust him at Tom with more force than I meant to, and Tom caught him, his eyes wide as he drew his son protectively toward his chest.

In that moment, I realized just how easily mistakes can happen, even big, bruising ones, and it shook me to the core.

By early morning, Henry is finally sleeping deeply, and Tom and I are both like zombies. I make coffee in the tiny kitchenette, and we drink it silently while Henry sleeps.

"I don't think I did that," Tom says after several minutes of silence, his voice low.

I stare at him, my mug halfway to my mouth. I know, of course, what he is talking about. "Then who did?" I ask quietly. "Diana? Or Andrew?" My mind is already racing through the possibilities. I realize I've been convinced of my son's guilt, simply by the wretched look on his face when he saw Henry. But what if he *hadn't* caused those bruises?

What if the Lawrences had?

"Diana?" Tom sounds doubtful. "Or Andrew? I don't know..." He sets down his coffee cup and scrubs his hands over his face. "I don't know," he admits on a moan. "Henry's been so fussy these last few weeks... Diana took care of him more than I did, but there were some nights... I was frustrated..."

He trails off, and I think of last night, when I felt overwhelmed with that exhausted frustration myself. But bruises? Bruises all over his body? Surely that takes more *effort*, deliberate or otherwise, which is terrible to consider.

I glance at Henry, asleep in his crib, one hand flung toward his face, his lips slightly pursed, and my heart aches with both love and fear. Who could hurt such a tiny, defenseless baby?

Was it my son? Could it have been me, under similar circumstances?

"I suppose," I tell Tom, "we need to talk to the Lawrences. They might be aware of the bruises, and if they're not—"

"They'll just use it as a reason to get custody," Tom finishes dully.

"They can't prove anything, Tom," I say swiftly. "No one can prove who caused those bruises, and considering Diana was the one who was taking care of him the most..." I let that idea trail away as Tom lifts his head to stare at me, eyes wide.

"I don't want to blame Diana," he says. "She's been nice to me. And she's had it hard, with Sophie..." He shakes his head, his expression firming. "No."

"It was someone," I tell him. "And if you don't think it was you..."

Tom lets out a groan as he covers his hands with his face. "I don't *know*," he admits on another moan. "I don't know, I just don't know..."

I fall silent. Tom's uncertainty is not a point in our favor, but I also know we can't continue like this. Not for our sakes, and certainly not for Henry's.

I just hope the Lawrences will be reasonable.

As if on cue, Tom's phone buzzes. He snatches it up before the sound can wake Henry, and then wordlessly he shows me the screen. It's Diana, calling yet again. This time, though, I think we need to answer.

I take the phone from Tom and slide to answer. "Diana?" My voice is terser than I meant for it to be.

"Audrey—"

"We're coming over," I tell her, and then I disconnect the call, because I'm too tired and emotional to get into some kind of argument over the phone. I hand Tom back his phone as he stares at me with wide, fear-filled eyes.

"Are we going to tell them...?"

"I think we have to," I say quietly. "But, Tom, remember, you don't know that it was you." I pause. "Surely you'd remember if you'd... *manhandled*... him like that?" I try to speak delicately, but Tom still flinches.

"I don't know," he admits again. "He's so small... maybe I don't know my own strength."

"I think you'd remember," I tell him. And so would Diana, if she'd gripped him hard enough to cause such marks. And so would Andrew, for that matter. No one, I remind myself, can prove anything.

Then Henry stirs in his crib and starts to cry.

Half an hour later, with both of us showered and Henry fed and mostly settled, we are in an Uber on our way back to Old Greenwich.

Neither of us speaks for the whole journey, tension banding my temples and clenching my gut. No matter what the crisis at work, I always have an action plan with careful, well-thought-out steps to achieve a stated goal. It's part of Crisis Action's whole mission to offer practical help in the worst of scenarios. And here I am, in the worst scenario of my own personal life, and I cannot think what to do.

It's humbling as well as frightening, and I feel woefully unprepared and vulnerable as the Uber pulls up into the Lawrences' driveway. I have no idea how to handle our upcoming interaction, and I know Tom is looking to me for leadership, the kind of leadership I normally thrive on providing. Why can't I manage it now? Instead, my mind is empty, my heart thudding.

I reach for the handle of the car seat as I murmur my thanks to the driver. The only thing I can think to do is keep going forward. Last night, I was full of self-righteous fury and indignant accusation; this morning, I decide, I'll be more measured, less defensive. I won't accuse anyone of anything. I'll look for solutions, a way we can bridge the chasm between our families.

Those resolutions last another ten seconds, until we reach the front door and Diana flings it open, looking harried.

"Where have you been?" she demands, and before I can reply, she steps forward and hisses, "A social worker is here. About Henry having *bruises*."

Something about her wild-eyed expression feels wrong, and it takes me a second to realize what it is. Diana looks *afraid*. She couldn't have called in the social worker, I think, and I'm guessing neither did Andrew. They've been as blindsided by these bruises as we have... which means they don't know who caused them, and they are second-guessing themselves just as Tom is. So who has called social services, I wonder. Does it even matter at this point?

The realization that we're all in the dark should bring some kind of relief, but instead I feel only sadness. Henry is eight weeks old. He deserves so much better than this motley group of adults who, in their grief and insecurity, struggle to manage his care, and may well have hurt him in the process.

"We know about the bruises," I tell Diana. "We saw them last night."

Her gaze narrows, and I know she is considering the implication of what I just said. That we didn't cause them. And as much as I don't want to throw accusations around, it's hard not to, because *someone* caused those bruises, and I am praying it wasn't my son.

"Come through to the kitchen," Diana says stiffly, and we follow her to that soaring space with so much marble and chrome—and a social worker sitting at the table who looks like every other social worker I've ever seen. The thought is unfair, I know, but I can't keep from thinking it because I recognize that calm yet supercilious expression—although maybe I'm projecting, because these people hold so much power and whenever I'm in front of them I feel my own failures so keenly.

I think of the interactions with Tom's caseworker, when he was staying with the Taylors. I don't think I was imagining the look of judgment in that woman's eyes when she told me my son preferred to live with strangers than his own mother, and, considering my circumstances, the court would uphold that decision, even if he was only fourteen years old.

Now, I put down Henry's car seat as I greet this woman who introduces herself as Naomi Bryson with a coolness I can't keep from my tone, even though I know I should. I need to appear friendly, but I'm too afraid.

Naomi Bryson launches into her explanation of how there has been a mandated report of bruising on Henry West, and she needs to investigate it. She looks between Tom and me. "I believe you've had the sole care of Henry since last night. Did you notice any bruising since you've been with him?"

"Yes, I observed it last night when I was changing him," I say woodenly. "On his arms and torso."

Naomi cocks her head. "And you didn't think to report it?"

Diana makes some little sound, and I turn to look at her, see how pale she is, her lips pressed firmly together.

"It was late," I tell Naomi, "and we wanted to talk to the Lawrences, which is why we came here," I reply, and I hear the self-defensiveness creeping into my tone and try to moderate it. "We didn't even know you were here."

I glance at Tom, willing him to say something, but he's cracking his knuckles as he stares at the floor. Despair floods through me, the acidic tang of bile on my tongue. They're going to think he caused the bruising. Of course they are.

"I'm glad you came," Naomi replies, and I am surprised to hear a hint of warmth in her voice. Maybe I'm misjudging her. Maybe she *isn't* judging us as much as I thought she was. "Why don't I have a quick look at Henry," Naomi suggests, "and then we can have a chat?"

I give a shrugging kind of nod, because what else can I do? In any case, it's not up to me. It's up to Tom, Henry's father, although maybe it's not up to him, either. Maybe this is going to happen no matter what any of us want.

"Yeah, okay," he mumbles, still looking at the floor.

Naomi eases Henry out of his car seat while we all watch, every single person holding their breath. I don't realize that I'm hoping I somehow imagined the bruises, or maybe they disappeared, until Naomi rolls up Henry's onesie and there they are, for all to see. Diana lets out a startled gasp and Andrew visibly deflates, his face ashen, while Tom and I remain stony-faced, seemingly unmoved, because we've seen them before.

The bruises have faded a little, paler at the edges, but even so, they still look starkly livid against Henry's pale, tender skin. I glance at Naomi, and see her face is suffused with sadness, and I imagine she has seen this type of situation far too many times before, and it never gets easier. I feel sorry for her, dealing with this day in day out, and then I feel sorry for us, because so are we.

But most of all, I feel sorry for Henry, who doesn't deserve any of this.

Slowly, Naomi rolls his onesie back down and rebuttons it. He is still dozing, and she carefully places him back in his car seat before she turns to look at all of us.

"So, obviously bruises like that are very concerning," she states in a careful tone. "And if it's okay, I'd like to ask you some questions about Henry's care." She glances around at all of us. "Should we all sit down? Is there somewhere more comfortable we could sit?"

"Over here, on the sofas..." Diana's voice is faint as she leads us to an adjoining sunroom with several sofas and armchairs, and a picture window overlooking a backyard resplendent with flowers, the sparkle of the Sound visible on the rolling horizon.

Naomi waits until we're all settled before she takes a notebook out of her bag. "I'm just going to take a few notes, if that's okay," she says, before glancing around at all of us. "I understand Henry's birth was traumatic," she states. "With his mother Sophie having an emergency caesarean and then going into septic shock...?"

Wordlessly, Diana nods.

Naomi glances at Tom in inquiry, and I resist the urge to give him a nudge, like he's a little boy who needs to remember his manners.

"Yeah," he says after a moment, his gaze on the floor. "Henry was in distress and the labor wasn't, you know, progressing, so they did the C-section. And then her scar got infected..." He trails off, seeming lost in the hard memories, and Naomi gives him a sad, sympathetic smile.

"That sounds incredibly difficult. And, of course, I'm so sorry for your loss." She glances around at all of us.

In response, we all murmur something unintelligible. It

feels like we're a bunch of unruly kids hauled before a headmistress, miserably waiting to be disciplined, and yet the stakes are so much higher than that. For all of us, and especially for this baby boy.

"So." Naomi draws a quick breath, and I brace myself. Again. "Who has had the primary care of Henry since his birth?"

Spots of color come into Diana's pale cheeks as she admits throatily, "I have. But Tom also helped." She glances at him apologetically, clearly worried that sounded like an accusation, and maybe it was one.

"And who has been living in the home?" Naomi asks in the same careful voice. "Just you, Tom, and Andrew?" Her gaze moves to me in query, and I give an instinctive shake of my head.

"I was in Chile until about ten days ago," I say, and then realize how defensive that sounds, as if I'm saying it couldn't possibly have been me that caused the bruising. "I'm staying in Stamford."

Naomi jots a few notes on her paper before the questions continue. Was Henry a difficult baby? Colicky? Did he feed well? Was anyone else ever alone with him, or responsible for his care? With the grief we were feeling, was caring for him challenging?

The questions all feel loaded, exposing our weaknesses and impossible to answer without giving something away. Diana and Andrew stammer through explanations as best as they can —he wasn't very difficult, not colicky but he has been a little fussier lately. There was a night nurse, but she was let go a few weeks ago, because they felt they could handle the nights. Last night, they hired a babysitter, someone off a respectable website...

Naomi nods, unsurprised by this information, and realization floods through me—and also Diana. We exchange a silent look of understanding as we both realize it must have been the babysitter who reported the bruises. I see a flash of something like apology in Diana's eyes, and I wonder if she thought it had been me.

I'm not sure what result to expect, but when the questions finally come to a close, Naomi gives us a somber look. "I'm going to need to take Henry to our approved pediatrician for a full exam," she states, and it's clearly not something we can argue with. "One of you is welcome to accompany me. When we've received a report from the pediatrician, we can consider next steps and how best to support you all in your parenting."

Support our parenting. Is that code for taking Henry away? Diana's face is deathly pale, and Andrew looks just as grim. Tom is still silent, staring at the floor. This doesn't feel like a positive development. At all.

"All right?" Naomi asks, although it's not really a question. Already she is standing, reaching for Henry's car seat. Diana opens her mouth like she wants to protest, and then closes it again. Tom gives a little shake of his head. "Is there someone who would like to accompany me?" she asks, glancing at Tom.

"I'll go," Andrew says. "Unless…?" He looks at Tom too, and my son shakes his head more firmly, looking both determined and defeated.

"You go."

We all stand as Naomi and Andrew prepare to leave, Andrew in his own car, Noami with Henry. It feels both surreal and shocking, to surrender our rights to a woman we've only met this morning, and yet that's how these things go.

No one speaks as they head out through the front door, Naomi carrying the car seat, Andrew looking terribly dejected. As the door clicks closed, they leave behind a silence that feels like grief, and an emptiness that reverberates through each one of us.

TWENTY-TWO

AUDREY

No one speaks for a long moment after Naomi and Andrew have gone with Henry. Then, abruptly, Tom rises and strides out of the room, his footsteps thudding up the stairs.

"Tom—" I call, and Diana flings out one hand, fluttering her fingers in appeal.

"Let him go."

I'd bristle at her advising me on how to handle my own son, but somehow I can't make myself be annoyed. Henry is gone. The time for self-defensiveness and angry accusations is surely over. Right now, in the aftermath, it feels like we're all to blame.

Upstairs, a door slams shut.

"Would you like a coffee?" Diana asks stiffly, and I let out a tired laugh, I don't know why.

"Yes, thank you."

She moves back to the kitchen, and I follow her, too tired to make conversation, to try. It doesn't feel like there's a point anymore, and yet I know the fight is just beginning. If Naomi Bryson decides Henry needs to be removed from his home... we all need to work together.

"I'm sorry," I finally say, because I decide I do need to try, after all. "I think I said some things last night that were... a little much." Which I suppose is an understatement, but I leave it at that, waiting for Diana to respond.

She is silent, her head bent as she spoons coffee into a French press. "I think we probably all did," she says at last, her gaze on the counter in front of her. "This situation has had... many challenges." A small, sad sigh escapes her, and she screws the lid onto the jar of coffee, her back to me.

"I always liked Sophie," I venture cautiously. "When I met her a year ago, after she'd reached out." I make a face, surprised by my own desire for honesty as I admit, "Tom wouldn't have. He never did."

Diana nods, unexpectedly sage. "Children can be so stubborn," she murmurs. "Especially when they're adults."

"Very true." I let out a huff of laughter as I consider all the times Tom refused to see me. "They think they know so much." In case I sound bitter, I add quickly, "Not that I've ever known that much. I think, as a mother, I always felt at a loss." Now I wonder if I've admitted too much, but I realize I'm tired of seeing Diana Lawrence as my enemy. Maybe we'll both fare better if we see each other as allies, mothers who have suffered and struggled and, hopefully, learned.

Diana smiles sadly. "That's certainly how I've always felt," she replies. "As a mother."

We are both silent, absorbing the weight of our mutual confessions.

"When Sophie was a baby," Diana says suddenly, "I had postnatal depression. Pretty badly." She pauses as she reaches for the kettle to finish making the coffee. "One day I walked out of the house. Just... walked out. Left her in her crib, for hours. Our landscaper heard her crying and called the police. Social workers got involved. Briefly, but still." She flutters her fingers toward the sofas where we'd all been sitting. "Having that woman here... it brought it all back. The sense of total *failure*.

Of judgment, both from within and without." A sigh escapes her as she pours the coffee into two mugs. "Motherhood is meant to be the most natural thing in the world, but it felt like a foreign country to me, one where I didn't speak the language or know the customs, and I was supposed to. Everyone expected me to, and thought it was strange and wrong that I didn't." She turns to me with a wry smile, although I can tell she's worried she's said too much. "Milk?"

I smile. "Please."

As she goes to the fridge to get some, it feels only fair and right to share some of my own story, and I find I want to. "I understand what you mean," I tell her. "Motherhood felt pretty foreign to me, too. Not the logistics of it—feeding, clothing, rocking, all that. I was... competent, I suppose, but I derived no joy from it. I felt empty inside, as well as restless." I pause, recalling those long, long days when everything felt like a chore. "When my husband and I agreed that he should stay at home and I should go to work—even in another country—it felt like such a relief, and that seemed abnormal. I think most people thought it was, including, unfortunately, Tom." I slip onto a stool as Diana hands me a mug of coffee. "But I still went."

"And judged yourself for it," she surmises. "As I did."

We lock gazes, silently acknowledging this unexpected point of sympathy, maybe one that mothers everywhere share. Is there *any* mother, I wonder, who doesn't feel guilty, like she's never done enough? I have yet to meet one.

Diana takes a sip of coffee, her gaze lowered. "I don't believe I hurt Henry," she says quietly, and before I can even begin to bristle, she adds, "and I don't think Tom did, either. Or Andrew. But he has those bruises, and the truth is—the truth I think we all have to face is..." She pauses to draw a breath and then says quietly, "*Any* of us could have done it. He was challenging these last few weeks. Once I snatched him out of his crib... maybe I was rough? I'm sure Tom could say the same. But I don't think any of us were being intentionally *abusive*. Not that that makes it much better. Those bruises..." Her voice wavers. "He's so little," she whispers as she struggles to compose herself. "So tiny. I absolutely hate the thought that one of us may have hurt him." Tears pool in her eyes and she blinks them back quickly. "But it seems like that's what happened," she continues, her voice wobbling all the more. "I don't know how else to make sense of it. I don't know how to *live* with it. I've second-guessed myself as a mother since Sophie was born, and I guess I won't stop now."

She shakes her head, wiping her eyes, and impulsively I reach over and grasp her hand. "I'm so sorry," I tell her. "For everything."

"So am I," she chokes. "I never wanted this to be a battle. I really meant what I said about working together, even if I don't know what that could possibly look like. But now I wonder if we'll even get the chance."

"They won't take him away," I say with more certainty than I feel. "For one infraction? You heard what she said, about supporting all of our parenting."

"Yeah, and what does that look like?" Diana mutters, sounding uncharacteristically cynical. She shakes her head as she takes a sip of coffee. "I just want another chance. With Sophie... I let my guilt paralyze me. Everything became an atonement, and it was never enough. I think it made motherhood a burden to me, *and* to Sophie. It was like we were always trying to make it up to each other, and we never could." She shakes her head again. "She could be so challenging... but then, so could I, in my own way. I couldn't let go of my guilt, and now I want to, but maybe I can't, because I have something else to feel guilty about." A sad smile quirks her mouth. "Does it ever end?"

"I don't think so," I tell her, and we both smile, another point of sympathy found.

"I'm sorry for the way things happened with Tom," Diana tells me. "Back when Sophie brought us to him. Maybe we overreacted—"

"From what Tom has told me," I interject dryly, "he didn't make a very good first impression."

"No," Diana agrees on a small, sad sigh. "But then, I suppose, neither did we."

"Tom seems to think pretty highly of you now," I tell Diana, and watch as a shy, pleased smile blooms across her face.

"I've tried—"

"Well, it's worked. I know he's appreciated your support. And he even has some sympathy with Andrew, whom I gather has been a little more..." I hesitate, trying to think of a neutral word, and come up empty.

"Andrew's been blindsided by all this," Diana tells me with a small, grimacing smile. "I know how he can come across, but he adored Sophie. He thought she'd respond to his ultimatums, out of love for him. The fact that she didn't..." She shakes her head. "It hurt him more than he was ever willing to admit, at least until recently. And..." She pauses, seeming to deliberate whether to say anything more. "We've both been afraid that Tom will take Henry and disappear from our lives. Grandparents have very few legal rights, you know. He could do that, to any of us, and there would be nothing we could do about it."

"I know." I felt as if I had precious few rights as a mother, so I can only imagine I'd have even less as a grandmother. "But," I tell Diana, "I don't think that's going to happen."

"If we get Henry back," she fills in unhappily, and I nod.

"If we get Henry back, and we *will*."

She lets out a broken little laugh. "You sound so sure."

"They don't take a child away over one infraction," I insist, as I did before. "We might get a warning, or have a report made, but we're not going to *lose* him, Diana. Not forever."

"I wish I had your certainty." Diana pauses, her hands

cradled around her coffee mug. "When Sophie was a baby, and social services got involved... they made a report as well." Her gaze is lowered, a spot of color in each pale cheek. "They didn't take her away from me, but there were follow-up checks, and Andrew hired a nanny and the whole thing just felt..." She blows out a breath. "Like it was all my fault—which, I suppose, it was."

"Diana." I rest my hand on her arm. "You can't keep blaming yourself for every mistake you've ever made," I say gently. "That's in the past. We need to focus on the future. Together."

She gives me a crooked smile and I drop my hand from her arm. "So how do you think that's going to work?" she asks. "For the four of us?"

"I don't know," I admit honestly. Even with the best of intentions, I suspect it will be fraught and at times painful. It might take a village to raise a child, but someone's still in charge.

"Are you planning on going back to work abroad?" For once, there's neither hope nor accusation in her voice.

"Probably not," I admit. As much as I loved it, I feel in my bones that my time there is over, and maybe, just maybe, there's important work for me to do *here*. I don't need to travel halfway across the world to feel needed.

Diana is silent for a long moment, her forehead pleated in thought, her gaze somber. "I don't want to take Henry away from Tom," she says at last. "I know tempers were running high last night, and we all said things we didn't truly mean. But I want to *support* Tom. When I had Sophie..." She pauses, her throat working. "My mother had died just a few weeks before. I felt anchorless... more than I needed to, because of my grief. But I don't want Tom to feel that way. I want to help him be the dad I know he can be. Whatever that looks like, and I'm not expecting prep school and sailing lessons and a golf club membership, if that's not what Tom wants for Henry.

I didn't come from that world, and Henry doesn't need to, either."

I laugh in surprise, because it's so along the lines of what I was thinking last night. "I don't know what Tom wants," I admit. "I don't think he knows, either. So maybe we need to talk to him, and ask him."

Diana nods slowly. "That sounds like a good idea."

We smile at each other, both of us, I suspect, feeling a little silly, as well as emotional. I don't know that I can call Diana my friend yet, but I think I probably could one day. One day soon, even.

"Shall I go find him?" she suggests, and I nod.

"Sure."

Diana heads out of the kitchen, and for a second I let my head drop into my hands. The sleepless night, the overload of emotion and anxiety this morning... I'm exhausted, but also hopeful. At least, I'm trying to be. It's a faint flicker inside me, longing to burst into flame.

For a few dazzling moments, I let myself imagine a future that I know, realistically, resembles more of a fairy tale than real life, and yet is all the more alluring for it. I imagine Tom and I in a cottage somewhere, maybe near the beach, the water sparkling like it does at the bottom of the Lawrences' lawn, Henry toddling through the long, green grass. I work at some local nonprofit, helping people part-time, smiling and relaxed and present. Tom goes back to school, maybe for art, something he's always loved, and thrives. The Lawrences are part of our lives, of *Henry's* life, offering childcare, weekend visits, relaxed dinners and birthday parties, trips to bowling alleys and beaches, all of us one big happy family.

It *could* happen, I tell myself. It doesn't have to be nothing more than a fantasy. If we work at it, if we *try*, we can make it happen. Why not? *Why not?*

Then I hear Diana's footsteps coming hurriedly down the

stairs, and I lift my head from my hands, my fairy tale fantasy disappearing like the ephemeral mist I knew it was all along. Already, just from the sound of her rushed footsteps on the stairs, I know something is wrong, although right now I can't even imagine what it is.

As Diana comes back into the kitchen, I see the worry writ large across her face, her eyes wide and blank with panic, and everything in me curdles with dread.

"What is it?" I ask, my heart already lurching with fear. "What's happened?"

"It's Tom," she says, her face pale, her hand fluttering by her throat. "He's… he's gone."

TWENTY-THREE

DIANA

"What do you mean, gone?"

Audrey sounds both disbelieving and angry, but I've come to realize that's her way of hiding her fear.

"He's not in his room, or anywhere in the house," I tell her. "I looked. And it looks like he's taken most of his clothes."

Audrey frowns, her forehead furrowed. "But—"

"He must have slipped out the front door while we were talking." It's the only thing I can think of, and it fills me with sadness. The only reason I can think of why Tom would leave like that is if he thought he was responsible.

"He told me he didn't cause those bruises," Audrey says, as if she can read my mind. "And I believe him."

I don't say anything, because it feels like there is nothing to say. Someone caused them. Maybe it was Tom, maybe it was Andrew, maybe it was me. There isn't anyone else.

Audrey shakes her head, despairing. "Do you know where he might have gone?"

"He left once before, to a friend in the Bronx," I admit. I am reluctant to recall that squalid place—the sweetish stench of cannabis, the crumpled beer cans on the floor. At least this time

Tom didn't take Henry with him, but maybe that's worse. The presence of his son might have acted like a check on him before, but now there's nothing to keep him from plunging into a pit of guilty despair. And what will he do then?

Audrey stares out the window, her gaze distant, her lips pressed together in a firm line. When I first saw her, in her utility clothes, her arms sinewy and strong, a sense of brisk capability emanating from every movement, I was intimidated. But now I just see a mother, who, like me, makes mistakes and isn't sure what to do, but like me wants to make amends and do her best. How can we help Tom now?

"I don't think we should chase after him," she finally says. "Or try to coax him back. He's an adult. He needs to make his own, adult decisions. The best thing we can do for him now is give him that space."

It sounds a bit too hands-off for me, considering the nature of our situation, and my impulse is to run out right now and find him, but... I suspect Audrey is right. If Tom is going to be a father to his son, he needs to face up to his responsibilities... as well as the consequences of his actions.

"He might not have caused those bruises," I tell her, "but judging by his actions, he's afraid he did."

"Yes," she agrees heavily. "That's what *I'm* afraid of." She stares outside at the spring afternoon, the bright blooms on rhododendron bushes just starting to wither and droop, and then she straightens, her gaze snapping to mine.

"I'll go back to my apartment. Maybe he's gone there."

"All right." I hesitate. "You'll keep in touch?"

"Yes, of course I will." She crosses to me and grasps my hand. "Whatever happens, Diana, we'll all get through this. *Together.*"

I nod, wanting to believe her. Yesterday it felt as if we were enemies, but now I would like to count Audrey as my friend, or at least my ally.

We exchange phone numbers, and then Audrey heads outside to wait for her Uber—I'd offered to drive her, but she refused, saying I should stay here in case Tom comes back—and I head upstairs, unsure what to do. I peek in Tom's room again, but there's nothing but a few clothes he left behind.

Then I head to Henry's nursery, breathing in the smell of baby powder that lingers in the air, like a ghostly memory. I picture him wrapped in the terrycloth towel with the teddy bear hood, all damp and rosy from a bath. The last time I changed him, he laughed when I tickled his tummy, a deep belly gurgle that made me laugh right back.

With a sigh, I collapse into the glider, resting my head in my hand. Now I am not picturing Henry in this room, but Sophie. Sophie as a baby, with her angelic blond ringlets and chubby pink cheeks. As a toddler, trying to climb out of her crib. A wave of longing and grief rushes through me and then subsides.

I will always miss my daughter. But I am learning to miss her without the accompanying soul-crushing guilt, and that makes it all easier to bear. I may not have been the best mother. I may not have even been a very good one. But I *tried*, and more and more I am realizing that is all you can do.

I want Tom to realize that too, but maybe that is something he has to come to understand for himself, just as I did, or at least am trying to. I think back to what Audrey said, and then I slip my phone from my pocket and send a quick text.

Tom, please come back. We want to support you.

I hesitate for a second, and then press send. Surely that's not too pushy, and Tom needs to know we don't blame him... if he even *did* cause those bruises. Secretly, I still doubt myself.

I don't know how long I sit in that glider, slowly rocking back and forth, letting the memories drift through, pulled by a tide of bittersweet longing. I think of Sophie, and then of

Henry, and back again—baby, toddler, child, teen. At some point, the shadows start to lengthen and I realize it is getting dark outside. I have been sitting in this room for most of the day.

I am just about to rise, aching with effort, when I hear a door open and close downstairs. Is Tom back? Or is it Andrew?

Footsteps sound on the stairs, slow and heavy. Then Andrew appears in the doorway of the nursery, looking haggard.

"Henry…?" I ask in a whisper, and he shakes his head.

"They took him. A ninety-six-hour emergency removal, which they can do without any paperwork. Because of the bruises." He slumps against the doorway. "I'm sorry, Diana."

"Ninety-six-hours…" Four endless days. "And what happens then?"

"A court hearing, to determine whether we—or Tom, really—can keep him. Since we can't prove who caused the bruises, we're all at risk."

I glance down at my lap. "Andrew," I whisper. "What if I did it?"

"Diana…"

I look up, blinking back tears, to see my husband gazing at me with both sorrow and sympathy, his blue eyes creased, his mouth turned down.

"If you'd caused them, you'd know it. Bruises like that on such a small baby? You'd have to have near-throttled him. It's not something that happens without realizing."

"I know, but…"

"I know how you doubt yourself," he says gently. "But not about this. Not about anything. We did the best we can—with Sophie, *and* with Henry. And we'll continue to do so… whatever that looks like."

I want to believe him, and more importantly I want to believe what he says matters. But what if we don't have a choice? What if that choice is taken away from us?

"Tom's gone," I tell Andrew. "He left when Audrey was still here, taking most of his stuff with him. We didn't see him go."

He frowns, seeming more unhappy than angry. "That suggests he knows he was to blame—"

"Not necessarily," I interject quietly. "He doubts himself too, Andrew. Just as I have."

Andrew sighs as he rakes a hand through his hair. "That might be," he says, "but it doesn't look good, to have him go AWOL like this. It won't help any of us."

"Once upon a time," I remind him gently, "you would have said that Tom doing something like this would help our case."

Andrew gives a grimace of acknowledgment. "Once upon a time," he agrees heavily. "I saw Tom as just an obstacle to overcome for far too long—first with Sophie, and then with Henry." He sighs, shaking his head. "He has his issues, God knows, but then we all do. And I've come to realize that taking Henry away from his father isn't necessarily the best plan for him, or for Tom, or for us. We all need to work together... if we can."

If we can.

Well, I think with a weary sort of hope, we can only try.

The next three days pass with painful slowness. I don't hear from Tom, and neither does Audrey. Naomi, now our assigned caseworker, tell us there will be a court hearing in Stamford to determine whether Henry should be returned to us or not.

"Naturally, we want to work toward an outcome where Henry can remain with his family," she assures me in her kind yet brisk way. "We just need to make sure that's in his best interest."

"Surely it's in his *better* interest," I say with quiet dignity, "than becoming a ward of the state?" The words alone sound awful and impersonal.

"That is what we will have to determine," Noami replies,

refusing to rise to my challenge. "The purpose of DCF is to *support* families, not tear them apart. I hope you can believe that."

"I want to," I tell her honestly. I'm just not sure that I can. Not when Henry has been apart from us for three days, and my arms ache and the house feels empty. And we still haven't heard from Tom.

Andrew has hired Claire, the family lawyer we spoke to back at the beginning, to represent us in court, and a petition comes through the mail, from Henry's state-appointed lawyer, informing us of our court date, in two days' time. It all feels far too official for an eight-week-old baby who hasn't known any home but this one.

I think of Henry and Tom constantly, wondering where they both are, if they're coping. Do the people taking care of Henry know that deep knee bends are what help him fall asleep? Do they realize that rubbing his back rather than patting it helps get a burp up? There are a thousand tiny things that I didn't realize I knew about my grandson, ways I cared for him that become instinctive and now make me ache with the loss of them.

As for Tom... has he fallen back into old, harmful ways? I picture him on some kind of bender with his nameless friend from the Bronx, and I want to both shake him by the shoulders and give him a hug. Doesn't he realize how much his abandonment could hurt his case? Doesn't he *care*?

I fear he does, and that he has somehow convinced himself that taking himself out of the picture is best for Henry.

"I don't know where he is," Audrey admits when I call her the night before the court hearing, in the hopes that she might have heard from Tom. "I've called and texted him so many times, and there's been nothing." She sounds both exhausted and anxious, and I know she is as worried for Tom as she is for Henry, just as I am.

"If he doesn't show up in court—" I begin.

"He'll forfeit his parental rights, at least for the time being," Audrey fills in flatly. "I know. It's why I keep calling him... I want him to step up to the challenge, but I also want to help him do it. But even without him there—*especially* without him there—you and Andrew should be able to regain custody." She speaks matter-of-factly, without any bitterness, for which I am grateful, because I know that even when we are trying to work together, this all feels fraught.

"We won't necessarily regain custody if they still can't determine who caused the bruises," I am compelled to remind her. "Right now, Andrew and I could be as guilty as Tom, at least in the court's eyes." I dread the thought of appearing in court, being accused, even if only by implication. The condemnation, the judgment, the shame... and worse, not getting my grandson back. Would he go to Audrey then? Is that something she's considered?

"I don't think that's likely to happen," Audrey replies quietly. "Especially if Tom is a no-show."

As we end the call, promising to be in touch if we hear anything, I realize that Andrew and I could be on the cusp of getting what we thought we wanted—custody of our grandson, with no son-in-law to complicate the situation.

But just as Andrew acknowledged, it doesn't feel the way we once might have thought it would. I don't just want Henry back, I want Tom back, too. The two of them together.

This won't be a happy ending, I realize, unless we have both our boys back home. But with the court hearing in just over twelve hours, that seems more unlikely than ever.

TWENTY-FOUR
AUDREY

I buy a new outfit for the court hearing, because I suspect cargo pants and a T-shirt won't cut it, although I'm sure there have been people appearing in court wearing worse. I, however, don't want to be one of them.

The last three days have felt endless, with no word from Tom. I can only imagine what he's thinking, how he's doing, and none of it seems like it could possibly be good. I hope he's read my texts, but there's no way to tell. He might not even know about the court hearing, much less be planning to appear.

And if he doesn't... like I told Diana, it won't look good, for him, or for me. I'm not sure what my chances are of gaining custody of Henry, considering I once lost custody of my own son, but I've already decided not to try. Diana and Andrew Lawrence are, I've come to realize, good people. They can give Henry a better home than I can. As for that dream I had, of Tom and I living together by the beach? I always knew that's all it ever was. A dream, lost like so many others.

And so, the morning of the court hearing, Diana and Andrew having arranged to give me a ride, I am staring at my reflection, hoping I don't look as uncomfortable as I feel, in a cotton blouse and dark skirt. I look, I realize, like a waitress. A tired, old one, the lines on my face more pronounced, my hair looking grayer than it did even a few weeks ago.

Every time I close my eyes, I see the bruises on Henry's arms, the dark banding his stomach. And then I think of my son causing them, and I feel sick with sorrow and grief. I do not want to think about what the judge hearing our case might say about them. I want us all to move past this, Tom included, but how can he if he won't even show up?

I am reaching for my purse, ready to go, when I hear a key in the door and then, to my amazement, Tom is there, looking both exhausted and resolute, in a black suit he must have worn for Sophie's funeral.

"*Tom.*" I start toward him, my arms outstretched for a hug, although I can't remember the last time my son and I embraced. He doesn't move and I hesitate, dropping my arms, trying to gauge his mood. "I'm so glad you're here."

"I'll come to court," he says, tossing his key on the table. "I'm going to give up custody to the Lawrences." His tone is both defeated and determined, brooking no argument.

"Tom..." I don't know what to say. I can understand why he feels like he should, but I hate the thought of him losing access to his own son... just as I lost him. "Are you sure?"

"Yes, I'm sure." His throat works, his forehead furrowing as he struggles to contain his emotions. "If I caused those bruises... I can't risk it again..." He draws a shuddering breath as he wipes his sleeve across his eyes. "It's better for Henry if I don't."

His shoulders start to shake, and this time I hold my arms out, walking over to him to wrap him in a hug. He comes willingly, his head on my shoulder as sobs wrack his body.

"Oh, Tom, Tom..." I murmur as I rub his back, like he's a child in need of comfort, and right now he *is*. I don't know how to make it better, only that I want to, but I can't. All I can do is offer comfort in the face of grief, of guilt. My poor son... and my poor grandson.

After another minute, Tom steps back, wiping his eyes again. "I talked to Uncle Jack," he tells me. "He might have a job for me out in Perth."

I gape for a few seconds. "You're going to go to *Australia?*"

He nods, resolute. "I think it's better if I get away from here. From all of it."

I can certainly understand that instinct, since it's one I've had many times before. "That's what I always thought," I tell him quietly. "And I believed it. But Tom... going away isn't always the right choice. Sometimes you need to stay and fight your battles. I often wish I had."

He sets his jaw. "This is different."

"Tom, you are *not* a danger to your son," I state firmly. "Whether you caused those bruises or not." He shakes his head, determined to deny it, and I roll right over him. "I mean it. The fact that you're thinking like this *proves* you're not. And you've been under enormous pressure... you need support. We all do. And we can give it to each other, if we stay and try. Henry needs a father—"

He shakes his head. "He has Andrew."

"Who is his grandfather," I say in agreement. "And that's good. But you'll leave a hole in his life, Tom, whether you realize it or not. Just like I left a hole in yours."

He stares at me for a long moment, and then a sigh escapes him in a gust of breath. "So what do you suggest I do? Go to court and say I'm sorry, I didn't mean it, I'll try harder next time?" His tone is sneering, dismissive.

"Yes, pretty much," I reply steadily. "One mistake doesn't have to define you, and that's if you even made it in the first place."

"Everybody thinks I did."

I recall my conversation with Diana, the doubts she had. "I

don't know about that," I tell my son. "I think you might be hardest on yourself."

He shakes his head in instinctive denial. "You can't tell me that Henry would have a better life with me than with the Lawrences."

"Define better," I reply, determined to meet every objection with one of my own. "Henry needs his father. No matter what material possessions or opportunities the Lawrences can give him, they can't give him that. I know that much, and I know it from experience, Tom, as do you."

His shoulders slump, his head bowed. "I just don't know if I can," he whispers. "I don't know if I have it in me."

I understand that too, because it was so often how I felt. Sometimes running away really is easier, but not, I've learned, in the long run.

"You have help," I tell him. "I'm not going anywhere, and neither are the Lawrences. You don't have to do this alone."

The decision crystallizes inside me; whether or not I'm reinstated with Crisis Action, I'm not going back. There are people right here, *important* people, who need me, more than anyone far away does. I'm not as indispensable as I'd believed with that organization, but maybe, just maybe, I'm more important to my son than I ever thought I was.

Before Tom can answer, there is a knock on the door. The Lawrences are here, and it's time to go to court. I glance at him before going to open the door; Diana stands there, looking tense and pale; her eyes widen as she catches sight of Tom, and he tenses.

"Tom..." Diana hurries toward him while he watches warily, and then jerks in surprise when she throws her arms around him. "I'm so glad you're back," she says, and tentatively, as if he can't quite believe it, my son returns the unexpected hug.

. . .

The courtroom isn't a grand space; it looks like a corporate meeting room, with a couple of tables and chairs.

Claire, the Lawrences' lawyer, met us outside, greeting us in a briskly professional way. She tells us what will happen—the social worker will describe the mandated report, the doctor will present his evidence, and then she'll make our case for Henry being returned, before the judge decides whether or not he can be.

"It shouldn't take very long, since there isn't much evidence to discuss," she says. "I feel confident Henry will be returned, especially as I am suggesting that we have a safety plan in place, with certain conditions."

"What conditions?" I ask. It's the first I've heard of them.

"Nothing too onerous," Claire tells me with a cool smile. "Weekly check-ins, Tom's attendance at a grief support group, that sort of thing."

"We're attending the group, as well," Diana inserts quickly. "This isn't just about Tom."

"It's all of us," Andrew agrees, putting his arm around his wife, and I feel a little better.

In the end, however, it doesn't even come to all that. Naomi describes the report of bruising on Henry's body and arms, and how she saw it herself the next day. She speaks matter-of-factly, without emotion, but it's still hard to hear. Bruises on a baby... can anyone hear that without making a judgment?

Diana and I exchange guilty, unhappy looks, while Tom stares down at his lap and Andrew looks straight ahead, all of us needing to brace ourselves to hear what happened. It feels like an indictment of all of us.

Then the doctor gives his evidence, first dryly stating where he saw the bruises, how they were the size of fingers, as if someone had held Henry too tightly, or even shaken him. Bile rises in my throat, and I have to swallow it down, force away the images of Tom or any one of us hurting Henry.

"There were no signs of fractures," he continues, glancing down at his notes, "or any other trauma. Furthermore, a blood test revealed that Henry West has a Vitamin K deficiency which would contribute to the bruising. Infants with such a deficiency tend to bruise very easily."

The judge, a woman in her fifties with curly, gray hair and a no-nonsense expression, takes off her glasses to stare at the doctor. "Are you saying the bruising was exacerbated by the vitamin deficiency?"

"That is certainly a distinct possibility," the doctor replies in his dry way. "Arguably, there should have been no bruising at all or cause for it, but the severity of the bruises would almost certainly have been amplified by the deficiency."

For a few seconds, the words don't penetrate. I simply stare at him, this innocuous-looking middle-aged man in a gray suit and striped tie who holds all our fates in his hands.

"*Tom*," I whisper. "Did you hear that? The bruises might have been caused by a *vitamin* deficiency."

It sounds too good to be true, and my son seems to think that too, because he gives a little shake of his head, looking torn between confusion and hope. "Still, he shouldn't have *any* bruising..."

"It makes a difference," I tell him in a hiss. "It must. You *must* let it." I stare at him fiercely, willing him to let go of the guilt. Willing for all of us to, so we can move toward a future... together.

"In light of these findings," the judge says, "I rule that Henry West be returned to his father and family." She drones on about the support plans in place and the conditions we'd discussed and then turns to address Tom directly. "You've had a very challenging start to fatherhood," she tells him with a small, sad smile. "And I would urge you to take advantage of the support that is being offered, both for your own sake as well as your son's. Parenting is difficult at the best of times, and we could all use a little help."

And then it's over, like a party that ends abruptly, leaving us reeling with disbelief and wonder.

"Congratulations," Naomi tells us warmly as she greets us afterward. "Henry is outside, with his carer. I'm sure you want to be reunited."

Tom nods jerkily, his expression uncertain, and then we follow her out to the hallway, where Henry is sitting in his car seat, sucking his fist, his eyes wide and bright with curiosity. A woman stands as we come forward, glancing uncertainly between us all.

"Henry is being returned to his family," Naomi explains, and then Tom is taking his son from his car seat, bringing him gently, so very gently, to his chest as he brushes a kiss across his downy head and Henry nestles in, like he knows exactly where he belongs.

I glance at Diana, and see she is wiping tears from her eyes, while I am blinking them back. Hours ago, this moment felt impossible, and yet now it has come to pass, and I am so very grateful.

Tom glances up at us, smiling, a look of relief breaking across his face like a wave.

"Welcome home," he says to his son, to all of us, and for the first time, it truly feels like that's where we are.

EPILOGUE
DIANA

Two years later

Sophie's headstone is simple, with her name, the dates of her birth and death, and then one word. Beloved.

Beloved daughter, wife, friend, mother. Henry might have never known her, but he knows of her. I tell him stories of Sophie as a little girl and when he comes over, as he does every Wednesday and Friday, I get out her toys. He loves the wooden blocks best; we can spend hours stacking towers. At least, I stack the towers, and Henry knocks them down, chortling with delight at my pretend gasps of surprised dismay.

Sometimes I take him out in the garden, or even down to the beach, where we stack pebbles and skim stones into the Sound. Andrew takes Friday afternoons off, and has "Grandpa time", which involves a lot of rough-and-tumble play in the yard. Next week, he's going to take Henry fishing.

Henry lives with Tom and Audrey in a little duplex on Shippan Point, near Stamford, in sight of the Sound. Audrey works for a local charity that supports disadvantaged women returning to the workforce, and Tom works in construction while also studying for a degree in graphic design.

I've gone back to school, too, at the grand old age of fifty-four to get a degree in counseling. I also volunteer with Holding Hands, a charity that supports new mothers, especially those who are finding the adjustment hard. Andrew has cut down his hours, and between us and Audrey and Tom, Henry always has someone watching him. It's not always easy, and everyone is juggling a lot, but we can make it work, by helping each other. It might not take a whole village to raise a child, but it definitely takes the four of us.

On this breezy spring day, the second anniversary of Sophie's death, I stare at her headstone and remember all the things I loved about her. That deep belly laugh. The way her eyes sparkled. The gusto she had for life, even when it felt like too much. How she'd curl into me for comfort. I miss her, and I'll always miss her, but at long last my grieving isn't tainted by guilt for not being good enough. It simply *is*, a weight I carry, will always carry, because it is part of me, and I can live with that.

A tiny hand slips in mine, and I gaze down at my grandson, my heart suffused with love. Henry has Tom's hazel eyes and Sophie's bright blond hair. He also has her dimples, which delight me every time he grins. Now he's looking serious; he might only be two, but already he senses the somber gravity of this moment.

"Your mama, Henry," I say gently, pointing to the headstone. "She loved you very much."

Henry frowns, his hand still in mine. "Mama," he says, and I smile.

"Yes. Mama." We won't ever forget her, because Sophie is part of who Henry is, even if he can't fully understand that yet. One day, he will. We will all make sure of it.

For now, though, I simply smile at my grandson, and then, with my hand enfolding his, I turn and walk back to the car, and the family waiting for us.

A LETTER FROM KATE

Dear reader,

I want to say a huge thank you for choosing to read *My Daughter's Baby*. If you enjoyed it, and would like to keep up to date with all my latest releases, just sign up at the following link. Your email address will never be shared, and you can unsubscribe at any time.

The idea for this story first came to me when my own daughter got married—fortunately to a lovely man we knew and loved! But it got my writer's brain thinking "what if…" and so this story was born. It's always my aim to explore any issue from both sides and find empathy and understanding wherever I can, which I hope I achieved with this novel.

www.bookouture.com/kate-hewitt

I hope you loved *My Daughter's Baby* and if you did, I would be very grateful if you could write a review. I'd love to hear what you think, and it makes such a difference helping new readers to discover one of my books for the first time.

I love hearing from my readers—you can get in touch with me on social media or through my website.

Thanks again for reading!

Kate

KEEP IN TOUCH WITH KATE

www.kate-hewitt.com

facebook.com/groups/KatesReads
goodreads.com/author/show/1269244.Kate_Hewitt
substack.com/@katehewitt

𝕏 x.com/author_kate

ACKNOWLEDGMENTS

As ever, there are so many people who are part of bringing a book to see the light of day! Thank you to the whole amazing team at Bookouture who have helped with this process, from editing, copyediting, and proofreading, to designing and marketing. In particular, I'd like to thank my editor, Jess Whitlum-Cooper, as well as Imogen Allport and Laura Deacon, and Sarah Hardy and Kim Nash in publicity, Melanie Price in marketing, Richard King and Saidah Graham in foreign rights, and Sinead O'Connor in audio. I have really appreciated everyone's positivity and proactiveness!

I'd also like to thank my writing friends who check in with me to make sure I'm making progress and give me plenty of encouragement and inspiration—Jenna Ness and Emma Robinson in particular. Thanks also to the lovely readers in my Facebook group, Kate's Reads, who are always so supportive and encouraging. You make it all worthwhile!

PUBLISHING TEAM

Turning a manuscript into a book requires the efforts of many people. The publishing team at Bookouture would like to acknowledge everyone who contributed to this publication.

Audio
Alba Proko
Melissa Tran
Sinead O'Connor

Commercial
Lauren Morrissette
Hannah Richmond
Imogen Allport

Cover design
Alice Moore

Data and analysis
Mark Alder
Mohamed Bussuri

Editorial
Jess Whitlum-Cooper
Imogen Allport

Copyeditor
Jade Craddock

Proofreader
Liz Hurst

Marketing
Alex Crow
Melanie Price
Occy Carr
Cíara Rosney
Martyna Młynarska

Operations and distribution
Marina Valles
Stephanie Straub
Joe Morris

Production
Hannah Snetsinger
Mandy Kullar
Nadia Michael
Charlotte Hegley

Publicity
Kim Nash
Noelle Holten
Jess Readett
Sarah Hardy

Rights and contracts
Peta Nightingale
Richard King
Saidah Graham

RAISING READERS
Books Build Bright Futures

Dear Reader,

We'd love your attention for one more page to tell you about the crisis in children's reading, and what we can all do.

Studies have shown that reading for fun is the **single biggest predictor of a child's future life chances** – more than family circumstance, parents' educational background or income. It improves academic results, mental health, wealth, communication skills, ambition and happiness.

The number of children reading for fun is in rapid decline. Young people have a lot of competition for their time, and a worryingly high number do not have a single book at home.

Hachette works extensively with schools, libraries and literacy charities, but here are some ways we can all raise more readers:

- Reading to children for just 10 minutes a day makes a difference
- Don't give up if children aren't regular readers – there will be books for them!

- Visit bookshops and libraries to get recommendations
- Encourage them to listen to audiobooks
- Support school libraries
- Give books as gifts

There's a lot more information about how to encourage children to read on our websites: **www.RaisingReaders.co.uk** and **www.JoinRaisingReaders.com**.

Thank you for reading.

Made in United States
North Haven, CT
24 November 2025